WHAT TOMORROW WILL BE

ALSO BY JULIANNE MACLEAN

WOMEN'S FICTION

Beyond the Moonlit Sea

These Tangled Vines

A Fire Sparkling

A Curve in the Road

All Our Beautiful Goodbyes

The Color of Heaven Series

The Color of Heaven

The Color of Destiny

The Color of Hope

The Color of a Dream

The Color of a Memory

The Color of Love

The Color of the Season

The Color of Joy

The Color of Time

The Color of Forever

The Color of a Promise

The Color of a Christmas Miracle

The Color of a Silver Lining

CONTEMPORARY ROMANCE

Promise You'll Stay

HISTORICAL ROMANCE

The American Heiress Series

To Marry the Duke

An Affair Most Wicked

My Own Private Hero

Love According to Lily

Portrait of a Lover

Surrender to a Scoundrel

The Pembroke Palace Series

In My Wildest Fantasies

The Mistress Diaries

When a Stranger Loves Me

Married by Midnight

A Kiss Before the Wedding (a Pembroke Palace short story)

Seduced at Sunset

The Highlander Series

Captured by the Highlander

Claimed by the Highlander

Seduced by the Highlander

Return of the Highlander

Taken by the Highlander

The Rebel (a Highland short story)

The Royal Trilogy

Be My Prince

Princess in Love

The Prince's Bride

Dodge City Brides Trilogy

Mail Order Prairie Bride

Tempting the Marshal

Taken by the Cowboy

STAND-ALONE HISTORICAL ROMANCE

Adam's Promise

A Storm of Infinite Beauty

WHAT TOMORROW WILL BE

A NOVEL

JULIANNE MACLEAN

This is a work of fiction. Names, characters, organizations, places, events, and incidents are either products of the author's imagination or are used fictitiously. Otherwise, any resemblance to actual persons, living or dead, is purely coincidental.

Published by Lake Union Publishing, Seattle
www.apub.com

EU product safety contact:
Amazon Media EU S. à r.l.
38, avenue John F. Kennedy, L-1855 Luxembourg
amazonpublishing-gpsr@amazon.com

ISBN-13: 9781662519123 (paperback)
ISBN-13: 9781662519130 (digital)

Cover design by Kathleen Lynch/Black Kat Design
Cover images: © shaunl, © fotograzia / Getty; © Mohamad Itani / ArcAngel Images

Printed in the United States of America

For my daughter, Laura

PROLOGUE

When I was nineteen, I thought I had it all figured out. I'd found my soulmate, the great love of my life, and I was on a clear, direct path to the career of my dreams. What could possibly go wrong? My life was golden—until I went for a hike in the winter sunshine and fell off a mountain.

I wish I could say I learned a lot from the ordeal—that when the ground collapsed under my feet and I tumbled down a vertical rock face, I came to understand that life isn't always steady or predictable. I also wish that afterward, I could have recognized the long-term power and potency of trauma. How, for the rest of your life, lingering scars can steer you off course and make you doubt that anything good is truly lasting.

I absorbed no such wisdom that day, nor in the months and years to come. Even when death came calling a second time, I had not yet recognized my ignorance.

But there I go again, dwelling on the past when this is supposed to be a story about love, forgiveness, and soulmates, and not just the human kind.

It's a story about lessons learned—that there can be joy after tragedy, and hope after forgiveness.

There is growth in the healing.

But maybe that's something you learn from life, over decades. Not from a fleeting encounter with death, however intense it may be.

PART ONE

THE MOUNTAIN

1998

CHAPTER ONE

Beautiful Dreams

Wolfville, Nova Scotia

"What are you doing here?" I ask as I descend the steps at the Manning School of Business, my heavy backpack slung over my left shoulder. It's a dreary, damp day, and the chill in the air makes me shiver. "Aren't you supposed to be in class?"

Jacob saunters toward me, and I can't believe how relieved I am to see him, because for the past twenty-four hours, I've been staring into the abyss. But here he is—the one person in the world who can save the day. And save *me*.

I pause at the bottom of the steps and watch him approach. He wears faded blue jeans with sneakers and the brown leather jacket I gave him for Christmas.

Though we've been together for almost two years, I still feel as if I could fall over backward at the sight of him. He's so beautiful in every way—especially when he appears unexpectedly as I'm walking out of the computer lab, about to suffer a nervous breakdown.

"The prof canceled at the last minute," he tells me. "So I figured I'd come and meet you."

I reach him on the asphalt path and kiss him on the cheek. "I'm happy to see you."

He looks down at me with a slight frown. "Everything okay?"

He knows me so well.

Two girls walk past on their way into the business school, and I nod silently because I can't tell Jacob the truth right now. Not here.

"Do you want to go to the cafeteria?" I ask. "I have an hour before Finance."

"I can't. I have to go back to the apartment for something, but I came to tell you that I have a surprise for you."

I raise an eyebrow and incline my head. "A surprise?"

"Yes. Can you come over after class? I've got supper planned, and afterward, we can go for a walk." He looks at me expectantly, and his boyish grin is so adorable that all the tension releases from my body.

"Supper and a walk sounds perfect."

He smiles and backs away. "Great. I'm making your favorite."

"Alphagetti?"

He laughs. "No. I got those frozen burgers you like. Sliced cheese. And sandwich pickles."

My eyebrows fly up. "Burgers with sandwich pickles? You're my hero."

"I got carrot cake too."

"You didn't."

"I did."

I give him a questioning but flirtatious look, because something about this feels special. But I don't pry. "I'll see you later, then."

Watching him walk off, I bury my stress until we can talk properly later, in private.

~

As soon as I enter my dorm room at Eaton House, I go straight to the phone on my desk. It's a long-distance call to Dalhousie University in Halifax, but I don't care. I need to talk to Becky.

Thankfully, she answers after the first ring. "Hello?"

"Hey, it's me. I'm glad I caught you."

Becky and I have been best friends since seventh grade, when her family moved to Halifax and bought a house a block away from ours. I was an only child, and at the time, all the kids in the neighborhood were older boys who played ball hockey in the street. When Becky moved in, we formed an immediate bond. Weekend sleepovers became the norm for the next six years.

"Sienna," she says. "This is unexpected. What's up?"

"Well . . ." I hesitate because I'm not sure how much to reveal. Part of me wants to tell her that I haven't slept alone a single night since November because I've been staying with her brother, in his apartment. And now my period is late.

But I can't tell her that, because Jacob needs to be the first to hear this. And he will. I swear, in a few hours, over burgers, I'll tell him. But right now, I'm craving information, and if anyone would know what his "surprise" is—and if it's what I hope—Becky is that person. She's his younger sister and greatest confidante.

But I can't simply launch into it. I learned a long time ago that in order for our friendship to survive, I need to make time for Becky outside of my relationship with her brother.

"How's it going with you?" I ask. "What happened with the volleyball player last weekend?"

Becky scoffs. "Oh, nothing. He was just a wicked flirt. God, I wish you were here to give me a good shake and remind me that not all guys who talk to me for more than ten seconds are Mr. Right."

I laugh, but she isn't exaggerating. Becky has always been a dreamer. She wants a house with a white picket fence, a husband, two kids, and a dog, so it takes nothing for her to fall head over heels in love with any potential Prince Charming at a Friday-night frat party.

But how can I criticize? I'm a dreamer too. I want to be an interior designer and own my own business, and like Becky, I often spend too much time mapping out my future. As a result, I forget to enjoy the present.

Becky's tone brightens. "But enough about me. Why are you calling in the middle of the day on a Wednesday?"

I pick up a pen and scribble aimlessly on a notepad. "Well . . . Jacob said he has a surprise for me. He's cooking my favorite supper tonight—burgers and pickles. He even got carrot cake, and he seemed a little . . . I don't know . . . coy. Do you know anything?"

"I wish I could help, but I don't know a thing. I swear."

I lay my hand on my belly. I look down at it and wonder if I'm just bloated. Then the dreadful worry returns.

"Maybe he's just in the mood for carrot cake," I say. "And I was looking for an excuse to call you anyway." I rest my forehead against the wall and let out a heavy sigh. "I wish you were here."

I also wish we could go back to the days when we were in total control of our futures.

"Is everything okay between you guys?" she asks. "Are you having relationship troubles?"

"No, it's nothing like that. We're fine." I pause. "I don't know what's wrong with me."

Except that I do. I'm terrified that I'm pregnant. How will Jacob take the news? He wants to be an engineer, and he has two more years of school. I don't want to get in the way of that.

And how will I tell my parents?

I bite my lower lip and wish I could keep this news to myself, at least until I tell Jacob, but my stomach is in knots, and I need to talk to someone. Not just someone. Becky. My best friend.

"I'm late," I say.

There's a weighted silence on the other end of the line.

"How late?" she finally asks.

"Ten days."

She ponders this for a few seconds. "But you've never been regular. You're always late."

"A few days maybe," I reply. "A week tops. But never *this* late."

"You use protection, though, I assume?"

"Of course. But it's not foolproof. I honestly don't know how this could have happened. We're always so careful."

"Have you told him yet?" Becky asks.

"No, I'm planning to do that tonight, so please keep this to yourself." The words spill out of me with desperate pleading.

"It's in the vault," she replies. "But you should get a pregnancy test. Like . . . right now."

I check my watch. "I can't. I have Finance in twenty minutes."

"Can you skip it?"

"No, I have to give a presentation, and it's worth thirty percent of my grade. But I'll go to the pharmacy right after. I'll take the test when I get to Jacob's place." I realize I'm on the verge of tears. "God, I'm a wreck." I twirl the phone cord around my finger.

"Try not to worry," she says. "Maybe it's just the stress from exams that's making you late. But if not, we'll figure it out. No matter what Jacob says, I'm here for you."

I want desperately to believe that everything will be okay and that I haven't ruined my life. Or Jacob's.

"Thank you. I don't know what I'd do without you." I really mean it. I love her like a sister. "And remember . . . please don't tell anyone."

"I won't breathe a word," she promises. "But call me later, after you take the test. I won't be able to sleep tonight if I don't know."

"I will—I promise."

"I'm glad you called," she says. "I miss you."

"I miss you too."

We say goodbye and hang up, and I hurry off to class.

~

"How did the presentation go?" Jacob asks. He's sitting outside the front door to his apartment, halfway down the wooden steps. He rises to meet me as I approach.

"Good." It's a struggle to sound cheerful.

"I'm sure you did great." Jacob pulls me into his arms, hugs me, and kisses the side of my head. "Remember when I said I have a surprise for you?"

How could I forget? I step back, nod, and pray it's a ring. At least that way, when we break the news to my parents—that I got knocked up at college—we could lead with an engagement. It would lessen the blow. The future would be settled, no more unknowns, and we could all start making plans. If I have to put my degree on hold, so be it. I'm young. I can readjust my career goals, maybe learn about business and interior design through a correspondence course.

Jacob leads me up the steps. "I haven't told a soul about this." We reach the landing outside his door. "Close your eyes."

"Okay." I shut them and listen to the sound of him opening the door. It squeaks on its hinges. Then he ushers me across the threshold, and I hear a whimper from inside.

I open my eyes, and what do I see? A puppy. A sweet little yellow Labrador retriever, staring at us from a gigantic red cushion on the floor.

I raise my hands to my mouth. "Oh, my goodness!"

The puppy's tail starts to wag, and my insides turn to jelly. All I want to do is pick him up and cuddle him.

"Where did you get him?" I slowly move closer to the cushion and get down on my knees.

Jacob kneels beside me. "A guy in my class was giving them away because his dog had a litter."

The puppy ambles toward me, and I sit cross-legged to welcome him onto my lap. I run my hand over his soft little body, and he licks my wrist. His tongue is soft, and it tickles. As I pat his small head, I can't stop smiling.

"What's his name?"

"Scooter," Jacob replies.

I snuggle Scooter close to my chest and kiss the top of his silky-soft head. "What a good name for you."

When I meet Jacob's gaze, I realize he's been watching me with affection. "Do you like him?"

"Do I like him? I *love* him." I start to giggle when Scooter licks my ear.

Jacob reaches out to pat him. "I thought we could raise him together."

I'm only half listening because Scooter is starting to chew on the string from my hoodie.

"If you want," Jacob continues, "we could consider him *our* dog, not just mine, since you're here so much anyway."

The suggestion finally filters through my brain. I'm already so in love with this little angel of a puppy that I lean toward Jacob and kiss him on the cheek. "I love that idea." Scooter wiggles in my arms. "Do you hear that? I'm gonna be your new mom."

Only then do my thoughts creep to the pregnancy test in my backpack, and the anxiety returns. "Is this the surprise you talked about?"

Jacob chuckles. "What . . . you were expecting more?"

I can't seem to smile or speak. My whole body has gone numb, and I feel foolish to have imagined that he was going to propose. What a stupid pipe dream. We're still in college. Getting married probably isn't even on Jacob's radar, nor should it be. He's a practical guy.

Scooter tries to wiggle out of my arms, so I set him down on the cushion. He staggers around the squishy surface on clumsy paws.

Jacob lays a hand on my shoulder. "Something's wrong. What is it?"

I shut my eyes and shake my head.

"Tell me."

I finally force myself to look at him. "I thought, coming over here, that . . ."

I can't continue. It's too embarrassing to admit that I was hoping for a ring. I'll have to explain this another way.

I swivel on my knees and face him. "I have to tell you something, but I don't want you to be upset." I can't find the right words, and I feel like I'm not making any sense. "I'm so sorry, Jacob. I'm not even sure how to . . ."

I notice the color draining from his face. "How to what? Are you not ready for a dog? Or are you talking about *us*? Are you having doubts or something?"

Oh, my God. He thinks I want to break up. But nothing could be further from the truth. I love him more than life itself. I can't even imagine being in this world without him.

"No, it's nothing like that," I assure him. "It's something else and . . ." I bury my face in my hands. "I don't know how to tell you this."

"Tell me what?" His words tumble out in a rush.

"My period's late."

Jacob stares at me blankly, and I understand that he's processing what I've just said.

"How late?" he asks.

"Ten days."

He sucks in a small breath, and I feel a sudden overwhelming need to ease his fears.

"I don't know for *sure* that I'm pregnant, because I'm always late. Just not *this* late. But I have a pregnancy test in my backpack. I thought I could take it here, and then we'll know for sure."

His lips are parted, and he wets them. "Are those tests reliable?"

"I think so."

"Then maybe we should do it now," he says, "before supper."

I'm relieved that he's not freaking out too much. At least not yet. But that's why I love him. He's never been a hothead.

I move to my backpack, unzip it, and withdraw the plastic bag with the test inside. "I'm nervous."

"Me too," Jacob says. "But everything's going to be okay." He gathers me into his arms and kisses the side of my head. "Whatever happens, we'll figure it out together. I'll marry you tomorrow if that's what you want."

I draw back, blinking in astonishment.

He shrugs and gives me a small smile. "I've always imagined us getting married anyway. We'd just have to move the date up—that's all."

I love him so much it hurts. This man is everything I've ever wanted.

"You're amazing," I say. "I love you."

"I love you too." He takes my hand, raises it to his lips, and kisses it. "If I had a ring right now, I'd get down on one knee."

I start to cry and laugh at the same time. "I might as well tell you . . . that's what I thought your surprise was."

"Really?" He glances at Scooter, who has fallen asleep on the cushion. "And it was just a dog." He kisses my hand again. "Next time it'll be a ring. I promise."

He walks me to the bathroom and ushers me inside, and I glance at him with unexpected anticipation before I close the door behind me.

~

Five minutes later, Jacob and I sit next to each other on the sofa, elbows on knees, watching the clock on the wall. Each minute ticks by like an hour, but we're almost there.

"Thirty more seconds," Jacob says.

The little plastic stick rests on the TV table across the room, and I wonder if it's already showing the result. I glance up at the clock again, and the second hand finally hits twelve.

"It's time." I breathe deeply.

Jacob wraps his arm around my shoulders and kisses my temple before he gets up to check the result. Heart racing, I sit and watch him pick up the stick and stare at it for a moment, his eyebrows drawn together, his brow furrowed.

"Two lines are positive, right?" he asks.

Oh, God. There it is. I'm going to have his baby. "Yes."

Jacob holds up the stick. "It's negative."

I stare at him with wide eyes, and the whole world goes quiet. Then my insides start buzzing.

"Are you sure?" I shoot off the sofa to check for myself. Jacob hands the stick to me, and I stare at the tiny window. There's only one pink line. "This can't be," I say. "Maybe I did it wrong."

"How many ways are there to pee on a stick?" Jacob asks.

I continue to stare at it in disbelief. "But I'm ten days late."

"Have you ever been that late before?"

I look up at him. "No. Never."

Scooter whimpers on the cushion. Then he squats and pees on it.

Jacob turns to him. "Oh no, Scooter. You're supposed to pee on the paper, remember?" He picks him up and gently deposits him on the newspaper by the front door, but it's too late and Scooter has no idea why he's over there, except maybe to be introduced to the scent of my shoes—an old, worn pair of loafers. He sniffs the left one and starts to chew on the tassel.

"No, Scooter," Jacob says. He scoops him up again and holds him like a football. "That's not for you."

Watching them, I realize I've been standing in a state of paralysis. In an attempt to shake myself out of my stupor, I look down at the test again. It wasn't the result I'd been expecting, and I feel completely unraveled.

Jacob moves closer. "Are you okay?"

"I don't know."

He sets Scooter on the floor and gives me his full attention. "Are you disappointed?"

There's nothing but compassion in his tone, and I'm grateful that he's always sensitive to my feelings. "Of course not," I reply. "I was terrified of being pregnant."

Yet something in me feels deflated, and I don't know what to make of it. I lift my watery gaze to meet his. "But maybe I am a *little* disappointed. When I started to imagine us getting married and living together . . ."

He nods. "I feel the same way. I kind of liked the idea. Although I don't know how our parents would have taken it."

"I'm pretty sure mine would have supported our decision, under the circumstances," I tell him. "They would have helped us."

We stand there in silence, our eyes locked, as if the world around us has faded away, and in that brief, fragile moment, a warmth swells in my chest. My heart feels full.

"Let's cook some burgers," he says. "I'm starving."

"Me too." I head for the kitchen. "Come on, Scooter. It's time for supper."

He trots happily to follow but stops when Jacob picks up the red cushion with pee on it and tosses it into the washing machine with some powdered detergent. He shuts the lid and presses the Start button, and when the water begins to hiss through the pipes, Scooter runs and tries to hide between my feet.

~

Before bed, we discuss the new sleeping arrangements and decide it would be best to train Scooter to sleep on his cushion on the floor in front of the closet. Not in bed with us, because we can't let him think he's king of the castle. Besides, he might pee on the blankets.

After I brush my teeth and change into my pajamas, I retrieve the red cushion from the dryer. It's still warm when I place it on the floor.

"Come on, Scooter. Time for bed. Lie down."

He seems to understand the command, or maybe he just wants to be close to me. Either way, I'm pleased when he curls up on the cushion.

"What a good boy." I pat him for a few minutes until his eyes close and his breathing slows. His little paws twitch, and I suspect he's dreaming about stinky shoes.

Jacob walks in with his toothbrush still in his mouth and gives me a thumbs-up for getting Scooter settled. He returns to the bathroom to finish brushing his teeth, and I quietly rise to my feet and crawl into bed.

Jacob joins me a moment later, slides under the covers, and switches off the lamp.

We face each other and embrace, our bodies linked by the emotional heights of the day. He inches closer and buries his face in the crook of my neck.

"It doesn't matter what the test said," he whispers. "I still want to marry you."

"I want to marry you too," I say breathlessly, because I never imagined I could love anyone like this.

His hand traces the curve of my hip, and his mouth is hungry for mine. I cling to him, this man who is the other half of my soul. I know he's the one I'm meant for—the only man I'll ever love.

~

I hear a noise in the night and wake groggily to realize it's Scooter, crying on the cushion. I nudge Jacob. He's asleep on his stomach, his cheek planted deep in the pillow.

He lifts his head. "What is it?"

Scooter bawls, and we both sit up.

"Do you need to go outside?" Jacob asks.

Scooter lets out another pitiful sob, and I lay a hand over my heart. "Oh no. He probably misses his mother. It's his first night away."

"Yeah." Jacob tosses the covers aside and pulls on his pajama bottoms. "I'll take him outside to distract him. Maybe he'll pee."

Jacob leads Scooter out of the bedroom, and I flop back onto the pillows and close my eyes. I try to go back to sleep, but I can't because I realize I, too, need to pee.

It's not easy to get out from under the warm covers, but I rise and make my way to the bathroom to take care of business. But as soon as I sit down on the toilet, I feel a familiar sensation that makes me gasp. I shift a little to peer into the toilet bowl, and I see red.

My thoughts become Ping-Pong balls. First, I'm relieved. Overwhelmingly so. But as I reach for the toilet paper, all I want to do is cry. There's no baby growing inside me, and Jacob and I won't get engaged anytime soon. Both realities make me wonder if I've ever known such disappointment in my life.

God, why did I let myself dream about holding our baby in my arms for the first time and sharing that moment with Jacob, making plans for the not-too-distant future? Wedding plans . . . financial plans . . . what color to paint the nursery . . .

After I flush the toilet, I stand at the sink and wash my hands. *This is a good thing,* I tell myself. I'm only nineteen. This isn't the time for marriage and a baby. Before I start that chapter of my life, I want to know how to run a business and learn the creative side of interior design. And it goes without saying that I'd prefer not to tell my parents that I have to quit school because I got pregnant.

I hear the front door of the apartment open, so I return to bed, where I listen to Jacob remove his jacket and talk to Scooter in hushed tones.

When they return, I sit up. "Did he pee?"

"He did," Jacob replies, "and I gave him a treat."

Scooter follows Jacob to the bed and barks when he gets in.

"No," Jacob firmly says. "This isn't your bed. You sleep over there." He points at the cushion, then gets up and leads Scooter toward it. "Good boy." He rubs Scooter's head, scratches behind his ears, and then joins me back under the covers.

I snuggle close. "Your hands are freezing."

"It was foggy out there. Cold and wet." He pulls me close. "I was wishing I had my long johns on."

"Ooh, sexy . . . a lumberjack vibe."

He laughs, and we snuggle close, but a pitiful wail causes both of us to sit up again.

Scooter peers at us with woeful puppy dog eyes, which rips my heart out. I clutch Jacob's forearm. "Maybe we could bring him up here with us. Just for tonight."

"There's no such thing as 'just for tonight.' If he sleeps on the bed, he'll expect to sleep with us forever."

I consider it for a moment. "Would that be so bad?"

Jacob looks down at Scooter, who's pulling out all the stops, his eyes full of hopeful desperation while he milks every ounce of sympathy he can muster.

Jacob starts to chuckle and hangs his head in defeat. "I guess this is it."

He gets up and lifts Scooter onto the bed, where he becomes a snuggly teddy bear between us. Later, Scooter burrows under the covers and earns his keep as the best foot warmer money can buy.

~

I wake to the sound of the telephone ringing in the kitchen. Sitting up in a panic, worried that I've overslept and missed my 8:30 class, I glance at the alarm clock. It's only 7:15, so I flop back down. Only then do I notice that I'm alone in bed.

The door opens, and Jacob walks in with the cordless telephone. "Yeah, just one sec. It's Becky."

He hands the phone to me, and I remember that I'd forgotten to call her the night before. "Hello?"

"Hey," she says with a note of concern. "What happened last night? You didn't call. Is everything okay?"

Jacob leaves the room, and I sit up on the edge of the bed. "I'm so sorry. I fell asleep."

"Did you take the test?"

"I did," I reply, "and it was negative."

She exhales with a whistle. "*Phew.* You must be so relieved."

"Yes, very," I lie, because I'm afraid I might cry if I start to talk about it. "Did Jacob tell you what the surprise was?"

"Yes—that he got you a puppy. Holy banana pants!"

I reach for my bathrobe on the back of the chair and pull it on. "I know, right? His name is Scooter, and he's *sooo* cute. Wait till you see him. But Jacob didn't get him for me. He's your brother's dog. I'm just helping out."

Becky laughs. "Sure. Just don't let him rope you into cleaning out the crate."

"I can't make any promises. Scooter's pretty hard to resist. He's even cute when he's pooping." I glance at my watch. "But listen, I really have to go. I have a class at eight thirty. Can I call you tonight?"

"Don't forget this time," she says.

"I promise I won't." I hang up and hurry to get in the shower.

A short while later, as I stand under the nozzle and shampoo my hair, I ponder, at length, what my life is supposed to look like from this day forward. Clearly a baby isn't in the cards, at least not this month, which is probably for the best because I still want to be an interior designer, and Jacob needs to finish his degree. I tell myself that we have plenty of time to build our lives together. We're only just getting started.

But as I step out of the shower and dry off, I experience a strange twinge of apprehension that prickles through me. Or is it a premonition? A sense that I may not always be in total control of my destiny? You'd think the past twenty-four hours might have taught me a lesson about that, but clearly they haven't. I still want what I want—a fulfilling career, children, a dog, and a nice country house in the valley, which I'll share with Jacob until death do us part.

CHAPTER TWO

Cape Split

January 1999

"Scooter, come!" Jacob picks up the leash and dangles it temptingly.

Scooter—now ten months old, fifty pounds, and clumsy on enormous paws—jumps off the sofa and gallops toward the door.

It's our first weekend back at school since Christmas vacation, and the weather is unseasonably mild. Earlier this morning, my mother called after church and referred to this as the "usual January thaw," but I cannot remember any day, in the dead of winter, when people walked around in shorts. It's an anomaly. What should have been snow over the last forty-eight hours had turned to rain, and the snowbanks along the streets melted and caused minor flooding in the ditches.

But today, the sun is out, and the weatherman is calling for record temperatures until Monday, so Jacob and I have decided to forgo an afternoon of studying in the library and go hiking at Cape Split.

"Do you have the backpack?" I ask as I finish wrapping our tuna sandwiches in cellophane and place them in the lunch bag.

"It's right here." Jacob tries to hook the leash onto Scooter's collar, but he spins wildly in a circle. "All right, all right. Hang on, buddy—we're going."

"He's so excited," I say, laughing.

Jacob opens the front door. "Let's bring that old beach towel in case he's dirty later."

"Good idea." After the rain, it's bound to be muddy on the trail, so I suspect that all three of us, together, will be one big hot mess.

~

The hiking trail at Cape Split begins at the inlet of Scots Bay. It's a pleasant and picturesque thirty-minute drive from the university, through the historic valley towns of Port Williams and Canning, past dykelands, cornfields, and apple farms. Naturally, it's less lush in the winter months. Today, the landscape is a soft palette of grays and browns. Nevertheless, I can't help but feel there's something special about this January day when we can drive with the windows down and feel the sun's warmth. Scooter is making the most of it in the back seat with his head out the window, the wind in his face, his tongue flapping like a ribbon on a kite.

We find a place to park not far from the trail entrance, and I get out, hook the leash on to Scooter's collar, and watch him jump out of the car. His tail wags while Jacob slings the backpack over his shoulder and locks the car doors.

"Let's go," Jacob says.

Scooter charges ahead, and I stumble forward. "Slow down, you rascal! You nearly pulled my arm out of the socket!" I turn to Jacob. "Sometimes I wonder if he's deaf. He doesn't seem to hear a word I say."

"He's just half husky," Jacob replies, in jest.

"Mush, mush!" I shout, and Scooter drags me harder and faster.

Jacob jogs ahead, grabs hold of Scooter's collar, and speaks firmly. "Scooter, stop. Sit."

Scooter's ears press back, and he immediately plants his bottom on the ground.

"Good boy." Jacob pats him on the head and turns to me. "You just have to be firm with him."

"I try, but he only listens to you. I think it's your deep voice."

"Maybe we should sign up for obedience classes."

I laugh. "For him or me?"

"Both," Jacob replies with a smile.

We start walking again, and Scooter trots beside me. He glances back at Jacob repeatedly, seeking approval and looking very eager to please.

"He worships you," I say.

I can't blame Scooter. I feel the same. Sometimes I wonder if Jacob's a saint.

~

The trail is steep and challenging, but it feels good to exert myself in the fresh air. I realize I've been hibernating since early November, when it became necessary to scrape ice off the car windshield every morning.

"This day doesn't feel real," I say as I step carefully over exposed tree roots and feel a strain in my calves on the upward climb.

"I know," Jacob replies. "I feel the same way. It's like we're in another universe." He's walking ahead of me, leading the way, while Scooter, off leash, follows behind me. I sense that he's being protective, which makes me love him more, even if he doesn't always listen to me.

"I'm glad we skipped the library," Jacob says. "Even if I flunk that quiz on Monday, this is worth it. Life is short. And I love this place."

"Me too." I've hiked Cape Split since I was a child, once a year with my parents. It was a summer highlight and a family tradition.

Jacob stops at the top of a steep cluster of boulders that function as steps. He turns around. "You doing okay?"

"I'm great," I reply, but that doesn't stop me from accepting his hand when he offers to pull me up and over the last big boulder. By this time, I'm perspiring, but it's rejuvenating with the wind in the trees and the distant roar of the ocean at the base of the mountain, the fragrance of mud and decaying leaves all around us. It's a two-hour hike to the top of the peninsula, but the payoff is worth every ounce of spent energy because the point at Cape Split is a natural wonder. It overlooks the Bay of Fundy from a height of two hundred feet. It's like standing on a narrow precipice at the edge of the world.

~

When at last we reach the summit, we emerge from the shade of the forest onto a hairpin turn around a narrow break in the cliff. We pause to stand at the wooden rail and look straight down a vertical drop to the pebbled beach below.

"This is giving me the creeps," I say. "Which is weird because it was always my favorite part of the hike when I was a kid."

Jacob lets the thought linger, turns it over in his mind. "Maybe, as we get older, we develop a clearer sense of danger because we become more aware of our mortality."

I feel a cool breeze blow across my forehead. "That's very deep thinking, but it makes sense." I back away from the rail. "Let's keep going."

Jacob follows with Scooter, and we emerge onto a field of grass, flaxen in its winter dormancy. I stop and gaze at the breathtaking views of the bay while Jacob hooks the leash on to Scooter's collar.

"I've never seen it like this before."

In summer, grass and wildflowers grow tall here. They dance and sway in the wind. But today, aside from the evergreens, all plant life seems dead. Blades of grass are flat, crisp, and darkened by rot.

But nothing is dead. I know this. Beneath the ground, the shoots are protecting themselves from freezing temperatures. They're conserving their energy during these shorter days and reduced sunlight. They are surviving. In time, the grass will green up. It will come alive with the arrival of spring.

Suddenly, laughter startles me out of my musings, and I turn. Others are sitting on camping chairs, enjoying a light lunch or taking photographs at the cliff's edge.

Jacob leads Scooter across the summit toward the point, but I hang back, watching them with nothing but love in my heart. I close my eyes for a moment and take in the scent of damp earth and spruce needles and the salty fragrance of the bay. I listen to the waves crashing steadily onto the beach below the cliffs, and I marvel at the miracle of this planet—the glaciers that formed the very ground I'm standing on, and the thousands of years of swirling waters that eroded this high curvature of land, turning it into something like a crooked finger, pointing west.

Jacob kneels and gives Scooter a good scratch behind both ears. Scooter leans into it, hard, and I smile.

I've been blessed. But why? Was I simply born under a shining star? Or did some powerful force from above consider me deserving? If so, I don't understand the reason. I only know that I've been incredibly lucky. I met the love of my life in my own neighborhood, at the exact right time. God has been very good to me.

~

It's not possible to sit on the grass because the ground is wet from the recent rain, so we find a fallen tree trunk to sit on. I open the backpack and dig for the water dish for Scooter. I peel off the plastic lid, and he laps greedily while I reach back into the bag for our tuna sandwiches. I pass one to Jacob and unwrap my own.

After a few bites, Jacob lays his hand on my knee. "Are you aware that it's been nine months to the day since you took that pregnancy test?"

I tip my head back to look skyward. "Yes. I thought about it a lot over Christmas. I wonder where we'd be right now if the test had been positive."

"Maybe we'd be in the hospital," he replies, "standing over an incubator. Or in the apartment, changing a diaper. Are you sorry it didn't work out that way?"

I pretend to consider it, but the truth is I've been reflecting on it for weeks. "I think we're exactly where we're meant to be. Otherwise, we'd be someplace else."

Jacob pats Scooter, who takes a seat on the grass beside him. "Yeah, but if it had happened, everything would've been fine. I think for you, it's possible to have everything you want."

I turn to him. "What do you mean?"

"A child and a career. Because you're a doer, Sienna. You don't let setbacks or obstacles get in your way. You figure out how to get around them."

I feel my cheeks flush at the compliment and realize that Jacob sees qualities in me I don't always see in myself. And he says the sweetest things.

I raise my sandwich to take a bite, but Scooter goes into begging mode. He rises up on his hind legs and drops his front paws onto my lap.

"Scooter . . . sit," Jacob warns with authority.

His floppy ears flatten. He drops his bum obediently but remains laser focused on my sandwich.

As soon as I finish the last bite, Jacob scans the horizon, and then he starts to pack up. "We should go. I don't want us to get stuck on the trail after dark."

I've never come to Cape Split in January, when the days are so short, and I wish we'd thought to bring flashlights. With a sense of urgency, I zip up my jacket, and we begin the trek across the summit, back to the trail.

~

I'm not yet aware that this is the end for us, our last moment together on this earth. I'm still feeling happy and energetic, eager to get my blood pumping. I'm also conscious of the distinctive beauty of this moment—the changing light in the sky and the movement of a thick white cloud directly above us. I glance up and wonder if it might be a sign of more rain, or perhaps snow if the temperature drops. I look ahead at the backpack on Jacob's shoulders, and Scooter in front of him, tugging on the leash.

Jacob whistles. "Slow down! No pulling."

It's remarkable, how every element of that final moment becomes imprinted on my brain.

~

Jacob stops at the fence. He wraps the leash around his fist to bring Scooter close and keep him secure because there are no pickets between the posts, just horizontal rails fashioned out of tree branches. He leans over and looks straight down. "The tide's gone out since we arrived."

I join him to look, and we say nothing as we study the sheer rock face and glance at spruce trees that cling to the top of the cliff by exposed roots.

Another young couple passes behind us on the trail. They say hello and continue on.

Feeling a potent urge to get going, I step back. "Ready?"

Still gripping the fence rail in one hand, Jacob turns. Almost immediately, the ground starts to give way beneath his feet. The fence tips forward, and in the space of a single heartbeat, he and Scooter abruptly drop.

Electrified by shock and terror, I rush forward to peer over the edge. The fence dangles by a single footing, and Jacob is hanging on. Scooter is yelping and screeching, scrambling to climb back up.

Our panicked eyes meet. "Hold on!" I scream as I drop to my hands and knees, but there's nothing I can do. They're both beyond my reach.

Jacob grunts and roars and kicks his toes against the rock face, in an attempt to run up it, but it's too steep and slippery, and he gains no traction. Pebbles pour down the side of the mountain, and the fence creaks and groans where it's held together with rusty nails. Scooter is almost to the top, but he's being strangled by Jacob's drag on the collar.

I'm vaguely aware of two people running toward us from the grassy summit. But it's too late. The ground beneath me starts to fall away. I slide forward, headfirst, the heels of my hands plowing through the earth as I fight to hold myself back from the edge. Scooter scratches his way up my arm. He tears my flesh to shreds.

Then suddenly, the post snaps. It splinters like a brittle twig, and we all descend together in a heap of flailing bodies, screams, and thuds as we bounce off the walls of earth and stone. There's a scraping of flesh and a smashing of bones. Blazing-hot terror until my bloodied, broken body hits the pebbly beach. The shock of impact leaves me breathless. All I can do is lie there, blinking up at the late-afternoon sky, confused and disoriented.

A white cloud passes over me. Brilliant rays of sunlight shoot out from behind. It's blinding, so I close my eyes. Only then do I begin to feel pain. Everywhere. In my guts, my bones, my cut flesh. Blood seeps from my nose, and I want to scream in agony, but I can't get a breath. My ribs feel like knives.

Jacob . . . I sense him beside me.

Please, God, let him be okay. I can't live without him.

Someone, please, help us.

I hear voices from above. "Hang in there! Help is coming!"

That's one prayer answered, at least.

Jacob's hand slides over mine, and I grab hold of it with every cell of my being. I hold tight and finally rest with some comfort.

"I'm here," he whispers. "Everything's going to be okay."

Thank you, Lord.

I want to tell Jacob that I won't give up, that we're going to make it out of here together, but I can't speak through my pain. Every bone, nerve, and muscle shrieks with agony. The most I can do is fight for one more breath. Then one more after that, until eventually I pass out.

~

A violent beating of helicopter blades from above. Jacob squeezes my hand. Images are sporadic. I feel myself rising up off the beach toward that loud, hovering machine, its engine roaring in the lingering glow of the sunset. I feel wind against my face. Only then do I become aware of foam blocks strapped to both sides of my head in a rescue basket.

I surrender to oblivion.

A sudden tug revives me. A man in a jumpsuit reaches out. He pulls me into the chopper. My gaze shifts wearily left and right in a grief-stricken search for Jacob, but all I can see is the roof of the chopper and a medic in a helmet, who leans over me. He shines a penlight at my pupils.

Where's Jacob? I want to ask, but I have no voice. I'm too weak even to open my mouth. Or maybe I'm dreaming and we're both still lying together on the beach, praying for rescue.

No, this is not a dream. People had called for help. Now I'm in a helicopter.

I manage to mumble, "Jacob?" but no one hears me above the clamor of the engine and rotor blades.

My eyes fall closed, and for some reason I'm not in pain anymore. I'm weightless. It doesn't occur to me that I might be dying. I think only of Jacob. I pray for his survival.

CHAPTER THREE

Soulmates

I've learned that pain comes in many forms. It has the power to immobilize, both physically and emotionally. It can wield this power temporarily and cause a brief paralysis, or it can apply a slow agony over minutes, hours, or weeks. Perhaps even a lifetime.

When consciousness returns, I'm in the hospital. I don't know what day it is, or what time. Intellectually, I'm cognizant of the fact that I've been in a terrible accident, but my thoughts are like pea soup, thick and goopy.

Later, I'm told that a team of surgeons used pins to stabilize a badly displaced pelvic fracture, and they removed my spleen. My shoulder was dislocated, and the flesh on my forearm had been torn off by Scooter's claws when he was clinging to me. A plastic surgeon was required to perform skin grafts. In addition, my rapid descent down the side of the mountain had scraped the top layer of flesh off my upper back, which, upon waking, is where most of my pain is centered. On top of all that, I have a concussion and three fractured ribs.

I come around slowly, gradually. Before I open my eyes, I hear monitors beeping and the soft voices of my parents keeping vigil, one on each side of my bed. They speak in hushed tones, not wanting to disturb me. I feel my mother's hand around mine. It's warm and loving.

That's the moment I fight like hell to open my eyes because I need to know about Jacob. Is he okay? And what about Scooter?

"Sienna?" My mother bends over me.

She knows I'm awake. I must have squeezed her hand, because I haven't moved otherwise, nor have I opened my eyes. I'm staring at darkness, thinking about Jacob.

The heart monitor beeps faster. I need to know where he is, and I'm so afraid.

"We're here, sweetheart," Mom says, squeezing my hand tighter. "You're going to be okay." A pause. "Are you awake? Can you hear me?"

At last, I open my eyes, and I see Mom's face, drawn with worry. She starts to cry with relief, and she bends to kiss my forehead while my father gets up and takes hold of my other hand.

"Thank God." He bows his head and weeps over me. I've never seen him cry, and it frightens me. It makes me understand how close to death I must have been.

I wet my parched lips and struggle to summon the capacity to speak so that someone will finally answer me. "Is Jacob okay?"

My parents, still leaning over me, say nothing. I glance from one to the other, but they won't look at me.

My mother shakes her head at my father. She doesn't want him to answer my question, which fills me with dread. Did the worst happen? I don't want it to be true, but I need someone to tell me.

"Take a moment to get your bearings," my father says. "You've been through a lot. Can we get you anything? Are you in pain?"

His reply confirms what I need to know, and tears pool in my eyes. "Just say it. Please . . . is Jacob here? Did he make it?"

My mother bends forward until her forehead is touching mine.

"I'm so sorry, sweetheart," my father says. "He didn't."

I hear the words, but they don't register. Nothing does. My heart is deadened, my body anesthetized.

Suddenly, I'm back on top of the mountain, handing Jacob the sandwich I'd made for him. I'm looking into his loving eyes, seeing our future together—an entire lifetime of undying love. Happiness. A home. Children. Grandchildren. Buried side by side.

Sickness rises in my abdomen. I need to vomit. My upper body convulses as I try to sit up. Mom grabs a stainless steel pan from the side table and shoves it under my chin just in time for me to expel the contents of my stomach, which is mostly nothing. But the convulsions are violent, and I feel like I'm choking.

When it's over, I lie back on the pillow and try to recover. What my father has just said to me still hasn't registered. It can't be right. Jacob can't be gone.

"What happened?" I ask. "Where did he die? In the helicopter? Or in the hospital? When? Just now?"

I need to know every detail before I can believe it. Until then, it's not true.

Both my parents sit down, hold my hands, and kiss them.

"He died instantly from the fall," Mom says. "He was gone when the rescue helicopters arrived. I'm so sorry, sweetheart."

I can't think or move. I'm confused because that's not right. "No," I say. "He was alive on the beach. He held my hand and talked to me until I was rescued. He can't be gone."

Suddenly I'm falling again. Down the mountain. The horrendous, unstoppable slide. Burning panic. The certainty that I'm going to die. My flesh tearing away, my heart on fire. *Jacob!*

Mom presses the call button, and a nurse runs into the room.

"She woke up," Dad says.

"I think she's having a panic attack," Mom adds.

I hear sobs and screams and realize they're coming from me. I'm shouting, "No!"

How could this have happened? We only wanted to enjoy a day outdoors instead of the library. Jacob has a quiz on Monday. This isn't happening!

A second nurse runs into the room. She picks up the tubing attached to my arm and inserts a needle into the injection port. Over the next few seconds, I begin to feel dizzy and displaced. I see Jacob's face and feel his hand on my cheek. He tells me that he loves me.

All I want is our beautiful life together, today and forever. I don't realize I'm sobbing and crying until the sedative takes effect and my breathing slows. My body shudders with relief, but I hate myself for giving in to this physical solace because it's artificial. It's not Jacob. He's gone. His life is over. Mine is too.

Oblivion comes quickly and blessedly, but I know that no medication can fix this. Emotionally, I am adrift in a cold sea where there's no rescue or remedy.

~

I'm not sure how long I've been lying here. I'm groggy from drugs, and I don't want to face reality. I just want to stare at the wall and pretend that this is a nightmare, one from which I will eventually wake.

Time passes. I don't care. Nothing matters.

Then the medications start to wear off, and I feel the ache and sting of a broad swath of bloody gashes down my back. *God, please help me . . .*

My head pounds, and my torso feels like a tractor trailer jackknifed into it.

"Is Scooter dead too?" I ask, my voice trembling.

Mom, unaware that I'd been awake for the past minute or so, sits forward in her chair. "He's at a vet hospital," she tells me. "But he's not doing well."

I turn my head on the pillow and look at her, detached. "What does that mean?"

She rubs my shoulder. "He was badly injured, sweetheart. They might have to put him down."

I become instantly alert. I try to sit up, but it hurts everywhere. "No!"

Mom tries to settle me, but I won't be settled.

"Don't let them do that!"

I'm staggered by the flash of a memory—the terror in Scooter's eyes, fixed on mine, when he was fighting to claw his way back to safety.

"They fixed *me*, didn't they?" I say. "They can fix him too."

"Yes, but—"

"But what? I'm human, and he's not? What are they going to do, shoot him?"

Mom turns desperately to my father for support. He's standing at the window, and I launch my ire at him too.

"He deserves a chance at life, just like me!"

"They won't shoot him," he replies. "But no one wants to see him suffer. It'll be handled humanely."

"What do you mean, suffer? I'm in pain, aren't I? I'm suffering, but you're not going to put *me* down."

My mother scoffs in horror.

"Of course not," Dad replies. He moves closer to the bed.

"Then what's there to talk about? Tell them to fix Scooter like they fixed me."

"It's not up to us," he replies. "He was Jacob's dog, and his family is making those decisions."

"Then call them. Please, Dad! I can't lose him too!"

I stare at my father intensely. He turns to my mother, and I watch their unspoken communication, a moment of shared deliberation.

Mom gets up from her chair. "I'll call Jacob's mother."

"Whatever it costs," Dad adds. "Tell her we'll pay the vet bills."

In that moment, I love them more than I've ever loved them in my life.

~

My parents' help should have satisfied me, but an hour later, I can't get Scooter out of my head. I'm consumed with thoughts of him at the vet hospital, alone in a cage, broken and bleeding, in pain, like me. Not knowing if Jacob or I have survived. Not knowing if we'll ever come back for him.

All I want to do is rip these tubes out of my veins and get discharged so that I can go find him. I need him, and he needs me—because he loved Jacob, just like I did. Our suffering is the same.

CHAPTER FOUR

The Dark Universe

It's three long days before I'm discharged. Meanwhile, my parents visit Scooter every afternoon at the vet hospital and get updates. Like me, he'd undergone surgery to fix a broken pelvis. He also had a shattered femur and internal bleeding. It's touch and go for the first two days, but on day three, we learn that he's sitting up and taking food.

For me, this news is the only glimmer of light in a world that's gone dark. I still feel as if I'm flat on my back on that beach, barely conscious, believing this is the end. Maybe it's the pain medication that keeps me numb, floating, and out of touch with reality, just above or below it. Whenever I doze off, I feel Jacob's hand wrap around mine. He squeezes it like he did on the beach, and he encourages me to hang on. His voice is soothing yet firm. But then I wake up, and I remember that he didn't make it, and no amount of morphine can touch the agony in my heart.

Flowers arrive. Friends and family call, but it's my mother who speaks to them because I'm not up to it. I can't listen to condolences about Jacob, and I certainly don't want to talk about the accident. I can't relive it. All I want to do is lie in bed and disappear, reach oblivion in sleep. But even that's taken away from me with the constant flow of hospital staff, in and out of the room.

Then Becky arrives. The second our eyes meet, we cry, and she rushes to the bed and hugs me. My parents leave us alone, and I'm glad because Becky is the only person I want to talk to about the accident. I tell her everything. I describe Jacob's last moments, and we sob and hold each other. Neither of us can believe he's truly gone.

The next day, a physiotherapist talks to me about my recovery, and I'm forced to get out of bed and start walking up and down the hospital corridors. I submit because I don't care, one way or another, about my recovery, and I can't be bothered to put up a fuss. I do what they tell me to do so that they won't keep harping and they'll leave me alone afterward.

Mostly, I feel anesthetized. When mindfulness happens, I cry, and my mother sits on the bed and holds me. She offers gentle words of comfort.

But sadly, comfort—even from my mother, who knows me best and loves me deeply and unconditionally—is a thousand miles away. Maybe a million. It's wherever Jacob is.

~

On the day of my discharge—after we're sent on our way with a set of crutches and a prescription for medications—we drive straight to the vet hospital to pick up Scooter.

My father pulls into the parking lot. Before he has a chance to shut off the engine, I open the back door and hobble out.

The weather is cold and gray, and the dampness seeps into my bones as I catch the scent of snow on the horizon. I can't help but think, grudgingly, as I assemble my crutches, about the sunshine and warmth on the summit of Cape Split five days ago.

Why did that happen? Was it a dirty trick from Mother Nature to lure us to a place we shouldn't have gone?

Mom scrambles to get out of the car and help me, but I wave her away. "I'm fine." I squeeze the handgrips, swing my body forward, and start toward the front entrance.

Mom jogs to keep up and overtakes me just in time to hold the glass door open. I hop into the reception area and make eye contact with the lady at the front desk. "We're here for Scooter."

Her expression warms. "Yes, he's been waiting for you. Have a seat, and we'll bring him out."

"How is he?" I ask impatiently, before she leaves.

"He's doing very well. He's quite a fighter. An incredible spirit."

I take from her response that she understands how stacked the odds had been against him. Clearly, no one believed that he would pull through, except for me. And I'm grateful that he has. He didn't give up. Maybe he's meant to be an example for me. If he could survive our ordeal, maybe I can too.

I move to a black leather chair, set my crutches aside, and sit down. My parents sit on chairs on either side of me. And we wait.

~

The door behind the reception desk opens, and a technician in navy blue scrubs brings Scooter out on a leash. "Here he is," she says cheerfully.

Scooter limps out with a cast on his back leg, and the sight of him tears me apart. He's wearing a plastic cone, and his back is marked with a grisly, stitched-up scar. There's a bandage over his left eye, and his head hangs low.

I watch him for a few seconds and feel sick to my stomach. I can't bear to imagine what he must have gone through on the beach and here in the hospital, alone.

"Scooter," I gently say as I sit forward and hold out my hands. God willing, the sound of my voice will help him remember his joyful life, from before.

His head lifts. He sniffs the air, and then his unbandaged eye finds me. His legs give out, and he falls onto the tile floor. I rise from the chair and hobble closer without my crutches. He sniffs my fingers, and his tail starts to wag. He licks my hands, and I nearly lose my balance.

Dad gets up to help steady me, and I start laughing and crying at the same time.

"There's my good boy. My sweet boy." I hug him and kiss his cheek over and over. "Everything's going to be okay now, my darling. I'm here." He keeps licking my cheeks, and it feels so good I can't stop crying.

~

Returning home from the hospital is harder than I expected. Physically, it's not easy for me or Scooter to climb the stairs to my bedroom, which is the first place I want to go. It's been an exhausting day, and all I want to do is curl up in bed with Scooter, hug him close, and sleep for a year. But when I walk into my room and rest my crutches against the dresser, I stare at the pink comforter, which I've had since junior high, and remember all the nights I talked to Jacob on the telephone. Back then, our relationship was new and exciting, full of promise. We never imagined that we wouldn't be together forever, or that one of us would die young.

Mom enters the room behind me, and I jump when she lays her hand on my shoulder.

"This room is full of memories," I say.

She nods slowly in agreement. "How can we make this easier for you? Would you like to sleep in the guest room? Or maybe we could think about redecorating, when you're ready."

"No," I reply. "I don't want to change a thing. I don't want to let anything go."

She touches my shoulder. "I understand, sweetheart. It's going to take time."

"*What's* going to take time?" I snap back, offended. "Forgetting about him? Moving on? Because I'm never going to do that. I *won't*." I limp to the bed and sit awkwardly on the edge of it. "He was it for me. The only one I wanted."

Tears come for me again. Panic, sorrow. I don't know how to handle it all.

"You're very young," Mom says. "You have your whole life ahead of you. Years and years to heal from this."

"But what if I don't want to forget him?" I reply, resisting the idea of an entire life, years and years, without Jacob.

Mom looks at me with sympathy and anguish and takes me into her arms. While she holds me, I try to imagine a future where I can laugh and feel joyful again, but I don't know how that will ever be possible. The only thing my heart knows, in this moment, is sadness.

PART TWO

YEARS AND YEARS

2006

CHAPTER FIVE

If the Ocean Was Beer

Halifax, Nova Scotia

It's a Saturday night, and I've let Becky talk me into going downtown, which means—in the language of Haligonians—pub-crawling or barhopping. I haven't had a night out in three months, and she's been after me to take some "me time" and consider the possibility that I've become a workaholic.

She's not wrong. After Jacob died, I couldn't face a return to university, where we'd shared our lives, so I dropped out of the business school permanently and set my sights on the University of Toronto, which offered a degree program in interior design. It had always been my end goal anyway, to learn the craft, and since my dad had been running the family business for decades without a business degree (he'd gone to community college to learn the plumbing trade and acquired management skills on the job), my parents supported my decision. Dad promised to help me with the business side of things if, and when, the time arrived.

So here I am, seven years later, president of my own fledgling interior design business. I have a modest office downtown on the historic Halifax Waterfront with two employees: a receptionist and bookkeeper named Gretchen, who keeps everything organized, and Jennie, my talented and creative assistant who shares my passion for decorating. She has an incredible work ethic, and sometimes I feel like she should be a full partner, but I'm the one with all the money at risk. It's my name on the lease and the line of credit.

Tonight, I'm meeting Becky for dinner at Salty's, a seafood restaurant with outdoor tables on the wharf overlooking the harbor. The hostess shows me to the table, where Becky is already seated with a glass of chilled chardonnay in front of her.

She removes her mirrored sunglasses, stands up, hugs me, and steps back to check out my outfit. "You came straight from work, didn't you. On a Saturday, no less."

"What gave me away?" I pull my chair out and hang my tote bag on the back of it.

"Hmm," she says, returning to her chair. "Could it be the blazer and button-down shirt? Or is it the loafers? It wouldn't hurt you to take your hair out of that tight ponytail every once in a while."

"It was a crazy day," I reply apologetically and settle into my chair. It's a gorgeous summer evening with a light breeze, and a sailboat is cruising by, heading toward open water. The aroma of fried crab cakes reaches my nose, and I realize I'm famished.

I return my attention to Becky. "You look gorgeous." She's wearing an off-the-shoulder, formfitting blue dress and dangly pearl earrings. Classy attire is one of the perks of her job managing a high-end clothing store in the Halifax Shopping Centre. "I can't believe how long your hair has gotten." It's shiny and wavy and reaches almost to her waist.

"That just goes to show how long it's been since we've seen each other." She takes hold of my hand from across the table. "How are you?"

"I'm good, actually," I reply with a slight frown, resenting the note of sympathy in her voice, which implies that I'm sad, lonely, and wasting away. "Something amazing happened at work," I tell her. "I got a call from Liz Tremblay's assistant, and she set up a time for us to chat on Tuesday."

My heart squeezes spasmodically at just the thought of it, because Liz and her husband, a major real estate developer, are local celebrities. They fight tirelessly for the rights of low-income homeowners and recently led a fundraising campaign to build a small apartment complex close to the children's hospital for family members who come from far away. The grand opening was all over the news last week.

"That sounds exciting," Becky says. "I wonder what she wants."

"I don't know, but I hope it involves decorating."

Becky reaches for her wine. "As long as you remember that there's more to life than work."

How can I forget when she's always trying to remind me that my life didn't end when Jacob died and that I still have plenty of living to do?

The problem is that her definition of living isn't the same as mine. She's been in high spirits lately because she's in a steady relationship with a guy named Mark, and she's optimistic about her future. I'm happy for her, of course, but I don't need that in my life right now. I don't want any complications. I just want to focus on growing my business.

"I appreciate the concern, but I'm perfectly fulfilled." I reach for my water glass and take a sip. "I wake up every morning and look forward to my day. Isn't that what matters?"

Becky sits back and folds her arms across her chest. "It depends on how big or small your bubble is."

The waiter's arrival couldn't come at a better time. He asks what I'll have to drink, and I point at Becky's wine. "I'll have whatever that is."

Becky rolls her eyes. "Seriously, do you not even care? Order what you want. They make a great cosmo here. You used to love cosmos."

I smile with resignation at the waiter. "Fine. Bring me a cosmo."

He disappears, and I pick up the menu. "I'm starving. What are you having?"

"The fish cakes, of course."

I slide the menu aside. "I'll get that too." I don't want to spend too much time thinking about food choices. I just want to talk to my friend about *her* life, not mine. "How's Mark?"

Her eyes light up. "Great. We're going whale watching next weekend."

"Oh, wow. Where?"

"Brier Island. He's had it booked for weeks. And we're going to Fredericton the week after that for his parents' thirtieth anniversary. His whole family's going to be there. I haven't met either of his brothers yet, so wish me luck." She reaches for her wine.

"They'll love you. Who wouldn't? You're wonderful."

She laughs. "And I love *you* for saying that."

We look at each other and sigh heavily, in perfect sync, and my mood takes a more serious turn. I'm not afraid to let it show, because Becky and I have always been open and honest with each other.

"I know we haven't seen each other much over the past few years," I say. "I was in Toronto, and you were here, and ever since I came back, I've been . . . well, you know . . . overwhelmed, trying to get the business going. But I just want you to know how important you are to me. You've been my rock ever since . . ." I lower my gaze to my lap because I can't say it.

"I understand." She looks toward the boats in the harbor. "We both went through hell together. But your hell was especially terrible, having been there and gone through it." She pauses and looks at me. "You're the only person, besides my parents, who really understands the weight of it all."

I nod, and my drink arrives in a fancy martini glass. I run my thumb and forefinger up and down the stem. "Do you ever talk to Mark about it?"

"I have," Becky replies. "And he's been wonderful. Very compassionate. But he never knew Jacob, so . . ."

"It's not something anyone can really share."

She reaches for her wine, and I raise my glass.

"To Jacob," she says in a somber tone. "And to us."

"May we all find happiness," I say.

It's only when I take the first sip that I realize I've included Jacob in my toast, as if we are, all three of us, still sitting together, on the Halifax Waterfront, looking forward to the unknown trajectory of our lives.

~

After a delicious dinner, which has included two more cosmos for me and two glasses of chardonnay for Becky, we find ourselves at the casino bar, where drinks are cheap. I've spent the evening venting about a client who can't make up her mind about modern rustic or a throwback to art deco, and Becky has opened up about Mark's obsession with *Star Wars* paraphernalia, predominantly Chewbacca but other characters as well from the original three films. Evidently, he has a small room in his basement with storage shelves and limited sunlight where he stores his dolls, though his preferred term is *action figures*. Becky is convinced he's in possession of a small fortune down there and that he should get everything insured.

Against our better judgment, Becky and I order a couple of dirty martinis, but we swear that these will be our last drinks of the night before we head home.

As the bartender slides the glasses toward us, Becky swivels on her stool, faces me, and raises her glass. "If the ocean was beer and I was a duck, I would swim to the bottom and drink myself up. But the ocean's not beer, and I'm not a duck, so let's drink these martinis and get totally messed up."

I tip my head back and laugh, but I reach my hand out before she takes a sip. "Wait, wait! I've got one." I raise my glass. "Pain makes you stronger. Tears make you braver. Heartbreak makes you wiser. And vodka makes you not remember any of that crap."

Becky laughs hysterically. "I love it! Bottoms up."

We sip our drinks, and then I slide off the barstool to hug her. "You're the best friend I've ever had." I have the uneasy feeling I might be slurring my words. "We'll be blood sisters forever. I love you so much."

"I love you too," she coos, and we hug cozily, swaying back and forth until her cell phone rings. She staggers back a little and rifles through her purse. "It must be Mark." She finds her phone and flips it open. "Hello? Hey, baby! You must be psychic. We just finished our drinks." She winks at me and nods. "Yes, we had a good time." She pauses. "We're at the casino bar. Okay. Sure. Yes, now's a good time to come. We'll meet you out front. Bye. I love you!" She snaps her phone shut and gives me a goofy smile. "He's the best."

"I'm so glad you're happy," I say drunkenly, fighting an urge to cry tears of joy, or maybe not joy.

She considers this, then grabs hold of my forearms and looks me straight in the eye. I find it hard to focus.

"But *you* need to be happy too!" she cries. "You need to love somebody again."

"I *do* love somebody," I reply. "I love *you*."

She smacks her forehead with her hand. "Oh, sweetheart. You're so awesome. You're my hero every day. But seriously . . . I don't want you to end up alone."

"I'm not alone," I explain. "I have Scooter, and my business, which I *love*. You have no idea, Becky. I'm serious. I want to marry it!"

She steps back and laughs. "You can't marry your business."

"Why not? We're perfect for each other. My business doesn't snore, and it pays all the bills."

I'm vaguely aware of a man on the barstool behind me. It's not until he rests his hand on my hip that I take notice, and my body clenches instantly with anger.

I turn around and take in his shaved head and pale, sweaty, pockmarked face. He's a big man, at least six feet tall, and thick around the middle.

"Ladies," he says. "You look like you're having a good time. Can I order us a fresh round?"

Suddenly, I feel completely sober, even though I'm not. "No thanks. We're just leaving."

He moves around us, casually, which blocks our exit from the barstools. "Don't break my heart. You girls can't leave when the night's still young." He rests his hand on his chest. "I'm Joe, and I've got a thousand dollars' worth of chips in my pocket. I could use the help of two beautiful women like you at the craps table. For luck."

Becky and I give each other a look, and I let out a breath of frustration. The night had been going so well. We'd been having such a good time.

"We're not here to gamble," Becky tells him.

"You don't have to gamble," he replies. "All you need to do is stand there and look pretty. Maybe blow on my dice." He wipes under his bulbous, oily nose and leers at Becky, which disgusts me. I glance uneasily around the bar. It's quite empty for a Saturday night.

"My boyfriend's on his way to get us," she says. "He'll be here any minute."

Joe grins and chuckles. "Yeah, sure. Any minute now." He waves his arm toward the casino. "Come on, ladies. One game. My friends are down there. We'll buy you drinks all night long. Everything on us. It'll be fun."

He puts his hand on my hip again, but this time I slap it away. "Do you *mind*?"

His bushy eyebrows lift, and when he talks, his breath stinks of onions and beer. "Don't be rude, sweetheart."

Honestly, I could barf. "I'm not your sweetheart."

While I wait for his stupid retort, something behind me distracts him. I glance over my shoulder, and there's a guy standing with his elbows on the bar, one foot planted on the brass rail. He's tall and younger than Joe, about my age. Broad shouldered. Has all his hair. He seems to be waiting to order a drink.

"How's it going?" he asks in a friendly tone as he turns toward us.

"All right," Joe replies uncertainly, which tells me that they've not met before. "What's it to you?"

The guy behind me shrugs. "I don't know. I was sitting over there watching the situation, and it seemed like you were being a bit pushy after the ladies said they were heading out."

Joe glares at him and rolls his thick neck. "Pushy."

"Yeah, just a bit." The guy seems totally relaxed and unthreatened. He speaks offhandedly. "I think these ladies just want to go home."

All my instincts are telling me to back away from this situation, but I can't move because the guy who has come to our rescue is standing directly behind me and I'm in the middle of this.

Suddenly the bartender, who looks more like an Olympic weight lifter, joins the conversation. He braces both fists on the bar.

"Everything all right over here?" His blue-eyed gaze swings from Joe to the guy behind me.

Joe downs the last of his beer. He sets the empty mug on the bar and wipes his thick hand across his mouth. "Thanks for the drink. I'll see you later."

He turns and stalks off. We all stand in silence, watching him go.

The guy behind me speaks to the bartender. "Thanks, Kev."

The bartender fills a mug of beer and slides it forward. "This one's on me."

Becky and I watch their exchange with interest.

"No, I still owe you from last night."

"You can fill up my gas tank—how about that?"

"You two know each other?" Becky asks.

I can't help but ask a follow-up question. "Or do you come here every night to defend unsuspecting women from annoying predators?"

The guy who came to our rescue takes a swig of beer. "Kevin and I used to be roommates. And sorry about that asshat. What was his name? Joe? He looked like a Joe. Nothing against Joes in general, but . . ." He sips his beer again and shakes his head. "I need to stop talking."

Maybe the martinis haven't completely worn off, because Becky starts laughing and can't seem to stop.

"You don't need to apologize for him," I say. "You're not responsible for who he is."

"If I was, I'd be very disappointed in myself."

We all chuckle, and Becky and I reclaim our seats at the bar. The bartender named Kevin claps his hands together. "How about two shots of tequila for you ladies, on the house."

Becky gives me a look. "Why not? How much worse can it get? Surely one shot of tequila won't put us over the edge."

"I'm not so sure about that," I reply with a dash of healthy skepticism.

Kevin fills two shot glasses, but at the last second, he adds a third for his friend and pushes forward a bowl of limes and a saltshaker.

I glance at Becky and shrug, lick my hand, sprinkle the salt, and toss back the shot. Hot fire torches my throat, so I quickly suck the lime and grimace. "I'm going to regret this in the morning."

"We all will," our heroic rescuer says. "Thank God for weekends." He smiles at me, and there's laughter in his eyes. All the tension from moments ago dissipates, and I lay my hand on his shoulder.

"Thank you. Really. That was so good of you . . . what you did."

"No worries," he says with ease and offers his hand. "I'm Nate."

"Sienna." I slide my hand into his and slowly shake it.

Our eyes remain fixed on each other's, and I feel a dizzying sensation—which I don't think is related to the tequila. Or the dirty martini. Or the cosmos. I haven't felt anything quite like it since Jacob and I first started looking at each other differently in high school.

Good God, how pathetic is it that my libido has been on hiatus for the past seven years? Not that I'm looking for anything, but this guy wakes me up to something—the long-lost thrill of certain feelings I've only ever experienced with Jacob. The sort of "complication" that I told Becky I wasn't interested in.

Becky's phone rings in her purse, and she pulls it out, flips it open. "Hey, baby." She listens for a moment. "No way. That's crazy." Another pause. "Yes, we're fine. We're just hanging out. Okay. Call me when you get here."

She drops her phone into her purse and turns to me. "A tractor trailer crashed on the Macdonald Bridge, so Mark's stuck there. Nothing's moving."

"Oh no," I reply.

"I hope no one was hurt," Kevin says. He looks to the far end of the bar, where an older couple had just sat down. "Excuse me." He slides a pen behind his ear and leaves us.

Becky and I reach for what's left in our martini glasses, when Nate says, "Hey, if you're hungry, I have a big plate of nachos at my table, and they're not going to eat themselves."

Becky looks at me and shrugs. "I could eat."

"Me too."

We follow Nate to a booth overlooking the water, which reflects the moon and the city lights. A gigantic plate of nachos is sitting there, barely touched. I stand for a few seconds, staring at it, wondering how he intended to eat all that by himself. More importantly, the melted cheese looks crusty and dry, and it doesn't take a rocket scientist to understand that he abandoned it when it was hot to help us get rid of Joe.

I feel guilty and grateful at the same time. I'm also ravenous, so I slide into the booth and rely on the good manners my mother taught me to make me wait until Nate digs in first.

Becky hesitates. "I need to use the ladies' room. You guys get started. I'll be back in a jiff."

I chuckle because I know her too well. She's playing matchmaker, but whatever. I pull a cheese-covered nacho from the plate and shove it into my mouth. It's a bit chewy after sitting out for too long, but it's still delicious, and I gobble greedily, then reach for another.

"So tell me, Sienna. What do you do?"

"I'm an interior designer."

"That sounds creative."

"It is, but I seem to spend most of my time worrying about bills, even though I have an office manager."

His eyebrows lift. "You own your own business?"

All I can do is nod because my mouth is full of cheese. I hold up a finger, then dig through my bag for my little stash of business cards and hand him one. By this time, I've finished chewing.

He reads it and lifts his gaze. His eyes are a mix of blue and gray with flecks of yellow, and I come to notice that his face is quite perfect—a strong jaw, straight nose, full lips. His teeth are perfect too. Clean and white.

"Sienna MacKay. Owner and creative director," he says, sounding impressed.

"Yes." I mention nothing more because I hate tooting my own horn. I was born missing whatever brain cells it requires to brag or bask in a spotlight. I prefer to let my work speak for itself. "It's a slow build," I tell him, "but we're getting there."

"I envy you." He holds up my card. "Can I keep this?"

"Of course."

He leans back, slides it into the front pocket of his faded blue jeans, and then reaches for a nacho chip and uses it to scoop some green peppers and sour cream.

"How about you?" I ask. "What do you do?"

"Law school," he replies flatly.

"Law school. Well done. And you envy *me*?"

He shakes his head. "Truth is I'm conflicted about it."

"Why?"

"Because it's not what I want to do with my life."

"Then why are you doing it?" I ask matter-of-factly.

"Because I'm a jellyfish."

I frown and wipe my mouth with a napkin. "You'll have to explain that to me."

"I'm not sure I can," he replies, "because I can't even explain it to myself. Ask Kevin. He'll give you a better answer."

I glance over at Kevin, who's scooping ice cubes into a cocktail shaker and hunting around for the right liquor bottle. "He looks busy."

"Yeah, well . . . the truth is I'm fighting to resist my basic impulses."

I chuckle. "I'm confused. But it sounds intriguing. What might those impulses be?"

He leans forward, rests his arms on the table, and gives me a slightly devious look, but it comes with a hint of a grin. "If it were up to me, I'd go to cooking school and become a chef."

I draw back slightly. "Wow. That's not the answer I was expecting."

He reaches for another nacho. "Eventually I'd open my own restaurant. Something classy. Fine dining. Creative presentations. Works of art on a plate, you know?"

"I *do* know. But why isn't it up to you?"

He wags his finger at me. "That's the burning question, right there. I've been asking myself that a lot lately, in my own mind, ever since I started an eight thirty a.m. class in corporate tax law, which I despise. I hate it more and more every day, and I'm not sure where it'll bottom out. Me flunking the exam, probably."

He sits back, reaches for the butter knife on the table, and pretends to slice his wrist.

I know he's joking, but still, it's sad. "So what's the solution?"

He sets the knife down and takes a deep breath, lets it out. "I don't want to disappoint my father. And therein lies the conflict. He's proud of me these days, which wasn't always the case."

"Meaning?"

He shrugs his very muscular shoulders. "My grades weren't good in high school, and what can I say? I hung out with a wild crowd. We skipped a lot of classes, and we liked to party."

"Yet you got into law school," I reply.

He glances at his reflection in the dark window. "I'm sure that came as a shock to many. My high school English teacher probably had a coronary."

I watch his expression for a moment while he stares out the window. "You must have found that satisfying on some level," I say.

"On every level imaginable." He looks at me again with an infectious grin, and I smile in return. "But I worked hard for it," he adds. "When I first started at Dal, for my undergrad, I took classes I actually found interesting."

"What was your major?"

"Psychology." He points at Kevin. "And now I have better friends, like that guy, who's super competitive, which rubbed off on me. I'd never met anyone who was competitive in the classroom before. Only in sports."

I nod with understanding.

A waiter comes by to check on us. Nate tells him he can bring the bill anytime, and I'm a little disappointed that the night is coming to an end. Then I wonder where Becky is. I spot her on a stool at the bar, talking to Kevin.

I return my attention to Nate. "So you enjoyed the path to law school," I say because I want to keep the conversation going. "But now that you're there, it's not what you thought it would be, and you don't want to disappoint your father. But maybe he'd be pleased to see you following your passion."

Nate shakes his head exaggeratingly. "Oh no. He's been grooming me to follow in his footsteps since I was . . . I can't even remember."

"What does he do?" I ask.

"He's a criminal lawyer and has done very well for himself—big house, fancy car. But he wants the same for me, and the truth is most restaurants fail."

I feel bad for Nate, because I know how good it feels to love your work. "Can't you just tell him that you don't need a fancy car and you'd prefer to go to work every day and love what you do? Maybe he'll surprise you and understand."

Nate scratches the back of his neck. "I highly doubt it." He stares at me for a moment, and I feel a strange fluttering in my belly. His eyes are wistful. "Did your parents ever give you trouble when you told them what you wanted to do?"

I feel a little guilty answering the question. "No, they were very supportive. Especially my dad because he runs his own business, and he was keen to help me out with that side of things."

"What kind of business?"

"He's a plumber," I reply. "And he, too, has done very well for himself. Big house and fancy car. That is, if you consider a Chevy Silverado fancy."

Nate laughs. "Beauty is in the eye of the beholder."

"Always."

The waiter comes by with the bill, and Nate thanks him, then reaches into the back pocket of his jeans for his wallet. He counts out a few bills and drops them onto the table.

I catch Becky in my peripheral vision, walking toward us. "Mark's out front," she says flatly.

My stomach drops. I'm not sure what's happening here. Or maybe I am. I'm feeling slightly infatuated, and it's a shock to my system because I haven't felt this way in ages and ages.

But how can this be anything but superficial when I've only just met the person sitting across from me?

I regard Nate with a tilt of my head. "Gotta go." I begin to slide across the leather bench. "Thanks for sharing your nachos."

Nate slides out of the booth as well. "My pleasure."

He's a gentleman. Polite and respectful. I feel another tug in the pit of my belly, followed by a wave of dread, knowing that I'll probably never see this man again.

"Well . . ." I sling my tote bag over my shoulder. "This was fun."

Becky starts to back away, and I wonder why she's so impatient to leave. "It was nice meeting you."

I have no choice but to follow her, until Nate calls after us. "Wait a second!" I stop and turn, and he approaches. "This probably sounds like a line after that jerk came on to you, but can I call you? Maybe we could have coffee sometime."

Trying not to sound flustered while my cheeks are flushing with heat, I say, "Sure. You have my card."

Nate smiles and starts to back away. "Get home safely."

"You too," I reply and follow Becky out of the bar and across the casino floor to the main entrance, where Mark is parked outside at the curb. I open the back door of his black Volkswagen Jetta and climb in.

He glances over his shoulder at me. "You called for a taxi?"

"We did."

Becky slides into the front seat and wraps her arms around his neck. "I'm so happy to see you."

"Someone's had a few too many margaritas," he mutters with humor as we pull away from the curb.

~

After the martinis and tequila shots, I'm shocked when I wake up the next morning with no headache. I've slept in a little, though. It's 9:30 a.m., which I consider to be wildly self-indulgent, at least for me, because I'm a morning person.

Scooter doesn't seem to mind. He's stretched out diagonally across my bed, snoring. I nudge him three times before he rolls over, yawns, and jumps to the floor for his morning walk around the neighborhood.

We live in an apartment in the South End of Halifax, in a historic building with marvelous character, but there's no elevator. It's a bit of a climb up a wide central staircase with wrought iron railings to reach our cozy abode, but Scooter and I can both use the exercise.

He's eight years old now and comes to work with me every day. I'm convinced he's proud of himself—as he should be—since earning the title of office mascot, which includes the perk of a dried liver treat upon arrival each morning. The clients adore him because not only is he a gorgeous blond Lab, but he's a charmer as well and a big old softy.

He treats everyone as if they're his long-lost best friend and makes them feel special. He wags his tail, but he's calm about it, and he doesn't create havoc like he once did when he was a puppy.

Quite frankly, he's my rock. I don't know how I could have survived the past seven years without him.

~

After Scooter and I return from our morning walk, I'm in the middle of spooning coffee grounds into the coffee machine when my cell phone rings. I retrieve it from the kitchen table and flip it open. "Hello?"

"Is this too soon to call?" a male voice asks, and I recognize it immediately.

"Yes, it is," I reply. "Have you no self-control?"

Nate chuckles. "Clearly not. It must have been the tequila shot."

"Tequila can make people do shocking things." I press the red button on my coffee maker, and it starts to gurgle. "I'm joking of course. It's nice to hear from you. What time did you get home last night?"

"I left not long after you did."

"You didn't hit the blackjack table?"

There's a pause. "I'm not much of a gambler."

"Yet you were in the casino bar on a Saturday night." I can admit to myself that I'm probing for information because I'm curious about this man. I want to know more about him—more than what he told me last night, which was quite a lot.

"I could say the same to you," he replies.

"Touché." I'm feeling impishly giddy.

"I'm calling to see if you'd like to go for a walk today," he says. "Point Pleasant Park? After lunch?"

I fight to stay quiet as I jump around my kitchen and make a screaming face. Then I stand still and take a breath. "That sounds like fun," I calmly reply. "Can I bring my dog?"

"Actually, I was going to ask you the same question."

"You have a dog?" My interest is piqued. "What kind?"

"She's a dachshund named Dolly. What's yours?"

"A big, adorable Labrador retriever. Sometimes he's clumsy and not too bright, but he loves little dogs. His name is Scooter."

"I can't wait to meet him."

We set a time to connect at the ice cream stand, and it's not until I hang up the phone and tell Scooter what's happening that I begin to feel strange about it. Scooter was Jacob's dog, and now I'm taking him to meet another man—a man whom I'm attracted to.

I remind myself that it's been seven years since the accident, and I should be ready to move on by now, like Becky says. But when I imagine walking in the park with Nate, talking and laughing and having a good time, I feel disloyal, along with a bone-deep sadness, followed by a heavy glut of guilt.

CHAPTER SIX

Lightheadedness

The parking lot is crammed with cars. It's a gorgeous, sun-drenched Sunday afternoon, and the park is teeming with young families, strollers, dogs, and runners. There's a long line at the ice cream stand.

I find a parking spot, shut off the engine, and check how I look in the rearview mirror. I've worn my hair down today, and I used my straightener, so it's smooth, dark, and shiny. My mascara hasn't smudged, but I need some lipstick. I dig into my purse to search for it, quickly apply it, and snap the top back on. With one last look at myself in the mirror, I grow self-conscious as I rub gently at the scar below my jawbone and the longer one down the left side of my neck to my collarbone. The scars on my forearm are especially grotesque, which is why I wear long sleeves most of the time, even on hot days like today. I wish they'd fade more with time, but they never seem to.

But whatever. There's not much I can do about that.

I turn to Scooter, who's sitting in the passenger seat beside me, grinning from ear to ear. "Ready for a walk?" His mouth snaps shut, and his eyes pin to mine. "Then let's get going."

I step out and move around to the passenger side, where I clip the leash on to his collar. He leaps out of the car and onto the asphalt and darts in multiple directions. He sniffs everywhere, dragging me forward, tail wagging. I barely have a chance to lock the car door.

Then I see Nate. He's walking toward me from a parking space near the stone wall along the water. Trotting beside him like a little queen—not dragging him—is an adorable long-haired dachshund.

"Hi there," Nate says. "This must be Scooter."

Scooter's tail starts wagging in double time as he sniffs Dolly's nose. They circle around each other and get tangled up in the leashes. Nate and I scramble to restore order. Only then do I focus my full attention on him. "Hi."

"Hi," he says with a grin.

If I'd entertained any notions that he might be less handsome in the light of day, when I'm sober, I was dead wrong. This guy could be a movie star.

"What a great day," I say, squinting up at the bright blue sky.

"Couldn't be better. Thanks for coming."

"Thanks for the invite."

We watch our dogs socialize and make sure they're okay with each other. Then our eyes meet again, and we smile. My cheeks are going to hurt if I keep this up.

"Shall we walk?" Nate asks.

I secretly love that he uses the word *shall.* "Sure." I head toward the path along the water. Scooter leads the way for all of us, his long tail wagging up a storm.

~

By the time we pass what was once known as Hangman's Beach and are heading toward the point, chatting, I'm consciously aware of my libido, which seems to be waking up after a long hibernation. Nate looks darn good as he stops to let Dolly do her business at the edge of the path. I can't help but admire his muscular physique under faded blue jeans and the way his white T-shirt stretches across his back and shoulders when he bends to pick up her droppings. A little shiver of excitement dances up my spine, and I'm strangely relieved—because I was beginning to fear that all my sexual impulses were long dead, never to be resurrected.

Unaware of my eyes on him, Nate straightens, ties a knot in the poop bag, and strolls along the path to drop it in a trash can. As I watch him, I think about Jacob, and I contemplate how young we were when we first fell in love. Jacob was never muscular like Nate. He was thin and lanky, but only because he'd never had the chance to mature and grow into a man's body.

I wonder what he might have looked like today if we'd never hiked up Cape Split . . .

Quickly, I shut my eyes and remind myself that it's not healthy to slide into that old pattern of obsessing over the unanswerable question: What if we hadn't gone?

Nate and Dolly return, and I steer my gaze toward the mouth of the harbor. The sky is blue, but a ribbon of fog hangs low over the horizon. It'll probably roll in later and bring a damp chill with it.

"Hey," Nate says. "You look lost in thought."

I force a smile. "Sorry. I was just thinking about something."

I glance down at Scooter, who's been sitting and staring at me anxiously for the past few minutes. Sometimes I wonder if he can read my mind. Maybe not in words but in feelings and memories.

I start to walk, and he remains at my side, glancing up at me frequently. Clearly he's worried.

"I hope this isn't too personal," Nate says, "but after you left last night, Kevin told me about a conversation he had with your friend."

My stomach drops, and I stare at the path in front of me. "With Becky?"

"Yeah. She mentioned that she lost her brother a few years ago at Cape Split, and that you were with him. That you both fell off the mountain. I'm so sorry. I can't even imagine that."

Becky, Becky, Becky. This always happens when she drinks. She talks about Jacob, even to strangers, and she cries.

"It's been more than a few years," I say. "Seven, actually."

We continue walking slowly onto a grassy area, where Scooter sniffs through a lush patch of clover.

"Can you talk about it?" Nate asks.

I can, but I don't like to. Nevertheless, I don't want to be rude. "A lot of what I remember about that day is blurred," I try to explain. "Like a fever dream. As if it wasn't real." I pause and glance up at him. "My parents sent me to a therapist after it happened, and he was very focused on getting me to understand the stages of grief. He wanted me to categorize every thought and feeling I had, to try and sort each emotion into one of the stages, like putting pills in a pillbox for each day of the week. Looking back on it, I think he wanted me to understand that my feelings were normal. But he constantly pushed me to move forward through each stage to reach the final state of acceptance."

"That sounds intense," Nate replies. "And did you? Reach that final state?"

"Back then?" I chuckle bitterly. "I don't think so. The whole process was too rigid, like a formula in a textbook. But I was all over the place emotionally, back and forth between denial and anger. I was a mess."

Scooter leads us toward an empty bench close to the water.

"I've never lost anyone important in my life," Nate tells me. "At least not yet. So I feel a bit . . . I don't know. Lucky. And at the same time wet behind the ears because I have no personal experience with death."

"Just enjoy the lucky part." I give him a sidelong glance. "Because that experience will come eventually, whether you like it or not. No one lives forever." We move around the bench, sit down, and get the dogs settled. "But grief isn't just limited to death," I add. "You can experience grief from all sorts of things—like the death of a dream. Becoming a chef, for instance. You might not even be aware that you're grieving about that."

Nate leans forward and scratches behind Dolly's ears. "What's your diagnosis, Dr. Sienna? Am I in a state of denial? Anger, more likely," he adds.

"I don't know. I'm not a psychologist. I was just thinking about you and your restaurant. I'm not sure why."

Dolly moves into the shade beneath the bench, and Nate sits back. "First of all, I love that you're thinking about me and my restaurant."

I chuckle.

"So let's talk about this," he continues. "Let's imagine that I let go of that dream, and I make it through law school. Then I finally conquer all the stages of grief and accept that this dream of mine is truly dead. No cooking school in Paris or Italy. No restaurant. No flavor creations with . . ." He pauses and looks up at the sky, thoughtfully. "Cilantro and cream. Or foie gras and mint."

"Yum," I say.

After a moment, he bends forward and rubs the top of Dolly's little head. "It'll be corporate tax law and calculators forever. A life of quiet, passive resignation." He regards me with humor. "I think I might prefer to hang out in the anger stage. Then at least I could keep blaming my dad for everything bad in my life."

I nod with understanding as I gaze out over the water. "That's one way of looking at it."

Nate lets out a groan. "Enough about my failed ambitions. I was hoping to impress you today. So much for that."

He crosses one leg over the other, faces me on the bench, and rests his arm along the back of it. I feel a tingling sensation on the side of my neck, as if his hand is creating static electricity there.

"Becky told Kevin that you haven't dated anyone since you lost your boyfriend," he says.

I shake my head derisively. "Becky has loose lips when she drinks."

"Will this get her in trouble?" he asks playfully.

"I suppose not. It's not as if it's classified information." The sun is hot on my shoulders under my white cotton sweater, and I fan myself with my hand. "But what she said isn't entirely correct. I *have* gone out on a bunch of dates, but none of them went anywhere."

He leans a little closer, looks me straight in the eye, and speaks softly. "Maybe you haven't gone out with the right person yet."

A thrilling energy dances across my skin. I don't think anyone has ever been so smooth and seductive with me. Not even Jacob. And I don't hate it.

"You could be right," I reply.

One side of his mouth curls up in a half smile, and he touches my shoulder with the tip of his forefinger. It's a gentle sweep, as if he's brushing a tiny blackfly away, but I feel it all the way down to my toes. The entire left side of my body erupts in goose bumps—the good kind—and I swallow heavily.

"If this were a first date," he says, "would you consider it worthy of a second?"

"I'm not sure yet." I check my watch. "We're only a half hour in, but so far so good."

He grins, and his cheerfulness reaches his eyes. "I think we have really good odds, because look . . ." He gestures toward Scooter and Dolly, who are now sitting beside each other at our feet, watching a tour boat go by. Their heads are moving in perfect unison.

I start to laugh. "They're so cute. They seem to like each other."

"How could they not?" He slides a glance at me. "Because they know *we* like each other."

"We do."

Nate smiles. "Shall we keep walking?"

There it is again. *Shall we . . .*

With a shiver of pleasure, I rise from the bench and follow him. All anxiety gone, Scooter follows too.

~

After our walk, Nate and I return to our cars and realize we're both famished.

"I'd suggest a restaurant," he says, "but we can't leave our dogs in the car."

"We could take them home and meet up somewhere," I propose.

"Or . . ." He gives it some thought. "Why don't you come over to my place. I could barbecue a couple of steaks. I live not far from here." He points toward town. "I'm on South Park."

"No kidding. I'm on South Park as well."

"Not Park Victoria . . ."

My shoulders slump. "No, but I'm only a few blocks away." Scooter tugs at his leash to reach a spilled ice cream cone on the asphalt. "That would have been weird if we lived in the same building."

"Very weird," Nate says while I gain control of Scooter. He looks down at Dolly, who's panting heavily. "I should get this gal back to the car and give her a drink."

"Same with this guy."

We stare at each other for a few seconds, and I feel the same excitement I felt when I was dancing around my kitchen.

"I'm on the sixteenth floor," he tells me as he backs away with Dolly trotting beside him. "Sixteen oh five. And bring Scooter, of course."

"Great. I'll see you in a bit."

I watch him walk off, but then I feel creepy staring at him, so I turn and get Scooter's water bowl out of the trunk. The poor boy is panting, and his tongue is hanging out. I laugh because I can totally relate.

~

I decide to make a quick pit stop at home to change out of this sweaty T-shirt, but I end up foraging frantically through my closet for something sexier. But not *too* sexy. It needs to look casual, like I just threw it on.

Sadly, nothing I own is quite right. If only Becky were here to put my look together. She'd know how to make great-tasting lemonade out of the rancid old fruit on these hangers.

I step back and concede that I own nothing a normal woman my age would wear to a hot guy's apartment for a steak dinner. But of course I'm not normal. All I do is work, so all I have are work clothes. Stylish, yes, but not great for hanging out on a sixteenth-floor balcony on a Sunday afternoon, sipping a beer.

In the end, I choose a sundress from a wedding I attended four years ago and a pair of well-worn flip-flops, with my white crocheted sweater.

Should I bring a bottle of wine?

Definitely yes. I turn from my pathetic excuse for a closet, because a bottle of something—anything—will help distract Nate from my frumpy dress. I dash to the pantry, open the door, and tip my head back to look up at the top shelf. Thank goodness. I just so happen to have a very decent bottle of red, which I've been saving for something special.

Next, I go to the bathroom and check myself out in the mirror. All I need to do is freshen up the foundation, add a little blush, brush my teeth, and we're off to the races.

A short time later, after walking two blocks in the heat, I'm buzzed into Nate's air-conditioned high-rise apartment building, and I step onto the elevator with Scooter. As soon as the doors slide closed in front of us, nervous butterflies invade my belly. I'm buzzing with excitement and anticipation as I ascend. How long has it been since I've felt like this?

But as I approach Nate's floor, those feelings are met by a surge of guilt and discomfort.

I can't bear the thought of Jacob seeing me with Nate. It's a ridiculous notion, and the rational part of my brain knows it. Jacob has been gone for many years, and I've accepted it. Truly, I have. I also understand, rationally, that it's important for me to move on and live a full life, which is why I'm riding up sixteen floors in this elevator.

But it doesn't change the fact that I've always felt like Jacob is "up there" somewhere, watching over me like a guardian angel, cheering me on or pulling strings to help me out. Occasionally, I still talk to him when I'm alone. I say things like, "Hey, babe, what did you think of that meeting today? Did I crush it?" And when I talk to Scooter, I often tell him how proud Jacob is of the wonderful dog he's become, and I look up and point at the ceiling. Scooter looks up, too, and he wags his tail.

The elevator slows, and *bing!*—the doors slide open. Scooter and I step off.

As we walk down the long carpeted corridor, I urge myself to accept that it's time for me to stop talking to my late boyfriend in the ceiling, or the sky, or wherever he is—because even if he's watching me, I'm fairly certain that he would want me to move on, to live a full life, and to be happy.

I reach apartment 1605 and knock. It takes a while for Nate to answer, and when he finally opens the door, he's not smiling.

"Sienna," he says in a cool tone.

I'm immediately unnerved, but I smile anyway and hold up the wine. "Hi. I brought this."

"Thanks. Come in." He takes it from me and turns away.

I hesitate briefly and wonder if he's one of those hot-and-cold people who make you feel constantly on edge, worrying that you did something wrong. But despite my reservations, I push on. I lead Scooter inside and unhook the leash from his collar. I kick off my flip-flops and walk into the bright, sunlit living room, where I see two people sitting at opposite ends of the sofa.

Nate gestures toward them. "Sienna, these are my parents, Bill and Joan Palmer. This is Sienna MacKay," he says to them.

They both rise, which gives me a moment to gather my composure as I move forward to shake their hands.

Joan is an attractive woman with impeccable taste and style. She wears her blond hair in a loose bun, and her pale-yellow dress complements her complexion. I'm guessing it's Italian linen.

As for Bill, based on Nate's description, he's not quite what I expected. He's partially bald and a few inches shorter than Joan. I can't help but think, as I hold my hand out across the coffee table, that Nate got his good looks from his mother's side of the family, while his controlling father looks like a little weasel.

"Mr. Palmer," I say. "It's a pleasure to meet you."

"Call me Bill." His handshake is firm.

I shake Joan's hand as well, and they both sit down again.

Sensing some bad energy in the room, I quietly take a seat.

"Can I get you a drink?" Nate asks as he examines the label on the bottle of wine I brought. "This looks good. We might as well open it now." He retreats to the kitchen and speaks over his shoulder. "Mom? Dad? Would you like some?"

"No thanks," Bill says. "We can't stay."

Yet they remain on the sofa, staring at me as if they're sizing me up.

I glance around the room politely. It doesn't look like a student apartment. All the furniture is crisp and new, and the walls are tastefully adorned with modern art. I wonder if Nate's parents hired a decorator, or perhaps Joan, with her exquisite taste, took care of furnishing the place.

"This is a lovely apartment," I say.

Thankfully, Joan initiates a conversation. "Nate tells us you're an interior designer."

"That's right." I relax a little and sit back. "I started my own company last year."

"That was ambitious of you," Joan replies, while Bill simply watches me with hard eyes.

I shrug a shoulder. "Not really. I come from a family of entrepreneurs, so it seemed like the right way to go."

"Your father's a plumber," Bill asserts.

I clear my throat. "Yes. That's his trade, but he runs his own company."

Bill lounges back on the sofa and scrutinizes me with narrow eyes, as if he wants to run me over with his car.

Thankfully, Nate returns with a glass of wine and hands it to me. I take hold but set it on the coffee table because I don't want to be the only one drinking.

Still standing, Nate glances at the gigantic clock on the wall. Then he looks at his mother. "You said you have to get going?"

Joan observes him for a few seconds, then taps her knee and speaks jauntily. "Yes, we're off to the Chester Yacht Club to meet some friends."

She and Bill rise and make their way around the coffee table. "It was nice to meet you," she says.

"You as well." I decide to stay put and let Nate escort them to the door, where they linger, speaking in hushed, angry tones.

I wish I could eavesdrop, but the balcony doors are wide open, and horns are honking in the street. It sounds like a wedding procession.

Eventually, Joan calls out to me. "Goodbye, Sienna!"

"Bye!" I reply with a pretense of gregariousness.

They leave, and Nate shuts the door gently behind them. He stands for a few seconds with his back to me, his hand on the doorknob.

When at last he turns around, he spreads his arms wide. "I apologize for that."

"For what?" I ask innocently.

He inclines his head and gives me a look. "You can be honest." He moves into the kitchen and emerges with another glass of wine. "You think my dad's a douchebag."

I laugh. "Not at all." It's a lie, but I don't want to insult his family. "He's intimidating—that's all."

"You picked up on that." Nate shakes his head at the situation and sips his wine.

"I take it you weren't expecting a visit from them?"

"No," he replies, "but they often do that—show up unannounced to make sure I'm not sleeping off a hangover in the middle of the day."

The rancor in his tone gives me a touch of unease. "Does that happen often?"

"Not since high school," Nate says, "but my dad's never going to let me forget it." He gestures toward the sliding glass door. "Let's go onto the balcony. I could use some fresh air."

I'm intensely aware that we're on the sixteenth floor, and my fear of heights causes my heart to race. I take a few calming breaths—one of many coping skills I've learned through years of exposure therapy—and follow him outside.

A small barbecue stands at one end of the balcony, and a bistro table with two chairs occupies the other. Nate moves to the railing, but the sight of him leaning over to look down at the treetops in Victoria Park is too much for me. I feel lightheaded, so I step sideways and press my back up against the glass door.

"I should apologize," Nate says, turning to face me. "I was inspired by our conversation earlier, but I shouldn't have gotten into it with my parents when you were on your way. It was bad timing."

"What do you mean . . . gotten into it?"

"I told them I wasn't enjoying law school," he explains, "and I floated the idea of dropping out and going to culinary school instead. Maybe Europe or Toronto."

I strive to focus on what Nate's saying to me and not the sixteen-story drop behind him. "How did they respond?"

He shakes his head. "Let's just say the idea was not well received."

"Did they *both* feel that way? What about your mom?"

"It doesn't matter because she'd never go against my dad. Not even privately, to me. They're old school that way. Dad's the head of the household, and Mom falls in line."

"I see."

Nate and I stand for a moment, staring at each other.

"Is *your* family like that?" he asks with drawn brows.

I don't want to rub salt in the wound, but I do want to be honest with him. "No, my father respects my mom's opinions. They don't always agree on everything, but they talk it out, and he'll admit if he's wrong. She's the same."

"Do they act like that with you too?"

I nod. "Yes. I always felt like I could win a debate with them if I could convince them to see my point of view. Usually, we'd come to a compromise."

Nate drops his gaze to his wine and sips it. "I shouldn't have mentioned you at all, but I was just so inspired by how you followed your dream and made it real, and how your family supported you. I told them all about that, but they just sat there, frowning."

"I guess that explains the chilly reception," I say. "They probably hate me now. Think I'm a bad influence."

"No, I've talked about quitting law school before. So don't worry about it."

"Easy for you to say."

He glances over his shoulder, down at the treetops. "It is, actually, because I can't keep letting my dad make decisions for me. If he's angry, that's his problem."

I shift my weight to brace both feet squarely on the concrete floor of the balcony. "Maybe he'll get over it eventually, if he sees that you're happy."

Nate sips his wine. "Not likely. He can't stomach defeat, and he holds a grudge like nobody's business. He has a cousin who backed out of a real estate deal they were considering together, and to this day, that cousin is dead to him. They were best friends when they were kids, but Dad hasn't spoken to him in over ten years."

"That's sad."

"Yes, but that's who he is. He's a stubborn son of a bitch, and he won't see anyone's point of view except his own. And I get the worst of it because . . . oh, I don't know. I think he wants sons he can brag about."

A cool breeze blows through the leafy trees below us, and an ambulance, siren blaring, makes its way along Tower Road toward the hospital.

"You'll figure it out," I say.

He smiles at me, and the moment feels intimate. "I guess I'll have to, before I flunk a class. I'm not sure which would be worse for my dad: his son getting a D in tax law or moving to Paris to learn how to cook." He chuckles cynically. "Honestly? I think he'd prefer the D. As long as I graduate."

I laugh as well, though it's not funny. It's incredibly sad.

"I envy you," he says. "I wish I had the support you got from your family."

"I'll never take it for granted," I reply. "This career—and the dream I had—is what got me through the past seven years. It gave me a reason to get out of bed in the mornings. And when you want to be creative and you can't be, it's like being deprived of oxygen."

Nate gestures toward me with a hand. "See? *You* get it. I wish *he* could."

Our gazes hold, and I feel a type of euphoria I'd forgotten existed. It's both emotional and physical, concurrently.

"What would you do if you were in my shoes?" he asks.

I shrug. "I can't answer that, because I don't know how badly you want to be a chef or how important it is for you to not disappoint your parents."

We look at each other with understanding until I take a brave step away from the wall. "Maybe I could provide better guidance if I could taste that steak you promised me."

Nate's expression brightens. "That sounds fair. But you'll be honest?"

I give him a questioning look. "About the steak or your future?"

"Both would be nice."

I consider this request. "For tonight, I promise to be honest about the steak."

"Fine," he says and rubs his hands together with enthusiasm. He turns to the barbecue, raises the lid, and begins to clean the grate with a wire brush. "I don't want to sound overconfident, but I think you should prepare to be amazed."

"I shall," I reply with anticipation.

I look down at the bistro table and chairs. In an effort to feel more relaxed, I slide the whole set away from the railing and closer to the wall so that I can sit down comfortably and watch him work.

CHAPTER SEVEN

Floating Out of My Chair

"You went to his apartment?" Becky asks the following morning when she calls me at work. "And he cooked dinner for you?"

"Not just dinner. It was the best friggin' steak I've ever tasted in my life. And I don't know what he did to those mushrooms, but I thought I was going to pass out."

She laughs. "You sure they weren't magic mushrooms?"

"Very funny. They were the normal kind, but the way he slowly sautéed them in butter with just a touch of cream . . . and he had a salad with a dressing that he made from scratch. I don't know what was in it, but . . . oh, my God . . . it was fantastic." My mouth waters at just the thought of it, and other things.

"Okay," Becky says, "enough about the food. How did it go otherwise? Did you make out?"

I grin as I flip through some fabric samples, but I can't bring myself to share those details with Becky, because she's Jacob's sister. "None of your business," I reply teasingly.

"Come on. Don't leave me hanging." When I don't respond, she lets out a sigh. "Fine. But at least tell me what you talked about."

I move from my desk to the sideboard against the wall, where I keep my paint chips. "We talked a lot about how I started my business. He had questions, so we're meeting for lunch tomorrow and he's coming to see my office."

"Oooh. Well played. He'll be impressed."

"I'm not trying to impress him," I tell her. "But I do want to help him out because he seems lost. He's not enjoying law school, because he wants to be a chef, and he's frustrated, which I totally understand. I can't imagine how I would have felt if my parents tried to talk me out of this career. If my dad had forced me to go to plumbing school."

"Oh, good Lord," she says. "No way. Just no."

I chuckle. "Nothing against the plumbing profession. Dad loves his work, and he's done well for himself, but I would have been miserable."

I lay a fabric sample next to a paint chip and dismiss the color combination.

"Now that we've gotten that out of the way," Becky says, "do you want to come over for dinner tonight? Mark left for Montreal this morning, and I'm on my own. He's not back until Thursday."

"How about tomorrow night instead?" I reply. "I have that phone call with Liz Tremblay in the morning, and so I'd like to prepare."

"Oh, I forgot about that. Let's do dinner tomorrow, and good luck."

"Thanks." We hang up, and I return to my paint and fabric samples, but it's no easy task to keep my focus when I can't stop thinking about Nate.

Because yes. We did make out on his sofa. And sweet Mary, Mother of God, it was even better than the mushrooms.

~

Twenty-four hours later, I take the call from Liz Tremblay, CEO at Ten Millennium, the leading real estate agency in the city.

"What can I do for you?" I ask after congratulating her on the grand opening of the apartment complex near the children's hospital that she and her husband had been working on.

She doesn't mince words and leads with a compliment. "You did some design work for friends of mine recently, and I love what you did. You have great style, Sienna."

My cheeks flush with heat, but I manage to keep my cool. "That's kind of you to say. Thank you."

"I've been obsessed with your website lately," she continues. "I can't stop looking at your photo gallery. You've got me totally inspired, which is why I'm calling—because I'd love for you to come by and discuss my decor. I've decided to change the whole look of my house from top to bottom, and you're the person I'd like to help me with that."

My belly explodes with butterflies because I know her house well, at least the exterior. It's a giant Victorian on a massive corner lot in the South End of the city. Every holiday season, the street becomes clogged with traffic when people drive by to view their Christmas decorations, including Santa's sleigh and reindeer in their front yard.

"I'd love to pop by and have a look," I say. "I'm inspired already. When would be a good time for you?"

We discuss our schedules, and she's keen to get started immediately, so we set up an appointment for the following afternoon.

"But before we hang up," she adds, "I'd like to float something else by you as well, and you don't have to decide anything today. We can talk about it in more detail tomorrow, but I'd like you to have some time to percolate."

Anticipation ripples through me. "I'm all ears."

Again, she gets right to the point. "My company could use a stager to get our properties ready for the market, but it's tough to find good people. There aren't many of you out there, and we can't always get someone when we need them. Half the time they're already booked up by Realtors from other agencies. So I'd like to offer you a retainer to be the exclusive stager for Ten Millennium."

Ten Millennium is the agency that handles everything for her husband's real estate development and construction firm. I'm in shock, unable to speak.

"I promise we'd keep you busy," she adds, "and you could of course continue doing work for other clients who aren't our competitors. By that I mean other Realtors selling houses and commercial properties."

I blink a few times as I ponder this. "Realtors all over the city make up more than half my clientele," I explain. "They're my bread and butter."

"I'm aware," she replies, "which is why I'm offering you a retainer. You can name your price, whatever you think is reasonable, and we'll negotiate from there. Take some time to think about that before we chat again tomorrow."

My stomach is backflipping. A regular retainer would take away the stress of slow periods, when I still have to pay rent for the office space, not to mention salaries and bank fees.

"It's an interesting proposition. I look forward to talking more about it."

Her voice takes on a light and cheerful note. "Great! I can't wait to meet you. I'm so excited to think about colors and fabrics and new furniture for this place. It's been feeling so drab lately. It's definitely in need of a facelift."

"I'm your girl," I tell her.

She thanks me, and we say goodbye. Slowly, I set the phone receiver back into its cradle on my desk and start to feel like I'm floating out of my chair. Did that really just happen? Did Liz Tremblay ask me to redecorate her South End mansion and do all the staging for Ten Millennium? With a retainer?

Then it hits me—that this is a total game changer for me. I leap out of my chair, run around my desk, and burst out of my office, into the reception area. "You're not going to believe what just happened," I say to Gretchen behind the front desk.

Jennie comes out of the studio. "What's going on?"

I look at them both in turn. "Liz Tremblay just called, and she wants us to decorate her house and, get this . . . to be the *exclusive stagers* for Ten Millennium. On retainer."

They each gape at me with wide eyes.

"Seriously?" Gretchen says.

"Seriously," I reply.

"That's not just residential houses," Jennie adds. "It'll include all her husband's commercial developments as well because she represents those too. We're talking office towers and conference centers."

"I know!" I reply with laughter.

They move in for a group hug, and we jump up and down in revelry. This goes on for a few fabulous seconds until the sound of the chime on the entrance door snaps us out of our merrymaking.

Quickly regaining a sense of professionalism, Jennie makes a U-turn toward the studio, and Gretchen returns to her chair behind the reception desk. With my back to the door, I tuck a lock of hair behind one ear, take a breath, and turn around.

It's Nate. He's twenty minutes early. I know this because I've been conscious of every second on the clock since 9:00 a.m., even while I was talking to Liz.

Wearing a black linen button-down shirt and faded blue jeans, his dark hair tousled from the wind, he's strikingly handsome. What is it about this man that arrests me on the spot? It's only been a few days since we met, but my blood is racing. Every minute I've spent with him has been intoxicating—from our deep conversations to the delicious food he's cooked for me and the way he kisses. I feel such a strong attraction to him it makes my head swim.

Still feeling giddy, I can't wait to tell him about the phone call with Liz Tremblay.

"Hi," he says, looking apologetic as he glances around the reception area. "I'm a bit early. I hope this isn't a bad time."

I smile broadly. "Your timing couldn't be better. Welcome." I approach him, rise up on my tiptoes, and kiss him on the cheek—which doesn't feel strange or inappropriate after our make-out session on his sofa the night before.

I turn to Gretchen. "This is Nate."

"You picked a good day to come for a tour," she says. "We're pretty happy around here."

Nate looks at me. "Happy is good. What's going on?"

I take him by the hand. "Come with me. We'll start the tour in my office, and I'll tell you all about it."

I feel Gretchen watching us with interest as I lead Nate across reception and into my office, where I close the door behind us. I turn and face him. "Do you know who Liz Tremblay is?"

"Of course. Santa Claus has a landing strip on her front lawn."

I smile. "That's right, and today feels like Christmas because she just called and asked me to decorate her whole house and . . ." I pause and hold my hands up. "Get this . . . she's offering me a retainer to be the *exclusive* stager for her real estate company."

Nate lays his hand over his chest, as if I've shot him with an arrow. "You're joking."

"I'm not."

"This is going to be huge for you." His eyes meet mine with amazement.

"Yes."

"Congratulations!"

His expression is joyful and genuine, and I begin to fall helplessly into the memory of kissing him on Sunday. I relive the sensation of his mouth on mine for the first time, his hands on my hips as he drew me close, and then the walk home in the fresh night air with our dogs while they sniffed flowers in gardens and peed on patches of dewy grass. We'd stood outside the entrance to my apartment building talking about our dreams and aspirations for another half hour before he kissed me good night.

After that, I went to bed happy, and now all I want to do is put my hands on his chest and feel his lips on mine again. But I'm at work, standing in my office, with two of my employees on the other side of the door, possibly with their ears pressed up against it.

"I had a great time on the weekend," Nate says, with a smile that makes me melt.

"So did I. I couldn't wait for you to get here this morning."

He stares at me, and I feel certain he's reading my thoughts. "I'd really like to kiss you right now, but I'm worried if I start, I won't be able to stop, and we'll end up on your couch."

I glance at the white leather sofa. "That could happen."

There's a humorous glimmer in his eyes. "You were supposed to give me a tour?"

"Yes." Pleased to have a reason to clear my head of images of us on my leather sofa, I let out a breath, but I still feel like a pressure cooker as I turn on my heel and gesture toward my white desk. "Here, we have mission control."

Nate checks out my sleek ergonomic chair and moves around it. "This is pretty cool. May I?"

"Be my guest."

He takes a seat and leans back, tests out the lumbar support. Then he glances around the room at the bookcases, carefully staged with a variety of personal items and plants. He takes in the tall weeping fig tree in a gigantic blue ceramic pot, the pewter framed mirror over the sideboard where I keep my paint chips and fabric samples, and the white filing cabinet.

"This is fantastic," he says. "You've really done it. Started your own company, took the bull by the horns."

I know he's happy for me, but at the same time, there's a sadness in his voice, which I understand deeply. "I hope you can figure things out too," I tell him.

The telephone rings, and I listen to Gretchen answer it out front.

"Shall we continue the tour?" I ask Nate.

"Let's do it." He rises from my chair and follows me out of my office.

As we make our way across reception to the design studio, I find it excruciating to resist the urge to take hold of his entire arm and rest my head on his shoulder. All I want to do is touch him.

We enter the studio, and I show him the gallery, which features some of our best recent work, and feel like I'm seventeen again, when I had no fears or reservations about falling in love and possessed the courage to jump in with both feet.

But I'm not seventeen anymore, and I don't have that same courage. Though I'm wildly attracted to this man, a part of me is terrified to become involved because I don't want to experience the kind of pain I felt when I lost Jacob. And I barely know Nate. Sure . . . he's handsome, and I feel an intimacy that shocks the hell out of me. For all I know, he could be my soulmate, the one I was always meant to be with.

On the other hand, he could be a reckless charmer who knows how to play this game really, really well. It would probably be wise to be cautious. Maybe sometimes, fear is good.

CHAPTER EIGHT

Nate

It's unusual that I haven't seen or spoken to my father in four weeks—not since the day he and Mom arrived unexpectedly at my apartment and met Sienna. The circumstances weren't ideal, and I've been kicking myself ever since, wishing I hadn't picked that day to bring up the possibility of quitting law school. I should have let them meet Sienna without any preconceived notions about her likability, according to their grand plan for my life.

But here we are, a month later, and it is what it is. Mom finally called me two days ago because she couldn't let my twenty-fifth birthday pass without the traditional Palmer Family Birthday Brunch.

As I wait for my older brother, Arthur, and his wife, Alex, to pick me up with their kids and chauffeur us to our childhood home at the head of St. Margaret's Bay, I wonder if my father expects me to bring Sienna. Mom said she was welcome, but I'd made a conscious decision to go alone. Not because I don't want to be with Sienna on my birthday. It's quite the opposite, and she'll be driving to St. Margaret's Bay later to pick me up. And that's when I'll feel better about turning twenty-five—when I see her face and hear her voice. But this morning . . . let's just say I want to keep her out of the eruption that is almost certainly going to occur.

Rain is falling hard when Arthur pulls up to the curb outside my building in his minivan. I venture outside and make a run for it, splashing through puddles until I reach the vehicle. As if by magic, the side door slides open, and I climb over the back seat to the rear. It takes a few seconds for me to get settled before I look up at my nine-year-old nephew, who's sitting beside me, staring.

"Hey, Andy," I say. "What do you think about this rain?"

"It's wet," he replies, and I laugh heartily.

"I can't argue." He's a good kid. Reminds me of myself at that age.

I sit forward to peer at the twins, my four-year-old nieces, in matching pink booster seats in the row in front of us. "Hey, girls."

"Hi, Uncle Nate," Jessie replies while Amy quietly draws a circle on the foggy window.

From the driver's seat, which seems a mile away, my brother glances over his shoulder at us. "It's time to wish Uncle Nate a happy birthday. Everybody ready?"

The whole family begins to sing. "Happy birthday to you . . ."

When they finish, my sister-in-law, who's a doctor of Shakespearean literature and bears a striking resemblance to a young Michelle Pfeiffer, turns in her seat. "Congratulations. Today, you've lived a quarter of a century. Something to think about."

"Believe me," I reply, "I've been thinking about it a lot lately."

"Yeah?" Arthur flicks the blinker, checks his mirrors, and pulls onto the wet street. "Digging deep, are we?"

"You could say that." I tug at the shoulder strap and buckle myself in.

Arthur glances at me in the rearview mirror. "Does it have anything to do with the plumber's daughter?"

Alex punches him in the arm. "Don't start."

"I'm just teasing," he replies, leaning away from her in defense of another blow.

My gut tightens into a knot. "Her name's Sienna, and she's an interior designer."

"I know, I know," Arthur replies. "We've heard all about her—that she started her own company, which I think is impressive for someone her age."

Working to ignore what I perceive as something patronizing in his tone, I follow Amy's lead and draw a face on the foggy window. But I make it frown.

Arthur increases the windshield wipers to full speed as he moves through a busy intersection. "Why didn't you bring her?" he asks.

He watches me in the rearview mirror, and I can tell he's fishing for dirt. I'm surprised he hasn't brought up the ugly sticking point of my desire to quit law school. Maybe he doesn't know. Maybe Dad was too embarrassed to mention it—because in his mind, it reflects badly on *him*. It makes him look like a failure as a father because somewhere along the line he missed the mark. He didn't instill the proper amount of discipline and ambition in his younger son, and now he's losing control of my trajectory through life.

I wonder if my father blames himself at all for how I turned out. I was the third child they'd never intended to have. A "happy accident," my mother always said. But most of the time I was left to my own devices, which I now see as a blessing. I was free to be creative and do my own thing—because Dad couldn't be bothered to be an influential presence. I was simply an afterthought, at least until I started rebelling in high school. Then he put me in the front seat with him, which worked for a while. I did what he wanted me to do. But it was never enough and never what I wanted.

"She had something for work," I lie. "But really, I just want to get through the day."

"That's probably wise," Arthur says, still fishing. "Wait until you're sure about this girl before you lock horns with Dad. Because if she's not the one, believe me, it's not worth it."

I listen to my brother's advice in silence, because I don't trust Arthur to take my side in anything. When it comes to Dad, he's always toed the line. Besides, I agree with him. Not much in life is worth going head-to-head with my father.

But some things are.

~

Clouds, dark and dense, hang low over the bay as we turn onto the long paved driveway to my parents' house. The twins have fallen asleep in their booster seats, and Andy is engrossed in a handheld Nintendo game.

I take a deep breath and close my eyes for a moment to summon the courage to face my father, which isn't an easy thing when I'm arriving in the back seat of my brother's perfect life. Arthur finished law school with honors and became the youngest partner of the criminal law division in my father's firm. The cherry on top was his marriage to a scholarly intellectual with the prestigious title of doctor. Alex may not have been a brain surgeon, but in my father's eyes, she was perfect because she was willing to stay home with the kids, teach them how to read above their grade level, make the house pretty, and look spectacular on Arthur's arm.

Sometimes when I've watched her leave their house to go running with her earbuds in, I've wondered if she's happy.

Meanwhile, my sister, Caroline, the eldest, left home at the age of twenty-four to marry an ambitious member of Parliament in England. Mom and Dad were very proud, and I've often wondered if *she's* been happy with that decision. Unfortunately, I've never had the chance to ask because she never comes home. Maybe that says it all.

Arthur pulls up in front of the massive oceanfront home. I look out the van window, streaked with water, at the gray cedar shakes, the broad windowpanes, and the landscaped, porticoed entrance with white columns and slate stairs leading to the front door.

I hate that I feel a surge of pride in the Palmer home and that, for a fleeting second, I wish I *had* brought Sienna—to show her everything I'm willing to give up for this crazy dream of mine. But the feeling soon passes when I imagine what's about to transpire. I don't want Sienna here for that.

It's still drizzly outside when both doors of the minivan slide open. Arthur and Alex pull the sleeping twins out of their booster seats. Then Andy and I climb out.

"Welcome, everyone," Mom says as we all pile up the stairs to the front veranda. She pinches the cheeks of each twin. "Come inside before you turn into a couple of ducks. I have crackers and cheese on the table."

"Thanks, Mom." Arthur gives her a kiss as he passes by.

Once everyone's inside, she and I face each other on the veranda. "Happy birthday, Flapjack," she says with affection. It's been her pet name for me for as long as I can remember.

We hug and make our way inside.

After we've all removed our wet shoes and rain jackets, Mom leads us to the kitchen, where she's prepared an incredible spread on the marble island—bunches of grapes and cheese on a bamboo platter, a bouquet of chocolate-dipped strawberries on sticks in a crystal vase, sweet Devonshire cream, and the sterling silver coffee service.

"Help yourselves," she says, "but don't fill up too much. We have eggs and bacon to come, and fresh blueberry waffles." She swings to Alex and speaks slyly. "Mimosas for the grown-ups?"

"That sounds marvelous," Alex replies and sets Jessie down.

Before I touch any food, I wander to the wide bank of windows and take in the view of the bay, ashen and thunderous with violent whitecaps. It's not lost on me that my father has not yet made an appearance.

Turning to the others, I ask, "Where's Dad?"

"In his office." Mom playfully rolls her eyes. "He had some work to finish, but I'm sure he'll be out as soon as he smells bacon."

~

At least twenty minutes pass before my father comes lumbering out of his office like a bear. Before saying hello to any of us, he complains to my mother about one of the partners at the firm. Then he waves Arthur to the back hall, where he vents for another five minutes. Eventually, he emerges to greet his grandchildren, his daughter-in-law, and lastly me. The birthday boy.

"Why didn't you bring your new girlfriend?" he demands to know, as if I've done something completely senseless.

"She had work," I reply. "A new client."

He slaps at the air dismissively and turns away. "Where's my mimosa?"

With flawless precision, my mother hands him his morning cocktail in a flute. "Here you are, darling."

He raises it in the air. "Welcome, all, and happy birthday to Flapjack."

"To Flapjack!" Arthur and Alex say in unison, also raising their glasses.

I paste on a smile. "Thanks, everyone."

"Now come on," Mom says and ushers us into the formal dining room, where the table is set with a white tablecloth, fine china, and fresh flowers. Helium balloons adorn all four corners of the room. A family tradition.

"Sit wherever you want," she adds. "Hot waffles are on the way."

~

I'm relieved, at first, when the conversation over brunch is directed at the grandchildren. Dad asks Andy about his soccer team, and Mom talks to the twins about their swimming lessons. Blueberry waffles and bacon arrive on shiny silver platters. (My parents employ a housekeeper named Jane, who also cooks and serves.) We talk about the rainy weather while we douse our plates in maple syrup and spoon dollops of fresh whipped cream on top of the waffles.

I'm comfortable keeping quiet, under the radar, because brunch is delicious and I'm starving. I help myself to a second waffle, spoon some mashed blueberries and whipped cream on top, drench it in maple syrup, and shovel it into my mouth. No sense letting the bacon go to waste. I grab some more of that too. And then the conversation takes a turn that I wasn't expecting.

Andy—my nephew, whose secret I promised to take to the grave when he clogged the toilet with his toy dinosaur—betrays me.

"What do you get when you cross a plumber with a jeweler?" he asks.

I glance up from my plate. My mouth is full, so I can't respond, but I stop chewing.

My father, clearly enthralled, sits back in his chair. "No idea, Andy. Do tell."

"A ring around the bathtub!" Andy shouts.

I direct my gaze to my brother. Arthur is beaming with pride, as if he fed the joke to his son at some point, probably when they were discussing me and my new girlfriend.

Everyone laughs, and my mother sits back in her chair and claps her hands. I immediately lose my appetite.

"Priceless!" she says with laughter.

Andy looks pleased with himself, and I worry for him.

"How about this one?" my father asks. He turns his sneering eyes to meet mine. "What do plumbers and economists all have in common?"

I sit back and toss my white linen napkin onto the table beside my plate. "No idea."

"They all deal with gross domestic product."

"Eww!" Alex cries, and everyone bursts into fits of laughter. My father grins with satisfaction as he reaches for more bacon.

"Why was the plumber depressed?" Andy asks. "Because his career was going down the toilet!"

My gaze sweeps around the table. For the life of me, I can't understand why my family is so intent on making fun of an amazing woman they've never met. A woman they know nothing about, except that her father is a plumber.

Are any of these people capable of acknowledging that Sienna's father built a thriving plumbing business from scratch, which now employs hundreds of workers? Would they appreciate that, at the family level, the MacKays are kind and loving toward each other? Sometimes they leave dirty dishes in the sink until the following morning, and no one gets yelled at. The dogs are allowed to jump on the furniture whenever they want. A scratch on the hardwood floor is considered a normal part of life.

I feel as if my heart has gone cold, and for the first time, I don't give a damn about my father's approval. Hell, I did what he wanted. I pulled myself up by my bootstraps and got into law school. But sitting here now, I feel like I'm still spinning my tires. What else do I have to do to earn this man's respect?

Funny. I used to think I had everything—because my parents were rich and there were no obvious struggles. But since meeting Sienna's family, I've come to realize that I was raised with a different sort of deprivation.

The persistent laughter sends my thoughts into a tailspin.

"Dad, can I talk to you?" I ask.

Laughter fades. Everyone's uneasy eyes land on me.

"I'm sitting right here, aren't I?" he replies.

"In private." My tone is hard, demanding, and I think he might be in shock because I've never stood up to him before. Certainly, I rebelled in my youth, but this is different. It's happening in front of the family at the Birthday Brunch table. His wife, his son, his daughter-in-law, and his grandchildren are all witnessing the event.

"Let's go into my office." He rises from his chair at the head of the table, and I follow. "This had better not be what I think it is," he warns as he shuts his office door behind us and strides heavily toward the credenza.

I glance around at the dark leather furniture and his monstrous mahogany desk. As children, we were rarely permitted to enter this room, but I try not to think about that. I'm not a child anymore.

"What if it is?" I ask with a note of challenge.

He pours scotch from the crystal decanter and hands the glass to me. Though I'm not normally a day drinker, I accept it and watch while he pours another for himself.

"Go on, then," he says, facing me. "Let's have it. Give me what you've got."

Suddenly I'm afflicted with some sort of emotional paralysis, or maybe it's just plain old terror because my father is a grizzly bear. He's bad tempered, loud, and hungry for blood. When he's angry and he speaks, he growls.

I down the scotch in a single gulp, and he laughs at me. "I figured you were going to need that."

As I wipe my mouth and set the crystal glass on the edge of his desk, I hate him for being right. "We spoke about it before," I say, "when I told you I didn't like law school."

"No one likes law school, you twit. But you man up and get through it. Like the rest of us."

"I don't want to get through it," I reply, "because I don't want to be a lawyer. I want to be a chef and open my own restaurant."

Dad glares, then stalks to the window, where he stands with feet apart, gazing out at the bay. I'm surprised at how relaxed he appears as he sips his drink. I suspect he's confident that I'm going to back down and give it another shot. At the very least, finish out the term.

"I sent notice to the registrar's office on Friday," I tell him. "I've informed them, in writing, that I'm quitting. Friday was my last day."

I might as well have dropped a grenade into the space between us. Dad swings around and roars at me. "You did *what*? Without speaking to me first?"

"I already spoke to you about it," I remind him, "and it was clear you didn't support the idea, so I didn't see the point."

His face reddens. His broad shoulders stiffen visibly. "I'm the one paying your bills. I deserved to know before the damned registrar."

"I knew you'd only try to talk me out of it."

"Damn right I would!" He waves his arm about. "I don't want my son throwing his life away to work in a kitchen, chopping onions for a living. Do you have any idea how much a cook makes?"

"It's not about the money."

He laughs bitterly, as if I'm a fool. "Everything's about the money eventually. You'll discover that in about five years when you're broke and living in a dump with cockroaches. Then you'll wish you'd listened to me."

"That's not going to happen," I tell him vehemently. "I'll make it work."

I want desperately to convince him that I can do it, even though, when I came here, I was certain that I'd never get his blessing. I had come prepared to accept that I'd have to make my own way, that he'd never support me or believe in me.

"I'm confident that I'll be more successful doing something I love," I try to explain. "Something I'm passionate about. Can you try to understand that?"

"Oh, for the love of God. You sound like an infant! The world doesn't work that way. And you'll get nowhere without my support."

"Financial support, you mean?"

He doesn't answer. He just stares at me with those black, beady eyes.

"Then give it to me," I say, point blank. "Give me a chance to prove myself. Fund my education. Send me to Europe to learn from the best, and I swear, Dad, I'll make you proud. I'll come home and make a name for myself. I'll open the best restaurant in the city."

My father's face hardens. His expression turns cold as stone. "You don't know the first damn thing about opening a business or running a restaurant. You don't know that it takes a lot more than knowing how to cook a decent steak. Frankly, it's beneath you."

My throat tightens, but I stand my ground. "It's beneath *you*, you mean. You want me in a suit, carrying a briefcase. Or maybe a surgeon's scrubs would have been good enough. But not much else."

We stare at each other intensely, and it takes every measure of courage and resolve I can muster to not look away.

"Is this about that girl?" he asks callously. "The plumber's daughter."

My hackles rise. "Stop calling her that."

"Sienna, then. Did she put these dreams in your head? Is she the one who made you think it was a good idea to quit law school?"

"No," I firmly reply. "I wanted to be a chef long before I met her."

"But you knew it wasn't an actual *career* option." He speaks with loathing and malice. "You always knew a law degree was the best path for you."

"No, Dad, I never thought that. *You* thought it was the right path for me, and I just didn't want to fight you. I wanted to make you happy."

As I speak the words, I hear traces of affection in my voice, a weakness.

He inclines his head, and something in his expression softens. "You *did*, son. You *did* make me happy. I was never more proud than I was on the day you received the acceptance letter from the law school." He sets his glass down on the desk, approaches me, and rests both hands on my shoulders. He looks me straight in the eye, and something inside me trembles. "You went through a bad time in high school," he says, "and it was rough, especially on your mother, but you came through it, and you were better for it."

My eyebrows pull together slightly, and I'm not sure what to say next. All I can do is stare at the patterned carpet because I can't seem to meet my father's gaze.

Then I realize that this has always been his boundless talent. He holds back love and doles out anger and displeasure. Then he throws you a crumb of praise, and you feel grateful for it. More than grateful. A kind word from him is like being touched by the hand of God. It's enough to make you weep.

My father is a master of manipulation.

And screw him for bringing Mom into this.

I lift my gaze. "I can't do it, Dad. I'm sorry. I don't want to be a lawyer."

He lowers his hands to his sides. For a few seconds, he watches me, wordlessly but with a scorching intensity that makes me want to flee the room. It's all I can do to take a breath and wait for him to respond.

"You'll regret this." His voice is low and threatening. "One day, and probably sooner than you think, you'll realize this was the biggest mistake of your life. When that day comes, don't come crying to me."

"Don't worry. I won't."

The silence between us becomes unbearable, so I begin to back away.

He strides forward and points his finger at me. "The minute you walk out that door," he bellows, "you won't get anything from me! Good luck paying rent on that swanky apartment your mother picked out for you. You'll be on your own!"

"That's exactly the way I want it."

Freedom. I need freedom to live my own life. I can't keep existing to please him, and I can't compete with Arthur. Arthur is everything I'm not, and I don't want to be like him anyway. I want to cook and create. I don't care about a big house or a fancy car. I want to see where things go with Sienna. I want to belong to a family that loves and supports one another.

I walk out of Dad's office, and he slams the door shut behind me.

The brunch table, when I return, is empty. Everyone has gone, except for Jane, who is clearing away the dishes. She doesn't look at me, and I feel like I've become invisible. Then I feel a vibration. Thunder from the floor beneath my feet. I look down and realize it's the bass speakers in the theater room downstairs.

My body is wound tight with stress, every muscle coiled like a spring on the verge of snapping. It's a stark contrast to the lightness I've known over the past month with Sienna.

I need to call her right away and tell her it's time to come and get me. I move quickly to the telephone in the kitchen and dial her number. She answers after the first ring. "Hello?"

"Hi, it's me. Can you come now?"

"Sure. But what happened? I didn't expect to hear from you for at least another hour. I just got here and ordered a coffee."

"I didn't waste any time," I explain. "My dad's in his office, frothing at the mouth, so I should get out of here before he decides to cook me for dinner."

"I'll be right there," she replies.

We say goodbye, and I dash down the wide, curving staircase to the entertainment room. I pass by the pool table to the home theater beyond, walk through the double doors, and find everyone seated, fully engrossed in the opening scene of *Monsters, Inc.*

My mother sits between the twins in the front row with an arm around each of them. Alex sits in the back row, filing her nails. I don't know where Arthur has gone.

"Hey guys," I say. "I have to get going."

Mom looks up. "But we haven't had your birthday cake yet."

I rub the back of my neck. "I'm sorry. Go ahead and enjoy it without me. Light the candles, and let the kids blow them out. Make a wish for me."

She frowns, and I suspect she knows what just happened.

Alex looks up from her nail filing. "You're going? But you don't have a car."

"Sienna's picking me up," I explain. "She's at the coffee shop down the road."

As I wave goodbye to Andy and the twins, I'm thankful that no one questions Sienna's convenient proximity, ten minutes away. They don't know that I came prepared for getting kicked out of the house before the cake was served.

~

The rain outside softens. Its pounding rhythm slows to a gentle patter on the long, tree-lined drive. I walk with my hood up, my head down, the tension in my chest slowly dissipating, leaving behind a strange emptiness. I'd expected to feel relieved—triumphant, even—but instead, all I feel is a hollow ache where the bond with my father should have been but never was. Still, there's no turning back now.

I look up and see Sienna's Audi Q7 pull into the driveway from the main road. Relief pours through me, and I start to jog toward her, my boots splashing through puddles. She stops and unlocks the passenger-side door for me. I quickly get in and lower the hood of my rain jacket.

We turn to each other, and our gazes lock. "How did it go?" she asks.

I lean back against the leather seat, close my eyes, and let the reality sink in. "Not great. But I haven't changed my mind. I'm quitting law school."

Sienna's voice becomes quiet. "How did he take it?"

My heart steadies as I look at her caring expression and feel her belief in me. "Exactly as I thought he would. First, he tried to intimidate me. Then he tried to make me feel worthy of his love if I caved. When that didn't work, he exploded. Textbook Dad."

Sienna lays her hand on my thigh. "I'm so sorry."

"Don't be. I'm used to it, and now I can do what I want. I don't have to worry about being good enough for him. It doesn't matter anymore, what he thinks."

She shifts into reverse and backs out of the driveway. I fasten my seat belt, and when we pick up speed on the road, I watch the windshield wipers whip back and forth. It starts to hit me that I'm on my own now. No more monthly allowance.

"I'll need to get a job," I say as I consider the logistics of my future. "Something to keep me going until I can start cooking school." She takes hold of my hand across the console. "I can't imagine where I'd be right now if I hadn't met you. I'd still be drowning. Suffocating."

"I just hope you don't regret your decision later," she replies, "and resent me for the rest of your life."

"Never." I lift her hand to my lips and kiss the back of it. "The only thing I'll regret is not doing this sooner. I wasted a lot of time preparing for the LSAT when I could have been starting cooking school."

"But if things were different," she says, "you and I might never have met."

I lean my head back against the seat. "You're right, so I shouldn't regret anything. Life is unfolding as it should. Which means I'm going to have to figure out how to get out of my lease. There's no way I can afford that apartment and save up for school at the same time."

We pass cozy houses along the rocky coastline and sailboats moored in the bay, bobbing up and down on heavy swells from the storm. I turn to Sienna and admire her profile as she keeps her eyes on the narrow, winding road.

"You should move in with me," I say before I consider the full ramifications of the suggestion. Is Sienna even ready for a step like that? I know she's crazy about me. We've spent every waking moment together over the past month. I'm head over heels in love with this girl, and I can't imagine what I'd do if I lost her now. But it's been only a month.

Sienna grins and gives me a sidelong glance. "Easy now. You've had a rough day. Maybe now's not the time to be making big decisions."

I turn in the seat to face her. "Yeah, but when you know, you know, and this is the real thing between you and me. Right?"

She smiles again, and I feel a burst of excitement that seems absurd after the argument I just had with my father. He just cut me off financially and disowned me. He'll probably call his lawyer in the morning and remove me from his will. I'll be dead to him.

Nevertheless, my heart is galloping with gusto into the future. Not only culinary school, but a possible life with Sienna.

"Just think about it," I say. "We could split the rent, and our dogs could be roomies . . . keep each other company when we're working."

Sienna keeps driving as she considers it. "It's a gorgeous apartment. A lot nicer than mine."

"We've practically been living together anyway. You sleep at my place every night, and your apartment's just sitting there empty. It's money out the window."

She laughs. "This is crazy, Nate! We only met last month!"

I face forward in the seat, tip my head back, and blink up at the roof of the car. "You're right. But I'm feeling wild, like somebody just cut shackles off my ankles, and all I want to do is run." I turn my head to look at her again. "I just want to be happy and stop worrying about what others think about my choices. And I want to wake up with you every morning and hear you talk about your work. I want to spend time with your family, who I love, by the way. And I want to cook for you. Every night."

She gives me a dazzling smile. "*That* sounds tempting. But I don't know if I can handle any more big changes right now, especially with all the extra workload. With those two new decorators I just hired, I might have to look for a new space to expand."

"Maybe living with me would help with all that." I face her more squarely. "Because we're good together. You know we are."

"I do, and it shocks the hell out of me because I never thought I'd ever want to be with someone again after . . ."

She doesn't finish the thought, but she doesn't have to. I know what she was about to say.

"But I do want to be with you," she adds.

I slant her a look and raise an eyebrow. "Is that a yes? Will you move in with me?"

She carefully considers it, then slowly nods her head. "I think I should."

And there it is. The start of something.

I take hold of her hand, raise it to my lips, and kiss it over and over until she starts laughing.

"This is going to be amazing," I tell her. And for the first time, I feel like I'm finally stepping into the life I'm meant to live, with the woman who woke me up to everything that truly matters.

As for my dad?

I don't care if I ever talk to him again. I don't need him or his money. I can do this on my own. He can go kick rocks.

CHAPTER NINE

The Guardian of My Soul

When Jacob and I fell in love, I was barely seventeen. Right away, there was friction with my parents because they worried about me moving too fast with an older boy, and they still saw me as a child. They set strict rules and curfews, which resulted in some sneaking around.

Looking back on it, I suppose that was probably part of the excitement. You know what they say: What is forbidden is coveted, and I definitely coveted time alone with Jacob. Whenever my parents dropped me off at the mall to meet friends, I would instead meet him in the parking lot, where we'd clutch on to each other, kiss passionately, and drive off together to a park or a hiking trail for privacy. I recall one memorable evening when we found a picnic table in a deserted playground and we sat talking, holding hands, watching the sunset. When it grew dark, we stretched out on the grass, stargazed, snuggled, and talked more about our hopes and dreams for the future. To this day, I consider that night to be the most romantic experience of my life.

I leap forward in my mind to the present day.

It's Christmas Eve, and Jacob has been dead for years. The fact that I'm reliving that night under the stars with him as I sit on the sofa in my parents' house—looking across the living room at Nate—fills me with confusion and guilt because I'm definitely falling in love with

Nate. But it's different from how I felt with Jacob. This doesn't feel as earth shattering. It's a quieter kind of love. There's no sneaking around to be alone together. Nate and I sleep together every night. It's easy and comfortable. But sometimes I worry that it's not the real thing because it's *too* comfortable. Or maybe this is how true love is supposed to feel. Hence the guilt and confusion.

Tonight, Nate is helping my father hook up a new thermostat with a timer that will help cut down on power bills in the future. My parents invited him to spend the holidays with us because he's been shut out of his own family gatherings. He still talks to his brother, Arthur, on the phone, but he hasn't seen his nephew or nieces since the disastrous Birthday Brunch when he stood up to his father. His mother occasionally reaches out to him with a phone call. Twice, she has sent money in the mail—cash that can't be traced to her bank account. Nate told her it wasn't necessary, but I know he appreciated it. He set it aside for culinary school next fall.

So here we all are. I'm sipping rum and eggnog on the sofa, and Scooter and Dolly are sleeping on the cushion beside me. Mom's in the kitchen puttering, snow has just begun to fall outside the window, and the weatherman has promised that we'll wake up to a white Christmas.

I bend to kiss Scooter on his cheek and inhale his familiar dog scent. "You're my favorite sweet boy," I softly say in his ear. "And, Dolly, you're my favorite girl," I add, not wanting to leave her out.

As I straighten and watch Nate and my father discuss the instruction booklet for the thermostat, I feel content, as if all is right with the world. My company is growing and thriving, and I know in my heart that Nate is wonderful. I can't imagine my life without him—which again fills me with confusion as to why I was thinking about Jacob earlier. Making comparisons I shouldn't make.

Absently, I stroke Scooter behind his soft ears, and I wonder if there will ever come a day when I don't think about Jacob at all. Will I ever cease to compare everything in my life with how it was when he and I were together? And what about all the years still to come? Will they stack up against the vision that Jacob and I, as a couple, had imagined for ourselves?

~

"This is so strange," I whisper to Nate as we climb the stairs to my bedroom, with Scooter and Dolly following close behind.

"Why?" he asks.

We reach the second floor, and I continue to whisper as I take his hand in mine and lead him down the hall. "Because my parents are okay with us sleeping together in my bedroom."

He chuckles. "It's cool that we're whispering. It makes things feel kinda naughty."

I smile as we enter my room, which hasn't changed much since I moved out after high school. Same bed, same comforter, same pictures on the walls. I close the door and immediately pull Nate into my arms for a proper kiss—the kind that makes me wish my parents weren't sleeping on the other side of the wall.

He holds me close, and I arch into him and the heat of his kiss. Somewhere outside, a snowblower revs its engine. I'm only vaguely aware of the colorful, flickering candolier on my windowsill.

Before things get out of hand, I peel myself away from Nate's warm body, smile coquettishly at him, and move to my open suitcase on top of my desk. "Just so you know, I left my black silk nightie at home and only brought my flannels."

"Totally understandable," he replies as he pulls his cashmere sweater off over his head and begins to unbutton his shirt.

Relaxed and easy, we get ready for bed, which should feel normal, but it doesn't because this is the room where, in high school, I wrote in my diary about my love for Jacob, which I vowed would last forever. It's also the place where I grieved the loss of him after Cape Split. A part of my heart died that day, and I never imagined I could love again, but here I am.

Yes, I still think of Jacob. Maybe I always will.

Scooter stretches out on the carpet at the foot of my bed while Dolly sniffs the perimeter of the room, taking in all the unfamiliar scents before she finds a cozy spot to lie down under my desk.

Wearing my flannel pj's, I slide into my double bed and hold the covers up for Nate to join me. He sits up against the pillows, and we snuggle close.

"I have to be honest," he says. "When we first arrived, I snooped around a little."

With sudden unease, I lift my head. "What do you mean?"

"I looked at a picture of you and Jacob with Scooter. It's on a shelf in your closet."

I know the picture. Of course I do. Becky took it when she came to visit, when Scooter was just a puppy. I had it framed, and it sat on my desk until recently. I only put it in the closet a few weeks ago when I was home and knew Nate would be here for Christmas.

"Did you see anything else?" I ask, because I still have everything from those years with Jacob—all the love letters we wrote to each other every day in class when we didn't have cell phones to communicate. I held on to ticket stubs to movies. I even kept his short stories from English class in high school. He'd wanted to throw them out when he graduated, but I demanded he hand them over so that we could read them together in rocking chairs on our back porch, when we were old and gray.

Nate looks down at me. "I saw a box on the top shelf that said *Memories*, and I was curious, but I didn't look inside."

I sit up. "I'm glad, because it's full of . . ." I'm not sure how to say it. "It's full of Jacob memorabilia, and I don't want you to see that stuff."

"Why not?"

I glance uncomfortably around my room, lit by the pink ceramic lamp next to my bed. "I don't know . . . I guess I don't want you to feel hurt, or jealous."

He strokes my hair away from my face. "I can't lie, I did feel a pain in my gut when I saw that picture of the two of you . . . with Scooter. You looked so happy."

"We were, but it was a long time ago. And he's gone now."

"Yes, but . . ." Nate's gaze lingers on mine, his eyes heavy with concern. "You never talk about him. And it's not like I'm blind to the fact that I'm the first person you've dated since then. Obviously, it took you a long time to get over him. So it must've been a pretty serious relationship."

I sit back. "It did take a long time because it was a very traumatic experience, and I'm not just talking about the physical scars, which you've seen, or my fear of heights. His death was a huge loss for me. But I don't want you to think that I'm not over him. I am."

I'm cognizant of the fact that my words are only half truths. Yes, I've begun to move on, but I've always believed that if heaven exists, Jacob and I will be together again. I've been imagining that happy reunion since the day he died.

"Sometimes I feel like you're hiding a part of yourself," Nate carefully says.

For a moment I can't speak. It's as if my secret has been discovered.

"He'll always know a part of you that I can never know," Nate continues, "because I don't know anything about your relationship with him, what he was like, or if you ever had arguments. I assume you lost your virginity to him . . . or maybe not. I don't know, but I *want* to know."

Suddenly, I feel splayed wide open and vulnerable. But maybe this is a good thing because Nate's curiosity is touching something deep in my heart, a place that's been covered up for a long time. And this is what I've been trying to drill into my brain over the past few years in therapy. I don't want to believe that nothing can ever be as good as it once was, or that I'll never feel that kind of love again.

I *have* been feeling it, and I want to open myself up to this man in my bed. I want to love him.

I cup Nate's cheek in my hand and speak with purpose. "I'll tell you anything you want to know. All you need to do is ask. And I love that you want to know, because I want us to be close."

"I want that too."

"We're in a perfect place," I assure him. "And if you want to go through that box on the top shelf in my closet, I'll bring it down, and we can look through everything. We can talk about it, because I don't want to hide anything from you. I want you to know that—for me—the past few months have felt like a new life, in the best way. I feel good about the future. A future with *you*."

The snowblower across the street shuts down, and the silence feels profound. I can almost hear the drumming of my heart.

"I can't imagine not having you in my life," Nate says with a glint of wonder in his eyes.

"I can't imagine it either." I'm astonished by a sense of awakening that leaves me reeling. Words come fast. They spill past my lips with open sincerity. "I love you."

He lets out a small breath, then cups the back of my head in his hand and pulls me close for a kiss. Within seconds, we're undressing each other, and I'm struggling to keep quiet because my parents are in the next room. I quickly switch off the lamp. Nate rolls on top of me, and the bed creaks noisily. We freeze and smile at each other, laugh quietly, and decide we don't care.

In the slow, steady flicker of the Christmas bulbs on my windowsill, behind the thin fabric of my pink curtains, I let myself go. At long last, I allow myself to fall willingly into pleasure with another man.

~

A few days later, after a whopping turkey dinner with all the fixings at Aunt Marie's house—with my grandparents and cousins at two tables stretched end to end—Nate and I usher Scooter and Dolly into the back seat of my SUV and drive home to our apartment.

It's dark when we pull into the underground garage. We park in our assigned spot, not far from the elevators, which is a good thing because we have boxes of gifts and scores of leftover food to unload.

"I feel like I'm going to burst," I say with a groan as I open the passenger-side door and roll myself out of the seat. "I shouldn't have had that second helping of sticky toffee pudding."

"There was enough food on that table to sink a cargo ship," Nate replies.

I shut the car door. "It's like that every year, and Gramma always brings that chocolate mint fudge you loved. It's her own special tradition, so you can look forward to that next year."

I reference next Christmas before I realize that I'm voicing an assumption that we'll still be together a year from now. But since Christmas Eve in my room, everything feels so much deeper and more real.

I open the door to the back seat, and Dolly jumps to her feet, tail wagging, eager to hop out, but Scooter is snoring and doesn't get up.

"Come on, ya big lug," I urge him with a gentle shove on the rump. "It's time for bed."

He lifts his head, looks at me for a second, and then goes back to sleep.

"Come on, Scooter. Chop-chop. You can't sleep down here all night."

He rolls to his side and lets out an enormous fart.

"Oh!" Nate calls out with a laugh. "Someone had too much sticky toffee pudding!"

"He didn't have any of that, did he?" I ask.

Nate comes around the back of the vehicle. "I saw Uncle George offering it to him under the table. Scooter didn't say no."

I click my tongue as I reach into the front seat for the bag of leftovers. "Scooter, you know better than that. Uncle George can't be trusted." I hand the bag to Nate. "Last year he gave him a bowl of whipped cream drizzled in Grand Marnier."

"He didn't," Nate replies. "How'd you like that, Scooter?"

Scooter doesn't respond.

"He loved it," I say, "but he had the runs for two days."

"Not surprised." Nate moves closer. "Let's go. Dolly's waiting at the elevator."

Scooter still doesn't move, and suddenly, the sticky-toffee-pudding story doesn't seem so funny anymore.

"Are you okay, buddy?" I ask, leaning in to rub his back. "Are you sick?"

He still doesn't respond, and I feel a tight squeeze in my chest that escalates to panic. Suddenly, I'm thrust back to the hospital where I've just learned that Jacob is dead. The sun is shooting toward the earth like a fiery cannonball. We're all done for. It's a familiar sensation that has required years of therapy to overcome.

But thank goodness, Scooter lifts his head. He rises on all fours, stretches, and lumbers toward me.

"You're okay," I say with relief, backing up to give him some room to jump out of the car. He walks nonchalantly toward the elevator, and I turn to Nate. "That scared me."

"Me too, a little," he replies. "But he's fine."

Nate and I gather everything we can and lock the vehicle. As we walk with our arms full of boxes and bags, I watch Scooter lie down in front of the elevator doors, and I'm not entirely confident that he's fine.

Sometimes I worry that I'm always going to feel like I'm standing on the edge of a high precipice, looking down with terror, forever teetering. Expecting to lose everyone I love.

~

I've often believed that the only other living being on this planet who truly understands my PTSD is Scooter.

Of course, my therapist and parents "understand" it. They offer intelligent advice, sympathy, and concern when warranted. But it's different with Scooter because he and I share it. Whenever I feel the oncoming trauma of a memory—as if I'm experiencing the fall from Cape Split all over again, in real time—I've been told that I appear to go into a trance.

Scooter does too. He stares at me intensely. But within seconds, his tail starts to wag. Then he whimpers anxiously and nuzzles the inside of my wrist with his nose until I, too, am released from the memory.

He's never been trained to be a service dog, but that's what he is to me. A quick snuggle with him, or the gentle lick of his tongue on my cheek, always calms me. He's the guardian of my soul, the protector of my heart and my physical body, and I don't know what I'd do without him.

~

"He just passed gas again," Nate tells me as I emerge from the bathroom, still brushing my teeth.

Scooter is stretched out on his side, dead center on our king-size bed. Nate draws the sheet up over his nose to mask the smell while he gives Scooter a gentle kick from under the covers. "Dude. What did you eat? A dead racoon?"

Scooter lifts his head with indifference, then flakes out again.

"He can't help it," I mutter through a frothy mouthful of toothpaste before I turn around and spit into the sink.

A moment later, I shut off the bathroom light, kick off my slippers, and climb into bed. I sit forward and rub Scooter's chest. "You'll feel better in the morning. And for the record, I feel bloated too. It's a good thing Christmas dinner comes only once a year."

When I look at Nate, he's still hiding his nose and mouth behind the sheet, and Dolly has hopped off the bed to sleep in the closet.

I can't help but laugh. "Come on, you guys. It's not *that* bad."

"We'll agree to disagree."

I switch off the light, lie down, roll to my side, and face Nate, with Scooter occupying the space between us.

Then I realize that Nate and Dolly were right. The stench truly is that bad, so I tug the duvet up over my head. "I think this is stretching the outer limits of unconditional love."

Nate laughs and pulls me close, but for some strange reason, I feel that familiar fear again—that this moment is too precious and, one of these days, I'm going to lose it all. Part of me wants to jump out of bed and flee, but I know there's no escape from this. It's my PTSD, so I focus on my breathing. I inhale slowly through my nose, count to four, and exhale slowly through my mouth. Then I tell myself that everything's fine. Nate loves me, Scooter is at my side, and, with the exception of the toxic cloud from the sticky toffee pudding he ate, life is good. I just have to keep breathing and stay grounded.

PART THREE

ON THE EDGE WITHIN

2025

CHAPTER TEN

A Fine Line

Halifax

My son, Connor, steals the puck at the blue line, and I rise to my feet in the bleachers. With astonishing speed and agility for a thirteen-year-old, he flies down the ice toward the goalie in the net.

It's the final playoff game of a weekend tournament, and the arena is raucous with shouts and cheers. Becky and I jump up and down as Connor navigates around a defenseman, then passes the puck across the ice to his teammate, who immediately casts it back. With lightning-fast reflexes and expert stick handling, Connor shoots and scores. The entire arena explodes with cheering and the clamor of noisemakers.

Ecstatic, I turn to Becky, who throws her arms around me. "He did it!" she shouts.

Other parents around us pat me on the back and shoulders. They're all good friends because most of us have known each other since our sons first learned to skate, and we've been hanging out in hockey rinks and traveling to tournaments for years, supporting our kids through this merry journey.

Connor is special, however, and everyone knows it. He's exceptionally talented, mostly because he works harder than any other kid in the league. It's obvious to me that he inherited a very intense competitive edge from his father.

There's still a minute left in the game, and the players get into position for a face-off, but everyone knows it's over. The score is 5–2, so there's no hope for the other team, but we all watch to the end and remain in our seats for the awards and presentations. No one is surprised when Connor wins MVP of the game as well as the entire tournament.

Later, Becky and I wait by the soda machines for Connor to emerge from the dressing room. He finally appears with Davey, his best friend on the team, the two of them sauntering out with their gigantic hockey bags slung over their shoulders, their hair wet from sweating under their helmets.

"Great game!" a parent says.

"Good job, guys!"

I can't help but notice a group of young girls in their path.

"Hi, Connor," one of them says. "Good game."

"Thanks." How aloof he is, oblivious to their swooning.

Becky nudges me, and we exchange a look of amusement.

"Thank goodness he thinks of nothing but hockey," I say privately to her as we zip up our parkas and follow him out of the arena.

It's cold and dark outside. With the windchill, it's minus 30 degrees Celsius, so Becky and I jog to the car. We scramble to get in, and I quickly press the ignition button and set the heat to full blast.

While we shiver, Connor takes his time crossing the parking lot with Davey. They stop and chat before Davey veers off toward his parents' minivan.

"He's coming," I say to Becky. I push the button to open the trunk, and he sets his hockey bag inside, shuts the trunk, and climbs into the back seat.

"Becky's coming home with us for dinner," I tell him as I watch him in the rearview mirror.

"Cool," he replies absently, with the glare of his cell phone lighting up his face. I'm not sure if he actually heard what I said, but that's how it is with teenagers these days, so I've learned not to take it personally.

I remind him to buckle his seat belt before I shift into drive, and as soon as we start moving, Becky flips through some radio stations until she lands on an old Gordon Lightfoot tune. As we make our way home, we talk about her workweek coming up. She's general manager of a downtown shopping mall and always has juicy stories to tell.

We're ten minutes away from home when Connor speaks up. "Did you hear from Dad?" he asks.

I glance at him again in the rearview mirror, and my heart sinks a little. "No, honey, I haven't. Did you text him about the game?"

"Yeah, but he hasn't responded." We stop at a red light, and Connor gazes out the window. Streetlights from the busy intersection illuminate his face, and I recognize his disappointment, clear as day to me. I see it in the way he rubs at his temple.

"He probably hasn't had a single minute to check his phone," I tell him. "You know what the restaurant's like at this hour."

"Yeah, it's busy." Connor picks up his phone again, and I hate that I must work constantly to convince my children that they matter to their father. I want them to feel confident about that, even though I'm not always sure I believe it myself. But at least *I'm* there for them. Every day. Devoted. One hundred and fifty percent.

~

When Nate and I first got married, he was still in cooking school, and I was working my butt off to support us and pay for his education after his father cut him off. Thankfully, money was never an issue because my company had taken off like a rocket. Back then, there weren't many designers doing home staging for the Realtors, and miraculously I'd had the foresight to hire a web guy to develop a software program to create virtual staging for homes, offices, and outdoor spaces. It was the first of its kind.

When Nate finally opened the restaurant of his dreams—an upscale fine-dining establishment on the Halifax Waterfront called Oblique—I began to find it difficult to juggle work and motherhood. Miraculously, a corporate buyer for my software program came along, so I took the offer and sold it—along with my business—for upward of three million dollars. The timing couldn't have been better because Nate started working twelve hours a day, six days a week, determined to be the first restaurant on the east coast of Canada to earn a Michelin star.

It was during that hectic time that I received the heartbreaking news of my mother's cancer diagnosis. A year later she was gone. Two years later, my father suffered a fatal heart attack, and Nate was so overwhelmed at the restaurant that he wasn't able to attend the funeral.

They were difficult years, but I'll always be grateful that the sale of my business had given me the freedom to stay home and take care of my family.

We pull into the driveway of our cozy house in the West End, a two-story craftsman with a low-pitched gable roof and a wide front porch with tapered columns on stone piers. Nate and I purchased it when I was pregnant with Amanda, but it was in dire need of TLC, so it came at a good price.

Over time, I've put my design skills to good use, and we've restored it to its former glory. It's in a sought-after neighborhood with expansive lots and mature trees, so today it's probably worth double what we paid for it. (Not that its market value matters to me, because I love this house, and I never want to move.)

I shut off the car and press the button to open the trunk. We all get out and hurry to the front door before our noses freeze off in the biting wind.

Connor disappears to the basement to dump his hockey gear while Becky and I ditch our coats and boots and make our way to the kitchen.

"Wine?" I ask.

"Yes, please," she replies.

I retrieve a bottle of white from the wine fridge and pour us each a glass.

"To hockey," Becky says, making a toast.

"And to us." We clink and sip.

"Can I do anything to help you with supper?" Becky asks.

"No need to lift a finger. I made a chicken lasagna this morning. All I have to do is stick it in the oven." I remove it from the refrigerator and peel back the aluminum foil.

While we wait for the oven to preheat, we sit on the stools at the kitchen island.

"It's a shame Nate missed the game," Becky says. "That was one for the record books."

"He did amazing, didn't he?" I reply, intentionally skipping over the reference to my husband's absence. I want only to celebrate Connor's clever leap over a defenseman's stick just before he caught a pass from his teammate and scored the final goal.

The TV comes on in the basement rec room, and I hear Connor talking to a friend on his cell phone.

Becky watches me for a moment, then asks carefully and quietly, "Has he been to a single game this year?"

Wishing that she'd let this pass, because I'm reaching the end of my tether and I don't want to be reminded of that, I pick up my wine and take a sip. "No, he hasn't," I admit.

She sits back and rests her fingers on the base of her wineglass. "Do you ever worry about how the kids feel about it? I know *you're* fine because you've always been supportive of his dreams, but Connor seemed a bit discouraged tonight."

"You noticed?" I take another swig of my wine.

"Yes." Becky sits forward. "You know that you can talk to me."

Explosions from the woofer speakers downstairs cause the floor to tremble. Obviously, Connor has found an action movie to watch.

"Yes, I do worry," I confess. "I hate that the kids don't feel important to their dad. And honestly, for years I've been feeling like a single mother."

It's the first time I've admitted this to anyone.

"Have you talked to him about it?"

"Yes, and he always apologizes and says he'll do better, but nothing ever changes." I pause and think about the many conversations we've had about the time he spends at the restaurant. "I want to be supportive of his career because I know what he went through with his father. I don't want him to ever regret quitting law school, because I'm the one who encouraged him—which ended up causing a permanent rift in his family."

"You blame yourself for that?" she asks with a touch of surprise.

"A little."

Becky shakes her head. "Well don't, because Nate wanted to be a chef long before he met you, so you can't take responsibility for a decision he made for himself. He was a grown-up."

"That's true," I reply. "But here we are, almost twenty years later, and I'm afraid he's turning into his father." I take another sip of wine. "Not because he's controlling or intimidating. He's not that way at all. It's kind of the opposite, actually. He's so obsessed with earning that Michelin star that he doesn't seem engaged in his kids' lives at all, which I'm afraid makes them feel like he doesn't care."

Becky fiddles with an earring. "Have Connor and Amanda ever expressed that to you?"

"Connor hasn't," I reply, "but I sense how he feels. You saw it in the car. And yes, Amanda has talked to me about it because she's sixteen, and as you know, she expresses her emotions openly."

"And dramatically," Becky replies with a wink.

The oven beeps to let me know it's reached the set temperature, so I rise from the stool and slide the casserole dish inside. I return to Becky and refill both our wineglasses.

She lets out a woeful sigh. "I'm sorry you're going through this. I wish you were married to someone who could put you first, like Jacob would have done."

I close my eyes for a moment, take a breath, and open them. "Please don't compare Nate to Jacob. That'll never be a fair fight."

Becky rubs the back of her neck. "Sorry. You're right. Because Jacob was a saint. We'll always think of him that way because he never had a chance to go through life and disappoint us."

We sit in silence, pondering the deeper connotations of that statement.

I sit forward and touch her knee. "Thank you for being here for me. But when it comes down to it, I can't bear to live with any more could-have-beens. I married Nate because I loved him, and I enjoyed giving him what I knew he was missing in his life—which was love and support. And I enjoyed watching him thrive when he worked for my dad and did well in cooking school. I was so proud of him. I'm *still* proud of him—that he overcame that awful pressure from his father. It's why I've let him get away with so much."

"I get it," Becky says. "You don't want to crush his dreams like his father did."

"I definitely don't." I sit for a moment and reconsider everything I just said. "But now it sounds like he was a project for me, but that's not how it was. We were both damaged, which is why we were good for each other. We were ready at the same time for a fresh start. That's why we connected so deeply and so fast. We helped each other through some big changes."

Becky listens to all this but doesn't let me off the hook. "Okay. I get all that. But that was then, and this is now, and it sounds like you both need to find a new common ground. And don't feel guilty about that. You're not Nate's father. You're his wife and the mother of his children, and his children need him."

I think about all this—about us being parents—as I fiddle with a hangnail on my thumb. "It's been years since Nate has spoken to his father," I tell her. "And I'm pretty sure the real reason he wants that Michelin star so badly is to impress him. I think, deep down, Nate's real dream is for his father to walk into Oblique, have the best meal of his life, pull Nate into his arms, and say, 'Well done, son. I'm proud of you.' But it bothers me that he's trying to fix something from the past instead of being grateful for what he has *today*."

The front door opens, and I jump.

"I'm home!" Amanda shouts from the front hall.

"We're in the kitchen!" I reply and speak quietly to Becky. "Let's talk about this later."

"I'll pencil it in."

I rise from the stool to greet my daughter, who has just come home from her part-time job lifeguarding at the indoor pool.

"Are you hungry?" I ask.

She stops and stares at me. "Not really."

"It's chicken lasagna," I reply, knowing it's her favorite, but I recognize that something's not right.

Amanda shrugs and continues to stare at me because she knows I can read her like a book.

"What's wrong?" I ask.

She quickly shakes her head.

"That girl again?"

"That girl" is the bully I want to strangle.

My daughter nods, and with a mixture of sympathy and rage, I pull her into my arms. "What happened?"

She buries her face in my shoulder and speaks angrily. "I don't want to talk about it."

There are times when my daughter speaks these words, but she means the opposite. Sometimes she wants me to drag the truth out of her. Other times, she wants to escape from the problem at hand and do something fun. I'm not sure which of those scenarios applies presently.

Amanda lifts her head, peers over my shoulder, and becomes instantly cheerful. "Is that Aunt Becky?" We step apart, and Amanda strides into the kitchen. "I didn't know you were coming over."

"I went to Connor's game." Becky stands up to hug Amanda. "I figured I might as well get a free meal out of it."

Amanda turns to me. "The chicken lasagna smells yummy. Can I help? I could make a salad."

"Music to my ears." I'm relieved that she's not dwelling on whatever happened with the malicious brat on Instagram. "Check the vegetable drawers. I've got cucumber and tomatoes that need to be chopped. And there's a can of black olives in the pantry cupboard if you want to go Greek."

"I'm on it." Amanda strides to the refrigerator just as the house shakes from the woofer speakers in the basement. More gunshots and explosions. People running and screaming.

This is my life. Teenagers. Food. Movies. Bullies.

Sadly, Nate has not been a part of it for a very long time. He has no idea what he's been missing.

~

The chicken lasagna, as always, is a hit, and Connor goes for a second helping, which he shovels into his mouth with the same speed and tenacity he exhibits on the ice.

I offer Moose Tracks ice cream for dessert, but Connor asks if he can take his bowl downstairs and finish watching the movie. I say yes because he asked nicely, but I also want some time alone with Becky and Amanda because I'm troubled by how quiet Amanda was during the meal. She barely touched her food.

"Two scoops or one?" I ask her and Becky.

"Two, please," Becky replies, and Amanda nods in agreement.

As I rise from the table, I'm aware that my daughter occasionally opens up to Becky about things she doesn't tell me. I once asked

Amanda about this, and she explained that it was because Becky was "single and stylish," and she had a different perspective about life compared with mine. I appreciated my daughter's honesty, but there have been instances where I've felt hurt by this. I try to resist any inclination to resent my best friend for this connection she has with my daughter because I'm conscious of Becky's disappointments in love. Her most serious relationship was with her boyfriend Mark, whom she'd wanted to marry, but after four years, it didn't work out. She's alone now, but she never complains. She's embraced her "single and stylish" life, so I'm grateful that Amanda has someone mature to talk to—someone I trust—about things she might not wish to reveal to me, her not-so-stylish mother.

A few minutes later, I return to the dining room with three bowls of ice cream on a tray. "Two scoops for all." I hand them out, and we all dig in.

We revel in the creamy vanilla ice cream, chocolate swirls, and peanut butter cups until we all sit back, groan over our full bellies, and push our bowls away.

"That was yummy," Becky says as she leans back in her chair and pushes out her belly. "I think I'm going to have a food baby."

Amanda laughs.

Becky sits forward again. "Now tell me what's been going on in your life, kiddo. It's got to be something because you barely ate your supper. What's up. Is it a boy? Are you failing geometry? Do you have a wart on your foot?"

Amanda glances at me. "Did you tell her?"

"I didn't say a word," I reply defensively, raising my hands in surrender.

Amanda exhales. "Okay, fine. Mom knows most of it, so you might as well hear it too."

"Spill it, kiddo. I'm all ears."

The floor rumbles with another explosion in the rec room below us, but we're immune to it now.

Amanda sits back and twirls her long dark hair around her index finger. "There's a guy at the pool that I like, and we've been flirting a bit."

Becky nods with approval. "Good job. Is he a hottie?"

Amanda and I both chuckle.

"Yes," she replies. "Very hot. His name is Jeff. But he goes to a different school, so I don't know any of his friends, but I can't imagine we'd ever be a thing if we went to the same school."

"Why not?"

"Because I can tell by his Instagram that he's super cool and popular, and . . . well, that's not me."

"You're super cool!" Becky replies, frowning and clearly offended by the idea.

Amanda grins. "I love that you think that. But anyway . . ."

Becky and I share a look as we wait for Amanda to continue. Most of the story I already know, except for whatever happened today that put her in a funk when she walked through the door.

"So we've been friendly at the pool . . ." Amanda continues. "We started following each other on Instagram, and he's been liking my stories. But then I started getting these rude DMs from some girl who starts calling me a bitch and a whore and—"

"I beg your pardon!" Becky sits forward in shock.

In an effort to keep silent, I rake my fingers through my hair, because I've already shared my opinions with Amanda on the matter and I don't need to do so again, but it's not easy to keep my mouth shut. But I'm interested in what my best friend has to say.

"What's her name?" Becky asks.

"Marissa."

"I hope you blocked her."

This is, of course, good advice.

"I did," Amanda replies. "But then she went old school and actually called me—I don't know how she got my number—and she threatened to cut me up if I kept talking to Jeff."

Becky clutches her forehead. "Holy banana pants."

"I know, right? It's crazy."

"It is," Becky says, "but seriously . . . if she threatened to cut you up, that's a crime. You need to call the police. At least file a report in case she ever actually does something."

I nod in agreement, but Amanda shakes her head. "I can't do that. It'll only piss her off more."

"Did something happen today?" I ask, still bothered by her mood when she walked in the door.

"Not exactly," Amanda replies. "She didn't call me, but I brought it up to Jeff in a private message."

I sit up with surprise because I had suggested she do that days ago, but she didn't want him to know that she had a crush on him. She wanted to play it cool and casual.

"How did he respond?" I ask.

Amanda fiddles with her spoon. "He apologized and said he was sorry that happened. He said they weren't a 'thing,' except for talking a few times at parties. According to him, she was into him, but he wasn't interested, and she's not his girlfriend, and she's borderline stalking him, so he basically thinks she's nuts."

"Great," Becky says and turns to me. "Remember back in the old days when bullies were just bullies? Now they have serious mental health issues, which is concerning for everyone."

"We had it so easy," I reply.

"You did," Amanda says reproachfully. "I wish I could have grown up in the eighties, before cell phones were invented."

"It was awesome, if I'm being honest," Becky replies. "If only we had a time machine and could go back and warn people about social media. Outlaw it while you have the chance!"

We all laugh, but I imagine what my life might have looked like if I could go back in time—if I could travel to the year 1999 and not hike up Cape Split. Jacob and I could have simply taken Scooter for a walk along the dykes, and that horrible thing . . . the three of us catapulting down the mountainside . . . would never have happened.

Then I think again. If that had been our choice, I wouldn't have Amanda or Connor. So I sweep that dream into the dustbin, as I always do whenever I'm plagued with regrets about that day.

"What are you going to do?" Becky asks Amanda.

She shrugs a shoulder. "I don't know. I like him, but maybe he's a player and I'll end up obsessed and crazy, too, just like her, stalking the *next* girl that goes after him."

"No!" I say, horror struck. "You'd never do that."

Amanda shivers theatrically. "Oh, God, I hope not. But you never know. Love makes people do crazy things."

I'm shocked that she feels so vulnerable to what fate might have in store for her.

"You guys have no idea what it's like," Amanda continues desperately. "High school is cutthroat for everyone, no matter where they come from. It's a big survival game."

I decide to button my lips because maybe she's right. What do I know about today's youth culture?

Becky interjects. "Well, if that's true, I still think you should call the cops. Because if that girl threatened to cut you up, she needs to learn that that's not okay and you're going to fight back."

"By sending the cops to her door?" Amanda asks. "Real brave of me."

"It *is* brave," I reply, presenting a united front with Becky because I agree with her wholeheartedly. "*Not* doing that is the cowardly thing because you're afraid of what the other kids might think. But the smart ones will respect you for it."

Amanda looks off to the side, her expression hollow, like something inside her has just given up. "Maybe. I don't know."

"You don't have to decide right now," I tell her in an effort to hold on to her fighting spirit. "See what happens this week, but if she keeps calling, you might reach your breaking point and be ready to do something about it. Keep me informed, okay?"

"I will." Amanda chews on her bottom lip. "May I be excused? I have homework."

I sit back with the pretense of letting it go and moving on. "Of course."

"I have to go home anyway," Becky adds. "I have an early meeting in the morning."

We all rise from the table, and Amanda circles around to give Becky a hug. "Thanks for the advice. I swear I won't let her walk all over me."

Becky gives Amanda a tight squeeze. "We know you won't, because you've got a backbone of steel." She turns and heads for the front hall. "And remember, there are plenty of other hot fish in the sea if Jeff doesn't work out. You're only sixteen. You're just getting started."

Amanda laughs as she heads up the stairs. "I'll remember that."

After she's gone, Becky pulls her parka from the coat-tree. "I don't envy her," she whispers. "I certainly wouldn't want to repeat that time in my life."

"Me neither."

Becky reaches for her purse and opens the front door. "Thanks for dinner. It was a great day. And keep me posted about the bully situation."

"I will."

I shut the door behind her and watch from the window as she gets into her car and pulls away from the curb.

The clock on the wall says it's almost eight thirty. I check my phone, but there are no texts or voicemail messages from Nate, which leaves me crestfallen.

I return to the kitchen to load the dishwasher, wishing he'd been present at dinner to hear about Connor's game and to learn what his daughter has been going through lately. It would have been nice if he could have offered some fatherly advice. But family time at the dinner table is a rare occurrence.

As I rinse the dishes, I decide that there's a fine line between being supportive of my husband's dreams and allowing him to take advantage of my self-sufficiency. Not only do I keep this family financially stable—because Oblique barely survived COVID—I also take care of all our children's needs, emotional and otherwise.

I think I'm beginning to harbor some resentment. Or perhaps it's been growing in me for quite some time.

~

After the kids are asleep, I pour a glass of wine for myself, just to finish off the bottle. Then I sit in front of the television for two hours, watching a true crime documentary about a woman who was killed by her philandering husband. By the end of the second hour, I'm fighting to stay awake, so I shut the TV off and head upstairs.

It's almost midnight, and Nate isn't home yet, but that's not unusual. He often lingers at the restaurant after closing to talk with his sous-chef, Graham, about the menu and oversee the bank deposits. He's very hands-on, which is why his staff respects him so much, but his dedication doesn't provide any leftovers for his wife and children at home.

After I change into my nightgown and brush my teeth, I'm too lazy to take off my makeup, so I crawl into bed, knowing that I'll wake up to mascara stains on the pillowcase. But what the hell? I don't care. It's time to wash the sheets anyway, and who's going to notice?

I switch off the lamp and snuggle under the covers, on my side, facing the window. My eyes are closed, but my mind races with images from the documentary, then thoughts of Amanda's threatening phone call. Before long, I'm filled with a dangerous desire to hunt that girl down and tell her to leave my daughter alone or else I'll rip her to shreds. It's satisfying to imagine, and with that in my mind, I start to drift off, but I'm soon awakened by the sound of a car in the driveway.

A moment later, the front door opens. Keys are tossed into the bowl in the hall. I listen to Nate's footsteps from the hall to the kitchen. The refrigerator door opens and closes. Then the TV comes on in the family room, and he lowers the volume.

I tell myself that I should probably get up and talk to him about what's been going on with Amanda, but since I've learned to handle most parenting issues on my own, I've given up relying on him for advice or support. And I'm tired. So I stay in bed, wondering when I stopped getting up to greet my husband late at night. It was probably when I was a new mother, exhausted from nursing Amanda for half the night. At any rate, it's been years, so he doesn't expect it now.

~

Shortly before dawn, I dream vividly that I'm back in my parents' house, but there are extra rooms that have turned the house into a maze. I find my way to the basement, which is packed to the ceiling with junk, and an eerie feeling comes over me, as if there are demons down there. Suddenly, I'm hurrying to the airport, but when I arrive, I discover my wallet isn't in my purse. Assuming I left it at my parents' house, I run back and find Scooter waiting in my bedroom. I'm so happy to see him I fall to my knees, hug him, and burst into tears. That's when I wake up.

I sit up in bed and glance quickly at Nate, who's sleeping soundly beside me. The memory of Scooter's tongue on my cheek, licking my tears away, still feels real, but he's been gone for years. I touch my face and try to hold on to the sensation, but it soon fades, as dreams always do.

I glance at my husband again. He's lying on his stomach with the pillow bunched up in his arms. I bend to kiss him on the back of his head.

"Good morning," he says, still half asleep, his words muffled in the thickness of the downy pillow.

"Good morning," I reply, feeling better than I felt the night before, when my mind was racing with thoughts of Amanda and the bully and the chilling documentary I watched on television.

I really need to avoid drinking wine before bed.

I toss the covers aside and get up to make breakfast for the kids.

CHAPTER ELEVEN

Where Dreams Go to Die

It's the Smiths' turn to drive the boys to hockey practice after school, so I'm at home in the kitchen when Amanda walks through the door. She pulls off her snowy boots, removes her coat, and drops her backpack on the floor.

"How was your day?" I ask from the table, where I've been sitting for the past hour, doing some research on my laptop.

"It sucked." She goes straight upstairs to her bedroom. Her door slams, and my stomach squinches. I shut my laptop, get up, and follow her.

I knock lightly on her door. "Can I come in?"

"Okay." Her voice is weepy. It reminds me of when she was three years old and accepted, stoically, that she couldn't have ice cream before dinner.

When I walk in, I find her curled up in a fetal position on her bed, hugging her furry pink pillow.

"What happened?" I ask.

"Nothing."

I gently close the door behind me and sit on the edge of her bed. "Did she call you again? Or do something else?"

Amanda doesn't reply. She lies still, so I sit, patiently rubbing her back.

After a moment, she rolls to face me and speaks with outrage. "One of her friends posted a comment on my Instagram about the play."

"The musical?" I think about the pictures Amanda had shared from rehearsals and opening night.

"She said I was desperate for attention. Then she took a screenshot of one of the pictures and photoshopped it with me . . ." Amanda stops talking and rolls away from me again. "I can't tell you."

I touch her shoulder and encourage her to face me again. "What did she do?"

Amanda finally rolls onto her back, sits up, and hugs her knees to her chest. Her eyes are puffy and red. "She made it look like I was . . . you know."

"No, I don't know. You have to tell me."

"It's that picture where I'm singing in the finale," she explains, "and she changed the microphone . . . she put a guy's . . ." She pauses. "She put a guy's *thing* in front of my mouth. Then Marissa posted it too. All my friends saw it."

It takes a few seconds for this to fully register in my brain as I stare at my daughter. When it hits me, my blood heats to a raging boil. "She did *what*?"

Amanda doesn't bother to repeat the information because she knows it's a rhetorical question, but she watches me with wide eyes when I rise to my feet.

"That's it," I say. "We're filing a report. Do you have a copy of the picture? Is it still online?"

"I have screenshots."

"Good. Grab your phone." I wave at her to follow me. "We're driving to the police station right now, and we'll get a restraining order if we have to."

"Mom . . ."

I stop and turn. "No. Listen. She can't get away with this kind of thing. She needs to learn a lesson about consequences and know that you're not going to take it. Get up. Let's go."

Amanda scrambles off her bed and follows me downstairs, where we pull on our coats and boots and march outside to the car.

~

It's not until afterward, when we're leaving the police station, that I think about calling Nate. I unlock the car door and get in, and that's when Amanda mentions it.

"Are we going to tell Dad about this?"

"Of course," I reply as I buckle my seat belt. "Do you want to call him right now? Or would you prefer that we tell him later, when he gets home?"

"You can tell him later," she replies, tipping her head back on the headrest and closing her eyes. "I'm not up for explaining it again. It sucks, and it's so embarrassing. I just want to go home and chill."

I glance at her and worry that this experience is going to damage her self-confidence—the kind of energy that drove her to try out for the high school musical. She was always fearless as a young child, adventurous and buoyant, but in this moment, I sense a gloom in her, a withdrawal I've never seen before, and I'm not sure how to handle it. Should I give her space to recover? Or encourage her to talk more about it and call her father? But if she called Nate right now, would he have time for her? It's past five o'clock, and Oblique has just opened its doors.

I press the ignition button and start the car, back out of our parking spot, and decide to leave it alone for now. Unfortunately, that decision amplifies my resentment.

As we cross town during rush hour, I wonder how Nate and I got here. I remember a time, early in our marriage, when I'd never hesitate to call him for anything, even just to chat. But as soon as he opened the restaurant, everything changed, and he started ignoring my calls. Not always, but often enough that I noticed. Or if he did pick up, he was distracted or even annoyed at me for interrupting him at work.

Eventually, I stopped calling, and over time, I learned how to deal with life's many challenges, big and small, on my own.

But today, the situation feels monumental. I just took our daughter to the police station to file a report about a crime committed against her, and she and I are both shaken up.

Nate is her father. He should know about this. And yet . . . *not* telling him feels strangely satisfying—because if he's unaware of what's going on, it shines a glaring spotlight on how negligent he's become as a parent. I almost feel like I'm rubbing it in his face, hoping that he'll wake up and feel guilty. It's the ultimate act of passive aggression.

I pull to a halt at a stop sign, flick the blinker, look both ways, and steer onto our street. Amanda has been quiet the entire way home, scrolling mindlessly through her Instagram feed. I've been quiet too, reflecting, simmering with my bottled-up hostilities, which seem to have come to a head.

In that moment I decide that I shouldn't let this fester. I've always prided myself on being a good communicator, so I resolve to call him as soon as we get home and tell him what happened today. I'll give him a chance to rise to the occasion. For once.

He'd better pick up, or at least return my call. If he doesn't . . .

I pull into our driveway and swear that if he fails this test, my resentments might explode in the deep, dark place where hopelessness lives—that old den inside me where I believe future happiness is beyond the realm of possibility.

I know that place. I lived there once, for a very long time.

It's the place where dreams go to die.

~

It's past midnight, and I'm waiting up for my husband. After Amanda and I arrived home, I called Nate, but unsurprisingly he didn't answer. I left a voicemail and told him it was about Amanda, and it was important, but he never called back.

Maybe I should have reached out to Martina, the restaurant manager, but every time I speak with her, she shares colorful details about incidents in the kitchen—things Nate clearly hasn't shared with me. She then responds with sympathy, as if she understands how painful it must be to be so out of touch with my husband. But I refuse to take her bait, even though I'm conscious of how much time they spend together. I feel like she can smell weakness, so the last thing I want her to know is that Nate doesn't return my calls.

When at last I hear his car in the driveway, I rise from the sofa to meet him at the door and will myself not to make this about me. Yes, I'm annoyed as hell at him for not calling, but this is about Amanda and what she needs from us. I'll address the broader subject of our relationship after we get that out of the way.

"You're still up," he says with surprise as he walks in.

"Didn't you get my voicemail?" I can't help it that my tone is full of accusation.

He sets his backpack on the floor and kicks the snow off his boots. "I saw that you called, but I didn't have a chance to listen to the message. It was a busy night."

I turn away from him and go to the kitchen. "It's always a busy night."

He removes his coat and boots and follows me. We end up standing across from each other at opposite ends of the kitchen island.

"Isn't that a good thing? That Oblique is busy again?"

I don't want to get into how long it took to revive the business after the COVID-19 closures, so I say nothing, because I want him to recognize that I'm miffed.

When he finally lets out a weary sigh, as if I'm the quintessential ball and chain, I want to climb over the kitchen island and shake him until his teeth rattle.

He drags a stool out to sit down. "What's wrong?"

I choose to remain standing. "You'd know what was going on if you'd listened to my message and called me back."

"I told you we were busy," he replies defensively. "You know I don't have time to talk on the phone once guests start to arrive."

I don't want to get into the weeds about restaurant operations. We've had this conversation too many times, most notably on the day he missed my father's funeral.

"Fine. You're here now, so I'll fill you in." I pull out a stool from my end of the island and sit down. "I took Amanda to the police station this afternoon—"

"What? Why?" he asks, interrupting before I have a chance to finish.

"To file a report because she's being bullied."

Nate frowns. "At school?"

"No, it's a girl from a different school, and it's happening online. She's posted some doctored images, but somehow she got ahold of Amanda's phone number and called her and made threats."

"What kind of threats? And why is she doing that?"

"She thinks Amanda's going after a guy she likes," I explain. "Amanda works with him at the pool on Saturdays. His name is Jeff."

Nate slowly nods. "I see." He sits quietly for a moment, taking it all in. "So is she actually going after this guy?" he asks with disbelief.

I scoff. "That's not really the point, is it? Even if she was, this girl has no right to call her and make threats. Did you not hear the part about us going to the police station today?"

He holds up a hand. "Okay, yes. I'm sorry. I'm just caught off guard with all this. Let's backtrack and start at the beginning."

I take a deep breath to try and relax and remember that he and I are on the same team. We both love Amanda, and we want her to be safe. I explain everything she told me about what's been going on, and I end with the phone call where Marissa used the words "cut you up."

"My God!" Nate shouts. "What the hell? You did the right thing, going to the cops. Jesus! Is Amanda okay?"

Finally, a reaction out of him, and it's genuine. A hopeful sign that he still cares about us.

"She's not great," I reply, "but she's keeping it together. I'm relieved that she agreed to file the report, because she didn't want to at first. She was worried about what Jeff might think, because she does like him. I had to talk her into it."

"I'm glad you did." He rubs his forehead. "Poor kid. She doesn't deserve that. And I'm sorry I missed your call." His eyes lift to meet mine. "I'm also sorry that you had to do that on your own. I wish I'd been here."

"Thank you," I reply with forbearance. "I appreciate that."

He regards me intently. "But you're still annoyed with me."

My heart feels cold, and I turn my face away. "Yes, because it's the same old thing. I understand that you want the restaurant to be a success, but to put it bluntly . . ." I meet his gaze. "You've become a workaholic, and you seem to have forgotten that you have a wife and two children at home who love you and miss you. And they're at an age where they need you."

He stares at me, speechless.

"When was the last time you came to the rink to see Connor play a game?" I ask.

He shakes his head because he has no answer.

"You have no idea how good he is. You'd be so proud."

His brow furrows as if he's in pain. "You and the kids are more important to me than anything. You know that."

"No, actually, I don't know that, because you're never here. It makes us feel like we don't matter to you."

He looks seriously worried now. "Have the kids said that to you?"

"No, not in so many words, but *I'm* saying it." I press my fist to my heart. "And this isn't the first time. Don't I deserve the same level of caring as they do?"

He rises from the stool and circles around the island toward me. "Of course you do, honey . . ." He takes me into his arms. "You know I love you. And you're right—I've been working too hard." He steps back and lays his hand on my cheek. "But please believe that I don't take you for granted, not ever. I know how much you do for this family. You take care of everything, and I could never have made it this far without you. You're my rock."

As I stare at the man who, years ago, pulled me out of my shell when no one else could, I believe him. Truly, I do. But I've also heard these words before, and nothing ever changes. He can't seem to leave the restaurant to anyone else to manage, not even for one night, and on the rare occasion when he's at home spending time with us, he can't purge the menu from his mind. He's on his phone, texting Graham about plate ideas or creeping the social media pages of his competitors.

If I were to tell Becky about this conversation, I know what she'd say. She'd tell me to give him an ultimatum: *Spend more time at home, or you'll lose me.*

But I don't want to say that because I still love my husband, and I don't want to leave him. I wouldn't have walked down the aisle and spoken vows before God if I'd considered this commitment to be optional.

"You're tired," he says, taking hold of my hand and kissing it. "Let's go to bed. We can talk more about the bully situation, and I swear, I'll do better and listen to your voicemails from now on. But if it's something really urgent, call the restaurant and tell Martina to deliver a message to me."

"Sure," I reply cynically. "Because Martina always has direct access to you. I wish I could say the same for me and the kids."

It's the first time I've ever expressed contention about Martina, and I don't regret it.

Nate absorbs my anger, but he brushes off my comment about Martina. "I promise I'll do better."

It amazes me that he can be so totally oblivious to the fact that Martina is beautiful and that his wife might find that threatening. But I'm tired of arguing, so I let it go. For now.

Later, after he showers and gets into bed and we switch off the lights, he faces me. "I'll get up early tomorrow and give Amanda a hug before she leaves for school. I want her to know that I'm here for her."

"That would mean a lot."

He holds me close, and though I'm not entirely confident anything will change, I forgive him. Because I love him, still.

~

Strangely, that night, I dream of Scooter again. While I'm sleeping, he pushes the bedroom door open, walks to my side of the bed, rises up on his hind legs, and rests his forelimbs on the edge of the mattress. I wake and blink a few times because I can barely comprehend that he's here. *My darling Scooter.* We stare at each other intensely, but then he begins to bark. It's a distress bark, a yelp that hurls me back to that moment on the cliff, when he was scrambling to save himself, just before the ground collapsed under my feet. My belly burns with terror, and I sit up in a panic—not because I'm afraid of falling down the mountainside. I know where I am. I'm in my bedroom with Nate.

But I'm also in a lucid dream. I'm somewhere between nightmare and reality. I don't want Scooter to wake Nate. Something is terribly wrong. It's those demons again. Scooter leaps onto the bed and lies down beside me. I hug him close, and he licks my face. I feel a tremendous sense of relief that we're both okay. The fear passes, and I fall back to sleep.

~

The next morning, I wake to a ray of sunshine piercing the crack between the drapes. It's blinding, so I squint and raise my hand to shade my eyes. When I roll to my side, away from it, Nate is gone. The bed is empty, and I wish my dream had been real, that Scooter was still lying here beside me. He was such a big part of my life, a lightness during my darkest days. Dolly was a great comfort after the loss of him, but sadly she passed away a year after Scooter. Both of them peacefully, at least.

All at once, I know what I need to do. Why didn't I think of it before?

I toss the covers aside and leap out of bed.

Thank you, Scooter, for the visit.

CHAPTER TWELVE

Somewhere Between Dreams and Reality

"Are you sure Dad's going to be okay with this?" Amanda asks after school when she pulls out a kitchen stool to sit beside me. "Remember when I begged for a puppy and he said no?"

"You were seven years old," I remind her as I open my laptop, "and Connor was a tyrant, in the throes of the terrible fours. It just wasn't the right time, but believe me, your father's a dog person. That's what we did on our first date. We took our dogs for a walk. I've told you that story."

She rolls her eyes. "Yes, but I try not to think about you guys being romantic. That's just gross."

I laugh and call up the SPCA website, which I've been staring at since breakfast. "Either way, he thinks it's a good idea, as long as you do your fair share and take him for walks."

"Dad or the dog?" she asks, and I laugh again.

"The dog, of course." I direct the mouse pointer to the adoptions page and bring up all dogs in the province.

"And how do you know it'll be a *him*?" Amanda asks. "Maybe we'll find a girl dog."

"I'm open to whatever you want," I reply. "We'll look at every dog that needs a home, regardless of gender. I was creeping the site earlier, and there's one in particular that spoke to me, but I don't want to influence you too much. This is supposed to be your dog, not mine, so it's your choice."

"Okay," she replies. "Let's have a look, and don't tell me which one you like. Let's see if we gravitate toward the same one."

"Good plan."

I click on the first page, which shows headshots of each dog with their age, gender, and location. From there we click on "View Details" for more pictures and to read a description of the dog's breed and personality.

"I'm going to look at all of them before I express an opinion," Amanda says, but as soon as we click on the first dog and read the description, she melts and thinks he's the one. This happens again for the next dog, and the one after that, so I quickly become immune to her decision-making and wait until we've seen all sixteen dogs.

"What do you think?" I ask.

She runs her middle finger over the touch pad and calls up a dog named Sniper. "I kind of like this guy," she says.

"He was my choice too!"

Sniper is a five-year-old cane corso mix weighing sixty-six pounds, described as calm and friendly, playful, and great on a leash.

"He looks like he always has a smile on his face," I add. "And it says he does a happy dance when he hears his name."

"Mom, he's at the Dartmouth shelter," she says. "We could go see him right now."

I check my watch and feel a rush of excitement. "They're open until five. Let's do it."

I shut my laptop, and we both vacate our stools, dash to the foyer, and grab our coats and purses.

"We're coming, Sniper!" Amanda says as we hurry out the front door.

~

"I'm so sorry," the volunteer at the front desk says to us when we burst through the shelter doors at 4:45 p.m. "Sniper was adopted today, and the new owners just picked him up."

Amanda seems unwilling to accept this. "But he was on the website a half hour ago. And we hit all green lights coming here."

The volunteer grimaces. "I'm sorry that you came all this way, but I didn't have time to update the website until ten minutes ago."

Amanda turns to me. "I'm so disappointed."

"Me too."

We just spent the entire car ride talking about Sniper and how he was perfect for us. We discussed sleeping arrangements and who would walk him at different times of the day.

"What kind of dog are you looking for?" the volunteer asks.

Her badge says Dolly, which strikes a chord in me because that was the name of Nate's dog when we first met. "We don't have any particular breed in mind. We're just looking for a dog that we feel a connection to."

Dolly comes around the front desk to talk to us. "It's hard to get a sense of that from a website," she says. "You really have to meet the dog in person."

I nod because I believe that's true.

"We do have another little guy who hasn't been added to the website yet, if you'd like to meet him," Dolly says.

I look at Amanda, and she shrugs a shoulder. "We might as well." She turns to Dolly. "What's his name?"

"Oscar. But I have to be up front with you. He has some health issues."

Amanda inclines her head. "What kind?"

I'm happy to let my daughter do the talking because this is supposed to be her dog. I want her to have the same sense of companionship and devotion that I'd had with Scooter, who had eased so much of my pain when I was younger.

"He just had surgery to remove a tumor in his abdomen," Dolly tells us. "But the good news is that it wasn't cancerous, so he's on the mend. But he's ten years old, and he has a heart murmur."

Amanda shakes her head. "What does that mean?"

"It means he has some abnormal blood flow in his heart. It could be caused by a few things—a leaky valve, or an enlarged ventricle. He'll need to be monitored, and he may eventually require daily medication. That can get pricey, and not everyone is up for that kind of commitment."

"Is that why he's here?" Amanda asks.

"No, not at all. Sadly, his owner was a senior citizen, living alone, and she passed away in her sleep. The neighbor heard Oscar howling and found him with her on the bed."

"Oh, God," I say, raising my hand to my mouth. "That's so sad."

"Yes, and it was difficult for the family because none of them was in a position to take him." She gives me a look. "Poor Oscar's been quite brokenhearted. He's been crying a lot, especially at night."

Amanda turns to me, and we exchange a look of shared understanding.

"Can we meet him?" I ask.

Dolly glances at the clock on the wall, and I know it's time for her to finish her shift and go home. Nevertheless, she speaks cheerfully. "Of course you can. He's out back. Come this way."

Amanda and I follow her through a glass door to a long narrow room with cages on either side. Oscar is inside a crate on the right. When we reach him, he's sitting up, with a plastic cone fastened around his neck. His glossy coat is gold and black with gray highlights, and his ears are perky. His short tail wags vigorously.

"This is why we don't have him on the website yet," Dolly says. "We need to wait for his stitches to heal."

At the sight of him, Amanda melts. "Oh, my goodness," she coos. "What kind of dog is he?"

"He's a Yorkshire terrier," Dolly replies.

I turn to her. "I thought Yorkies were small."

"You're thinking of the teacup size," Dolly replies. "Oscar is a giant Yorkie. He weighs sixteen pounds."

I kneel beside Amanda in front of the crate, and Dolly stands back to give us a moment to say hello to Oscar, who sniffs the backs of our hands through the cage door.

"Aren't you a sweetheart," I say lovingly, because I'm falling fast for this little guy, who peers up at me with sad, chocolate brown eyes. I feel like I might dissolve into a sticky puddle of pity for this poor creature who has lost his beloved person and was removed from his home, taken to a shelter, and operated on. I want desperately to take him into my arms and hug him.

"We can bring him out if you'd like," Dolly says.

"Yes, please," Amanda replies.

Dolly unlatches the door and pulls it open. Oscar slowly, hesitatingly, ambles out.

"He's a very special boy," Dolly says. "He's loyal and sociable, and he has the bladder of a heavyweight champ. I really want him to find a good home."

"He deserves nothing less." I run my hand down his smooth, glossy coat and give him a good scratch. He looks up at me with gleaming eyes and whimpers, and my heart throbs agonizingly in my chest because I swear I can feel his grief.

I glance up at Dolly. "When will he be ready to leave the shelter?"

"Any time after the vet sees him tomorrow," she says, "as long as there are no surprises. Though he'll need some follow-up care."

"And how does the adoption process work?" I ask.

There are no other questions in my mind because I already know that this is our dog. I wish we could take him home right now. I hate that he has to spend another night in the shelter alone, without us.

"First, you'll need to fill out an application online," Dolly explains, "and if you're approved, you can come and get him right away."

"We'll do that tonight," I reply.

"Wonderful. My supervisor will be here at eight thirty tomorrow morning, and I'll let her know you've already met Oscar, and I'll put in a good word for you."

Amanda, while scratching behind Oscar's ears inside the cone, looks up at Dolly with tears and laughter in her eyes. "Thank you so much. I really love him."

After that, it's not easy to leave, but it's past five o'clock. We get up off the floor, back away, and watch Dolly guide Oscar back into his cage. As soon as the cage door swings shut, he begins to whimper, and it breaks me in half.

"Don't worry—he'll be okay," Dolly assures us as we return to the reception area. "We have a volunteer who comes in at six, and she stays until nine. She's wonderful, and she'll take him out and spend time with him in the playroom. She'll tire him out, and he'll sleep well until morning."

~

When Oscar enters our house for the first time, he seems to already know this is his forever home and we are his new pack. He leads the way up the front steps, tugging at the leash and wagging his tail continuously. I unlock the front door and push it open, and he trots inside, where he waits for Amanda to unhook the leash from his harness.

Still wearing the plastic cone around his head, he sniffs his way from room to room, and we follow him with amusement and delight.

After he gets a sense of the place, Amanda shows him his water bowl and fills his food bowl with kibble that the shelter gave us. He immediately gobbles it down but looks up at us repeatedly as he chews, as if to assure himself that we won't disappear while he's distracted.

We then present some toys, and Oscar likes the squeaky ones best—in particular the blue tennis ball. We bounce it on the kitchen floor and play fetch in the family room until he wears himself out, plunks down on the carpet, and chews the squeaky ball until blue fuzz is littered everywhere.

"He's so perfect," Amanda says as she drops to her hands and knees and scratches his back. "I can't believe he's ours."

"Me neither," I reply, because he's precious and I love him already with all my heart.

When Connor arrives home from hockey practice, he, too, falls hard for Oscar. He sits down on the sofa and rubs his belly.

Later, after dinner, as I'm washing dishes and Amanda is doing her homework at the kitchen table, I mention that Oscar will need to go outside and do his business before bed.

"I'll do it," she shouts, raising her hand, and fetches Oscar's harness from the basket in the family room. She clips it on, hooks the leash, and then calls out to her brother in the basement. "Connor! I'm going to walk Oscar! Do you want to come?"

"Yes!" He runs up, taking two stairs at a time. They put on their coats and venture out the front door.

As their mom, I'm pleased to see them doing something together, because they're at an age where they don't have much in common. I watch them from the front window as they pass under the fluorescent glow of the streetlight at the end of our driveway, and I wish Nate were here to share in this moment.

~

By the time Nate pulls into the driveway, it's past midnight, and I'm lying on the family room sofa. Oscar is asleep in Amanda's room, stretched out beside her with his head on her pillow, snoring. I know this because I've peered in more than once to check on them, and I left the door ajar in case Oscar decides he needs to exit the room for any reason.

At the sound of a car door slamming shut, Oscar wakes and jumps off Amanda's bed. He lands with a thump and races downstairs. Nate's key in the door sends Oscar into a frenzy. He barks ferociously at the intruder who is entering our house.

In my bathrobe and slippers, I rise quickly because I don't want him to wake the kids, but it's probably too late for that. "It's okay, Oscar," I tell him as Nate walks in, but Oscar won't stop barking. I squat down and stroke his back to calm him.

I look up at Nate. "Welcome home. This is Oscar, who is clearly a good guard dog."

He's still barking, so Nate squats down and offers the back of his hand for Oscar to sniff. "Hey, buddy. It's okay. I live here too. It's nice to meet you."

I feel a twinge of nostalgia at the reminder of how Nate used to connect with Scooter and Dolly, but it seems so distant now, like another life.

Oscar stops barking but continues to growl. He refuses to approach Nate or sniff his hand.

"This is so strange," I say, still working to calm him. "He's been incredibly sweet all day. He must be scared. This is all a big change for him."

Amanda appears at the top of the stairs in her pajamas, rubbing her eyes. "What's going on?"

"Nothing," I reply. "Dad just came home, and Oscar's being protective. Sorry he woke you. You can go back to bed."

Without a word, she turns and leaves.

Nate rises, removes his coat, and hangs it on the coat-tree. "Let's give him a minute to get used to me. I'll get a drink. We can ignore him and act normal."

"All right." I lead the way to the kitchen, and Oscar follows me like a shadow, keeping close.

Nate moves to the liquor cupboard and withdraws the bottle of Bumbu rum we've had since Christmas.

"Really?" I ask. "On a Wednesday night?"

He gives me a look, brings out a small crystal tumbler, and opens the freezer door to scoop out some ice. "It's been one of those days. Would you like one?"

"No, thanks."

I stand at the kitchen island and watch him pour his drink, swirl it around until the ice cubes clink together, and then take a sip.

"I need to watch some TV," he says.

This means sports. He tells me it calms his brain after a busy night.

"Do you want to talk about it?" I ask, curious about what might have occurred at the restaurant.

He exhales heavily. "There was an electrical fire this afternoon. Thank God it happened before we opened, but still."

"Oh, my gosh. Was anyone hurt?"

He waves a hand dismissively through the air. "No, it was nothing like that. It was just some sparks from the outlet in the office." He moves toward the sofa. "But we lost power and had to get an electrician in pronto."

"That's horrible," I reply. "Was he able to fix everything?"

"Yes, after tearing out part of the wall. I guess that's what you get for buying an old building. We were able to open on time for dinner, but now we need to replace all the wiring—everything—to bring it up to code."

Nate collapses onto the sofa and picks up the remote control.

"It definitely sounds like one of those days," I reply and wonder about the cost of something like that, which worries me because the restaurant's profit margin is slim at the best of times. "Can you get a few different quotes?"

"I will, but the guy today gave me a ballpark figure." Nate sips his drink, then tips his head back against the sofa and blinks up at the ceiling for a few seconds. "It's a lot."

"I'm afraid to ask."

"Good, because you don't want to know."

Slowly, I move to the chair across from him and sit down. "Can you use the restaurant's line of credit?"

"I can," he replies, "but we're barely keeping our heads above water as it is. Sometimes, if we have a slow week, I've had to dip into that to pay my employees, so there's not much room left for a renovation."

I swallow with unease. "Are there any areas where you could cut back on expenses? I mean . . . some of your menu items are pretty extravagant."

He frowns. "I'm not going to start serving beans on toast, if that's what you're getting at."

I hate it when he gets like this.

"I'm not suggesting that at all. But surely there are other things . . . fixed costs you could trim. Or maybe you could get by with fewer employees. I could help out. Don't forget I built a successful business in a previous life, and I was a waitress in high school."

Nate sits forward and rests his elbows on his knees. "If I laid people off and started relying on my wife to greet guests at the door, tongues would wag. I don't want to risk the restaurant's reputation. I've worked too hard to get here, and we're so close."

"To getting a Michelin star?" I ask, feeling certain he's been living in a fantasy world, because Canada's east coast is not even on their radar. I know because I monitor these things.

Nevertheless, he nods and sips his drink.

"Does it really matter that much?" I ask impetuously. "You get great reviews, and you're considered one of the best restaurants in the city. Can't that be enough? Because there's a lot of politics involved in getting a Michelin rating. It's not just about the food."

His eyes are bloodshot when they meet mine. "Trust me, I know how difficult it is, but that's why I'm working so hard for it. I want to be the first. Then we wouldn't have to worry about paying employees. The increase in revenue would take care of everything."

Feeling deflated, I sit back in the chair and rub the back of my head. Oscar has lain down on top of my feet.

"If I can reach that goal," Nate continues, "*then* I can think about slowing down and spending more time with you and the kids. I'd have the funds to hire the right people to maintain my vision."

I feel as if we've been going around in circles. We're back to that same old conversation we've had a hundred times before—when he promises to slow down when he reaches a certain goal. But the goalposts keep moving. This time, there's a renovation to consider.

"So what are you going to do?" I ask while struggling to suppress my frustration. "Can you ask the bank to increase your credit limit?"

He finishes his drink and sets the glass on the coffee table. "I can, if I have to, but interest rates are killing me right now. It's like one step forward, two steps back."

My stomach starts to churn because I sense where this conversation is going.

He looks at me. "Would you consider loaning me the money? If I get that star, I'll have no trouble paying it back."

All the muscles in my body tense. He's my husband, and I love him. I've supported him up and down every path of this career journey, and I have no regrets about that. I was thrilled the day he purchased the building (for which I provided the down payment, and my name is on the deed). When he hung his sign out front, we celebrated with champagne. And on the first night he opened his doors, I took my parents, and we all ordered the most expensive items on the menu. But that was then, and the journey has been arduous ever since.

I'm not just referring to Nate's obsession with the restaurant, or the fact that I lost both my parents in the first few years of business. Then COVID-19 was especially difficult. Nate wasn't easy to live with during Oblique's closure. He became irritable and closed off, and he still hasn't returned to his old self.

"I'm not sure about that," I reply, because in all honesty, I'm not confident that he'll ever be able to pay it back. Maybe if he gets the star, it'll all work out, but I can't help but feel it's a pipe dream. "That money is our nest egg for retirement," I remind him. "And it's meant to cover the kids' education."

"Yes, of course we want to do that," he replies. "And we will. But that's at least two years away."

"Time moves quickly," I remind him.

We stare at each other across the width of the family room, and I hate this. I can't bear to say no to him, but I don't want to be irresponsible with the money I've set aside for the future. The money that came from the sale of my company.

"Is that a firm no?" he asks, sounding disappointed, which makes me feel like a greedy old miser.

"It's late," I reply. "You know I can't make important decisions past midnight, when my brain stops working. Let me think about it, okay? We'll talk again tomorrow."

"All right." He gestures toward Oscar. "You should go to bed and take that little guy. He needs a good night's sleep so that we can start fresh in the morning."

I take a deep breath to ease the tension in my body. "Yes, you guys definitely got off on the wrong foot." I sit forward and pat Oscar's head. "Can I do anything for you?" I ask Nate. "Freshen up your drink? Make you a plate of nachos?"

"No, thanks. I just need to chill and watch some basketball."

This all feels terribly superficial, as if we're both uneasy with the conversation we've just had and we're keeping our emotional cards close to our chests.

I wish it wasn't like this, and I still don't know how in the world we got here.

I rise from the chair. "Don't stay up too late."

"I won't."

"And I'm sorry about that fire today, but we'll figure it out."

He meets my gaze intensely. "We have to, because I can't lose Oblique, Sienna. You *know* I can't."

As I stare at him, I feel an immense pressure to help him get through this ordeal—because I understand who he is. Nate needs his restaurant to succeed because he can't give his father the satisfaction of saying "I told you so."

But then I remind myself that Nate hasn't spoken to that wretched man in years. Bill hasn't even met his grandchildren. At this point, I don't know why it matters to Nate what his father thinks. I certainly don't care. As far as I'm concerned, Bill Palmer is persona non grata.

But I keep this to myself, which only serves to accentuate the deep emotional chasm between my husband and me.

"We'll talk again tomorrow," I say as I lead Oscar from the room. I walk him to Amanda's door, where I pick him up, carry him inside to her bed, and set him down gently beside her.

"Go to sleep," I whisper and give Oscar a kiss on the head before placing one on Amanda's head as well.

Oscar drops his chin to his front paws and, with those big, beautiful brown eyes, watches me back out of the room.

~

At some point during the night, long after Nate has crawled into bed beside me and fallen into a deep slumber, I wake to a presence and the strong sense that I'm being watched. The room is pitch black, so I reach for my phone on the bedside table and raise it to check the time. It's 2:48 a.m. As I set it back down, the bluish light from the screen shines on a pair of big brown eyes staring up at me.

It's Oscar, and I wonder how long he's been sitting there.

"Hey," I whisper as I lower my hand to let him sniff it.

He whimpers softly, as if he doesn't want to wake anyone, but it's enough to let me know that he's anxious.

"Are you lonely?" I ask. "Do you want to come up?"

I slide out of bed and carefully lift him onto the mattress. He waits for me to settle under the covers before he snuggles next to me. Soon, we're spooning like I used to do with Scooter.

"I know you miss your person," I whisper in his ear as I move my hand to his chest and feel his little heart beating beneath my palm. "I know what that feels like, but you're in a safe place now. I promise we'll love you and take good care of you. For the rest of your days."

I fall asleep with tenderness in my heart but at the same time wishing solemnly that Nate could let go of his burning need to prove himself to someone who doesn't deserve his consideration. I wish Nate could focus instead on those of us who are proud of him no matter what. Whether the restaurant succeeds or fails, we will always love him. Why can't he appreciate that?

CHAPTER THIRTEEN

Dogs

I'm sitting in my car with the heat blasting, waiting for Amanda to finish her shift at the swimming pool. Oscar sleeps on my lap, like a baby in my arms, his heavy head resting in the crook of my elbow. How peaceful he looks in slumber. I stroke his head and finger his soft, velvety ear, then bend forward to kiss the top of his head.

In the next instant, I jump with fright when Amanda opens the car door and drops onto the seat like a bag of bricks.

Oscar startles awake and scrambles to stand on my lap, tail wagging.

"Hello, Oscar!" she coos and scratches behind his ears.

I recover my calm and watch her buckle her seat belt. "How was your shift?" This was the first time she'd seen Jeff since we filed the police report, so I'm more than a little curious.

"Great," she replies, eyes smiling. "It was amazing, actually."

My daughter's happiness is like a drug to me, and euphoria surges through my bloodstream. It's especially intoxicating after our stressful conversation this morning when she was worked up, afraid of what Jeff might think of her.

I pass Oscar across the console so she can hold him while we drive. "What happened?"

"As soon as I walked onto the pool deck," Amanda explains, "Jeff came straight over to tell me that he heard I went to the cops."

My eyebrows fly up. "Really? How did he know?"

"He said Marissa texted him and went on a crazy rant, calling him a . . . let's just say *loser*, but that's not the word she used. Anyway, she told him that I went to the cops and that I was the crazy one, but he doesn't think so." Amanda clasps my forearm. "Mom. He actually *thanked* me."

Overcome with relief, I meet her gaze. "No way."

"Yes, because she's been harassing him too, and he didn't know how to make her stop. He said he wished he had 'balls as big as' mine."

I laugh. "I love it."

Amanda laughs too. "I know, right? He's awesome. And just now we were talking, and he was really understanding, and he said it must have been tough on me, and he apologized for it happening. I told him it was definitely tough but that it turned out to be a good thing because I got a dog out of it." She rubs Oscar's belly, kisses the top of his head, and speaks baby talk. "You're worth every minute of the hell I went through."

"Every cloud has a silver lining." I chuckle as I watch her snuggle with Oscar.

"But there's more," she says, giving me a coy look.

"Do tell." I shift into drive and head for home.

"Jeff has a dog too," she says. "And guess what kind."

"I don't know."

She pauses for dramatic effect. "A giant Yorkie."

"No way!"

"Her name is Tootsie, and she's eight years old."

"Maybe they'll be best friends." I wink at her, and she smiles.

We reach a busy intersection, and when the light turns yellow, I consider hitting the brakes but decide to speed up.

"Here's the best part," Amanda adds. "Jeff asked if I wanted to meet up tomorrow and take the dogs for a walk."

I glance briefly at her. "Interesting. Is this a first date?"

"Mom. Don't."

"Don't what?" I ask innocently.

"Don't call it a date. We're just hanging out. But can I go? He said he could drive to our house."

I put on a serious face. "He drives? How old is this boy?"

"Seventeen."

I digest that. "Would Dad and I get to meet him?"

"I guess. If you want to."

"Of course we'd want to," I reply.

We drive in silence for a moment.

"Will Dad even be there?" Amanda asks.

I tap my thumb a few times on the steering wheel. "I'm not sure. What time would Jeff arrive?"

"Around noon."

I slowly nod. "Then Dad should be home, so it sounds fine. Tell Jeff to come to the front door and ring the bell."

We drive the next two blocks in a second round of silence, so I decide to scale back on the strict parenting routine. I nudge Amanda with my elbow and give her a look. "I can't wait to meet Tootsie."

She grins and immediately texts Jeff.

This improvement in her mood since breakfast comes as a great relief to me. I glance down at Oscar on her lap and feel rejuvenated.

~

The doorbell rings the next day. Oscar barks and runs to the front hall. There's a great hullabaloo, but I remain in the kitchen to give Amanda a chance to greet Jeff.

Naturally, I eavesdrop.

"Settle down, Oscar," Amanda says before she opens the door. "You made it."

They supervise the meeting of Tootsie and Oscar, and I'm pleased that the barking has ceased and neither dog is growling or yelping. I dry my hands at the kitchen sink and move to the foyer.

"Hi," I say. "You must be Jeff." He's a handsome boy, about five foot eleven, with honey-brown hair and blue eyes. He looks nervous. "I'm Sienna."

"It's a pleasure to meet you," he politely replies.

I turn my attention to the dogs, who are sniffing each other's behinds.

"This must be Tootsie," I say. "She's so adorable. They could be twins."

"Oscar's a bit bigger," Amanda mentions, and we all watch them interact for a few seconds.

"Amanda tells me you work at the pool," I say to Jeff, wanting to get to know him a little. "Have you been working there long?"

"This is my second year," he replies. "It's a good job. It's helping me save for university."

"Good for you. Do you know where you might like to go?"

"Probably Dal so that I can keep living at home and save money."

"That sounds like a good plan," I reply.

Oscar barks twice, and Amanda pulls his leash from the basket. "He needs to pee, so we should get going."

While Amanda pulls on her coat and boots, I glance toward the den, where Nate had disappeared immediately after breakfast. It grates on my nerves that he hasn't come out to say hello to his daughter's potential first boyfriend. He couldn't have failed to notice the doorbell ringing and the barking. But I don't want to call out to him and make a big deal out of it. That would be awkward for Amanda, so I let it be.

I move forward and hold the door open for her, Jeff, and the two dogs as they make their way outside and down the front steps.

After I shut the door behind them, I discreetly tug the curtain aside and peek out the window to spy. They're talking and laughing as they walk down the street, and I'm relieved to see Amanda smiling again after such a bad week.

But as I let the curtain fall closed, my feelings take a sharp turn, and there's a noisy pounding in my ears. I realize I've become a pressure cooker, and my lid is about to fly off.

Before I even realize what the hell I'm doing, I march down the hall to the den, where I find the door shut. I stop and stare at it for a few scorching seconds. Then I push forward and walk in without knocking.

Nate is talking on his cell phone, pacing around the room, arguing with someone about the wiring at the restaurant. He glances up at me briefly and holds up a finger to let me know that he can't talk to me right now.

I wrestle my emotions into a stranglehold, back out of the room, and return to the kitchen.

~

A few minutes later, Nate finds me at the counter, making a sandwich for myself.

"They left already?" he asks.

I slather mayonnaise on two slices of bread. "Yes. They went out to walk the dogs. Maybe you can meet Jeff when they come back."

He knows me well enough to recognize the anger in my tone. "Sorry. I wanted to meet him, but I couldn't get off the phone. I was putting out a few fires. Not literal fires. You know what I mean."

"I do." I slap ham and cheese on one slice of bread, cover it with the other, and cut it in half. I set the knife down with a clatter, then swing around to face him. "I can't do this anymore."

All color drains from his face. "Do what?"

"Support you and the restaurant."

He stares with wide eyes. "You mean financially? Babe, I haven't asked you for money since we opened, except for last week, but that was a special circumstance."

I shake my head. "You haven't been able to take a salary in years, and I'm covering all our expenses. I've had to dip into our nest egg more than once to cover extra things for the kids. And now it looks like I'm going to have to cover this electrical fire, and I'm starting to worry that the restaurant is going to bankrupt us."

"It's not," he assures me with a look of shock. "We have plenty of money in the bank."

"We *don't* have plenty of money!" I counter. "Not if I have to keep funneling it into the restaurant, and you know I've wanted to keep enough to cover the kids' educations. When I sold my company, that money was supposed to be our retirement fund, but at this rate, we'll blow through everything before Connor graduates from high school. Trust me, I did the math."

Suddenly he looks worried. He pulls out a stool at the kitchen island and sits down. "You're angry."

"Yes."

The lengthy silence between us is full of contentious energy.

"You've been angry a lot lately." He shuts his eyes and shakes his head at himself. "I'm sorry I didn't come out to meet Jeff earlier. I swear to you, I had every intention of it, and I promise I'll stay home until they get back. I'll meet him then."

His words are hollow in my ears. "Every time you say you'll do something or be somewhere . . . in my mind, I'm thinking, 'Yeah, sure.' And that's exactly what I'm thinking right now."

He bows his head. "If we can just get over this hump with the wiring . . . I promise you, things will get better."

I throw my hands up in the air. "Seriously? You're not hearing a word I'm saying! And I'm not just talking about money. I'm talking about your commitment as a husband and father because I might as well be a single parent. Me and the kids are at the bottom of your list of priorities."

"That's not true."

I take a few seconds to try and settle down. Then I continue in a calmer voice. "I've been disappointed too many times, and every day, I feel like I'm being lied to . . . taken advantage of—financially and in other ways too. I'm here to do your laundry and raise your kids and keep the house nice for when you come home. But what do you ever give back to me or the kids? Nothing."

Though I've lost my appetite, I pick up the plate with my sandwich on it and carry it to the sofa in the family room, because I need an excuse to walk away from him.

"Sienna . . ." He watches me sit down. "What can I do to fix this?"

I regard him with dismay. "Do you really need to ask that question? We've had this conversation a thousand times."

Thankfully, he owns up to that. "I know. I'm sorry."

I take a bite of my sandwich, chew, and swallow.

"At this point, something has to change because I feel angry at you all the time, and I don't want to live that way."

Neither of us speaks for at least a full minute, and the weight of our silence is oppressive.

"I love you," he finally says.

I look at him directly, and exhale. "You know, that's the first thing you've said today that I actually believe. Because I know you love me and the kids, and you don't want to lose us. But you're oblivious to our needs because you're so totally consumed by the success of Oblique. And we both know why."

I stare at him intensely and wait for him to admit what has been driving him all these years, since the day we met. But he just sits there, motionless, with dread in his eyes.

"It's because you don't want your father to see you fail," I tell him. "Which I don't understand because he's made it clear he doesn't care about us. Why does he matter to you? He cut you off years ago and hasn't even met our children. The man has a heart of stone, but still, you bend over backward to get his attention and prove yourself to him."

Nate says nothing. He just stares at the floor. Then I realize this conversation is too much for him. He has completely shut down.

I stand, walk to him, and lay my hand on his shoulder. "Will you at least admit this to yourself? Because I hate that he still has this power over you. I wish you could just live for your own happiness and not care what he thinks."

Nate finally looks up. "That's exactly what I did twenty years ago. It's why I quit law school."

"Yes, and that took courage," I concede. "But he still matters to you. More than *we* do, I think."

He scoffs. "Now you're being ridiculous."

"Am I? I don't think so."

Nate shakes his head, gets up, and strides to the bedroom.

I follow because I'm not ready to let this go. "Why is it so necessary for you to have a Michelin star? For that matter, why can't we cut our losses, close the restaurant, and you could work at any restaurant in the city? You've been getting offers for years. Then you could focus on your first love, which is being a chef, instead of worrying about bills and payroll and electrical fires."

He searches angrily through the shirts hanging in his closet. "I'm not going to shut it down. Please don't suggest that."

"Why not? Just consider it. That's all I ask. You'd have far less stress in your life, you'd make good money, and you wouldn't miss out on Connor's hockey games. You'd be around if Amanda is getting bullied."

He glares at me. "Stop throwing guilt at me." He pulls a wool sweater over his head and rolls the sleeves up to his elbows, then stalks out of the bedroom.

Again, I follow.

"I have to go to work," he tells me. He searches for his boots in the front hall closet and pulls them on.

"I thought you were going to stay to meet Jeff."

"Do you want him to meet us together like this?" he asks. "When we're at each other's throats?"

"Nate, come on . . ."

"No, listen. You don't get it. It's not just about my father. There's a whole staff depending on me for their livelihood." He pulls on his coat. "I have to go. I'll meet Amanda's friend another time." He walks out the door, gets in his car, and drives off.

I stand in the doorway and watch him disappear down the street.

There's a numbness in my veins. I don't know how to get through to him. What's it going to take? The restaurant falls deeper into debt every day, but he won't see it. And the kids are constantly disappointed. They don't feel close to him, or loved by him.

Perhaps the time has come to talk to a lawyer, because I can't let this continue. I can't just stand back and let him bleed this family dry.

PART FOUR

THE POWER OF LOVE

CHAPTER FOURTEEN

I Want to Believe

I am weeping. Crying my eyes out.

It's been two hours since I sat down in my lawyer's office and discussed the implications of a divorce—financial and otherwise.

I still haven't made up my mind. I was there only to seek information about what that path might look like, but now I can't stop thinking about our wedding day and how crazy in love we were. Back then, I believed that Nate was my knight in shining armor because he'd scooped me out of darkness and delivered me from my bottomless pit of grief. But everything between us is so different now.

This is why I weep. I don't want to believe that our love wasn't real or that it wasn't meant to be.

~

Days later, Nate walks into the kitchen. "Good morning," I say.

"Morning."

Freshly showered and dressed for the day, he pours himself a coffee from the French press and notices that I've cooked scrambled eggs and bacon, which is not something I normally do on weekdays. Bacon is reserved for weekends, but this morning I don't want Nate to simply grab his coffee and go.

"Have a seat, because there's something I want to talk to you about," I say.

He checks his watch—to signal that I'm making him late—but I try to not let it bother me. I don't want this to get ugly.

I bring the skillet from the stove to his plate at the island and serve up the eggs, which forces him to pull out a stool and sit down. Then I serve myself and sit beside him. Oscar lies down at my feet.

Nate digs in, and I pick up my fork, but all I can do is poke at my eggs.

"I went to see a lawyer," I finally confess.

Nate stops chewing. He turns his head and looks at me. "A lawyer? What about? Is Amanda still having trouble with that girl?"

"No." I swivel on the stool to face him. "I went to see someone to find out what a separation or divorce might look like."

Nate gulps down his eggs. "Sienna . . ."

"Please don't act like you're surprised." Steeling myself against the tenderness in his tone, I fight to be strong. "You know I haven't been happy."

He wipes his mouth with a napkin. "Yes, and I agree that we haven't been on the same page lately . . ." His tone becomes laced with pleading, and he starts working hard to talk sense into me. "But every marriage has rough patches." He reaches for my hand. "That doesn't mean we should throw in the towel."

"It's more than a rough patch," I argue. "I feel like you've lost interest in me, and it's been that way for a long time. We've become strangers, and . . ." I pause and keep my eyes downcast because I'm afraid that if I look directly at him, I'll start crying again. "I don't feel loved. At least not by you."

He blinks a few times in disbelief. "You're the love of my life. You know that."

I shake my head. "I used to know it, but I'm not so sure anymore, because you talk to Martina more than you talk to me. I think the restaurant has become the love of your life. That's where your passions are."

Nate takes my other hand, so he now holds both in his grasp. "I love you. Don't ever doubt that."

I give him a skeptical glance.

"Okay . . . yes," he says, conceding a little. "I've probably been a bad husband lately, but I did hear what you said before, about my father. I've been thinking about it, and . . . you're right. Maybe he's the reason I don't want to fail."

I say nothing because I want to hear more from him. I want to believe that this marriage is still salvageable.

"I just want him to know that he was wrong," Nate explains. "And I'd love to rub it in his face."

I slowly nod because I'd enjoy seeing that as well. "I get it. Honestly, I do. But chasing that dream has come at a high price. I still can't believe that I went to see a lawyer, which was never something I imagined would happen to us. *Ever.*"

"Me neither." He closes his eyes. "There must be something wrong with me, because I don't want to lose you and the kids, but I also need the restaurant to succeed. It's like an addiction."

Realizing that we're going around in circles again, I turn back to my eggs and take the first bite.

Nate watches me for a moment. "Sienna . . . are you actually serious? About separating?"

"Yes," I reply.

He leans back on the stool while I eat my breakfast, but at this point, I'm force-feeding myself.

"Please . . . we can work things out," he says.

I reach for my glass of orange juice and take a sip. "I've been trying to work it out with you for more than a year, but nothing ever changes."

"I'll do whatever you want," he quickly replies.

Sensing that he's finally starting to take this seriously, I set down my fork and lean back also. "And what do you think that is?"

"I'll shut down the restaurant."

My breath hitches. It's an enormous concession, and we both know it.

"And I'll get a job," he adds. "I don't know where but . . . somewhere."

Nate looks away. He seems lost, as if he's drowning in that image, and though he's finally agreeing to make a change, I take no pleasure in this. None of it feels right.

I get up and carry the dirty dishes to the sink and rinse them. When I turn around, Nate is still seated. He's staring intensely at the floral centerpiece. Then his cell phone rings. He picks it up, checks the display, and says to me, "I have to take this." He rises and heads for the den while I begin to load the dishwasher.

A moment later, he returns. "Sorry about that. I swear I wasn't ditching this conversation, but it was Martina. I told her I won't be working tonight. Graham can manage the kitchen on his own."

I blink a few times and wonder if I've fallen into an alternate universe.

"I still have to go in this morning," Nate adds, "just to prep Graham and make sure everything will run smoothly without me, but we can't leave things like this. We should spend time together and talk some more." He pauses. "Like we used to."

I'm caught off guard. "Today?"

"Yes, this afternoon. Let's go somewhere. To the South Shore. We could drive to Peggy's Cove and have lunch."

We haven't been to the lighthouse at Peggy's Cove in years—not since the kids were small. "I'd like that," I reply, feeling the first traces of hope.

Nate gives me a small smile. "Good." Then he checks his watch again. "I need to go and meet Graham, but I'll let everyone know that I'm taking the whole day off. They'll have to figure it out."

When his eyes meet mine, I see where his thoughts have already gone—to the restaurant, tonight's menu, the challenge of staff management. He's becoming stressed, and my hopes wane.

"I'll be back by noon," he assures me.

"Sure."

Remaining cool, I vow to myself that this will be the last chance I give him—because I've been down this road of empty promises too many times, and I'm almost certain that he's not going to show up today.

CHAPTER FIFTEEN

A Warmth That Beckons

I am wrong. At precisely 11:55 a.m., Oscar goes ballistic when Nate walks through the front door.

In a way, it feels like some sort of genesis, yet I know that we are far from resurrected. It's been ages since Nate and I have been affectionate with each other. I can't even remember the last time we snuggled on the sofa. We've been detached, physically and emotionally, and though I'm pleased that he's made this effort to come home today, I don't know how we can ever find our way back to what we once were. There's too much animosity between us now. Imitation smiles and awkwardness.

When he finally enters the kitchen with Oscar following excitedly, sniffing at his pant leg, I don't have the first clue what to say to him. For a few clumsy seconds, we stand and stare.

"Do you still want to go to Peggy's Cove?" he asks.

I force myself to snap out of this inertia. "Yes. Just give me a minute to change."

~

We decide to leave Oscar at home so that we can focus on each other. This is Nate's suggestion, not mine.

In the car, after we exhaust the conversation about what happened that morning at the restaurant (the electrician's visit and the all-important staff meeting with Graham in charge), Nate turns on the radio. From that moment on, we drive in silence, as if we are both relying on the destination to provide the solution to our marital troubles. That's where we will finally reconnect. The journey to get there is merely incidental.

But for me, the lack of conversation in this enclosed space becomes as aggravating as a pair of tight shoes. My nerves are strained. I'm trying not to feel angry again, but my thoughts race dangerously. Nate knows I'm considering a separation, and he admits he must do better for us. Yet he's staring at the road, probably obsessing about the restaurant, worrying about the staff's performance, and wishing he were there to manage them, instead of sitting in this car with me.

As the miles pass, I grow increasingly frustrated. This excursion feels pointless. I want to sort things out, but I'm tired of rowing this boat, and I refuse to be the only one in this relationship who ever picks up the oars. I'm done with that. So I don't initiate conversation. I simply gaze out the window.

~

Peggy's Cove is a small, picturesque fishing village, best known for its famed, iconic lighthouse, which sits atop a rugged granite outcrop overlooking the Atlantic Ocean. It's crowded today because of a recent storm. The locals have come out to watch the cove's wild waters, with waves crashing violently against the rocks.

Nate gets lucky and finds a parking spot on the upper lot behind the Sou'Wester restaurant. As soon as I open the car door, I hear the ferocious roar of the ocean beyond. I step out and breathe in the fresh, salty fragrance of the sea. Then I take in the small fishing village with its colorful boats, weathered buildings, lobster traps, and nets piled on the wharf. Seagulls squawk and spiral above us. I look up. The air is cold. I can see my breath, but the winter sun is bright and warm on my face.

Nate locks the car. "I can't believe how much this place has changed." He's referring to the freshly paved road to the restaurant, the modern sidewalks, and the public washrooms, which have made the village more accessible and tourist friendly.

We walk to the front of the restaurant for our first proper view of the ocean, where monstrous waves explode against the rocks, shooting foamy plumes fifty feet into the air.

"My God, look at that." Nate stares, awestruck. "It's like a volcanic eruption." He then turns his attention to the new viewing deck that juts out over the rocks. "That's impressive."

"The safety railings are a good thing," I say as I walk toward it. "But half the fun of coming here is rock hopping."

"No one's stopping us." He glances to the left, where the granite boulders are crawling with visitors.

We stroll to the wooden deck and marvel at the mighty power of the North Atlantic. For a fleeting second, I forget the problems in my marriage because my daily life seems insignificant compared to these breathtaking forces.

An older couple approaches, and the woman asks me to take their picture. I happily comply and wait while they pose in front of the rail. I arrange the proper frame and the right composition and wait for a wave to break in the background. I even take a quick video that I know they'll appreciate when they review their photo gallery later.

"Here you go." I hand their phone back to them, and they thank me. I then discover that Nate has wandered off. He's standing at the edge of the deck, near the path to the lighthouse, waving at me to join him.

Moments later, we step from the well-maintained gravel path onto the uneven granite. We pick our way over patches of ice in hollows where the sun has yet to reach.

It's a short walk to the lighthouse, but in front of it, the north wind hits us with a sharp bite, so we decide to not linger but to venture onto the crests and valleys of the sloping granite landscape. We stroll to the highest point where we can watch the waves crash and explode below us, as loud as cannon fire.

"It's unbelievable!" I shout.

He nods, and again I grow frustrated with his silence.

The wind off the water is frigid, so I gather my wool scarf tighter around my neck. My nose runs, and I sniffle. "Should we head back to the restaurant?" I ask.

"Sure." He pauses. "But I'd like to get something off my chest first."

"All right." I tug my scarf higher to cover my mouth and ears and hunch my shoulders stiffly because I'm starting to shiver.

The wind whips at Nate's hair. "I want you to know that I don't want a divorce. I love you."

I'm pleased to hear it, and my stiff muscles relax slightly.

"But I don't want to shut down the restaurant either," he says.

Another wave crashes onto the shoreline, and my heart sinks.

"I did a lot of thinking this morning," he says, "and if you could just give me one more year. If you could help me get through this reno . . ."

"Nate . . ."

"No, listen . . . please, hear me out. I talked to the electrician this morning, and it turns out it's not as bad as I thought it would be, and the building will be worth a lot more if we do some upgrades. I talked to Martina about things we can do in terms of operations, and if I haven't turned the situation around a year from now, I promise I'll shut it down. And just so you know that I'm serious about making our marriage work, I'd like us to go to couples counseling. You suggested it once, and I wasn't ready, but I am now."

I stare at him in shock, and I'm certain that he's just saying what he thinks I want to hear. He's dangling a carrot to get me on board with the restaurant renovations and prevent me from leaving him.

"No," I say, flat out. "You know how I feel, and I can't take another year of this. I'm seriously worried that if the restaurant goes bankrupt, they'll come after our house."

He speaks reassuringly. "That's not going to happen."

"How do you know? The lawyer said it was a possibility."

With diminishing hope, I face the raging ocean, the violent swells, and the foaming whitecaps. The sky is blue, and the sun is beaming on the water, but the world is a tempest right now. I'm freezing, and I want to scream. I don't want lunch or hot chocolate. I just want to get back in the car and drive home alone. Nate can call an Uber.

I turn and start hopping down the sloping rocks.

"Sienna, wait!" Nate calls after me. "Just let me tell you about the plan!"

"No! You need therapy!" I shout over my shoulder, but I feel him chasing after me.

Suddenly, I'm knocked off my feet. It's as if I've been bodychecked. The next instant, I'm spinning in the churning, ice-cold water. The temperature takes my breath away, and I gasp. Frigid salt water pours into my lungs. It burns my chest and stings my flesh, like a steel cheese grater scouring my entire body.

I struggle to kick and swim to the surface, but I'm powerless against the currents. My body is flung into a series of barrel rolls. I can't breathe. I'm disoriented. My heart is about to explode.

Then I slam against a rock-solid wall. The impact paralyzes me, and I go limp as I'm swept away. There's red in the water. It's my blood, but I don't know where it's coming from because I feel bone-numbing pain everywhere.

Miraculously, I break the surface, catch a brief glimpse of blue sky, and cough water out of my lungs. But I have only seconds to take a breath before I'm struck by a massive wave and sucked under again, into the bubbles and cold, rolling deep.

Down I go . . .

There's no hope for me.

No one can save me now. I know it.

I become drowsy . . . confused . . . numb.

There's no more pain.

My children . . . *God in heaven, my children.*

I think of them with heartache. I don't want to leave them alone in the world, but there's nothing I can do. This is the end. I'm about to die here.

Yet the will to survive is steadfast. As I'm dragged down by the undertow, my body craves oxygen. I open my mouth and draw in an enormous breath of water.

The shock of it entering my lungs sends me into a fresh panic. My body twitches and seizes convulsively. The loss of control is devastating. This goes on and on.

Eventually, my panic recedes. I am thrust upward again, toward the surface. I see bubbles, glistening in the sun, rising, and I kick hard and shoot like a rocket toward the light.

~

I need to get home. I need to see my children one more time. Warn them that I won't be around after today. They'll need to rely on their father and Becky. Most of all, I want them to know they're loved.

I fly through the front door of my house and reach the kitchen. Oscar is asleep on his bed next to the sofa. He stirs. His tail starts wagging, and he barks with distress, so I comfort him. I kiss his sweet, furry cheek, and he nuzzles my neck.

"What a good boy you are."

He prances in circles.

Amanda runs down the stairs, and I'm overjoyed to see her.

"Oscar, what is it?" She kneels beside him and tries to scratch behind his ears, but he darts away and twirls, as if he's chasing his tail. He stops, and his ears perk up. He looks intently at me, then at her, then back at me again.

Amanda laughs and gets up off the floor. "What's wrong with you?"

"Sweetheart," I say to her, but she ignores me. "Amanda, you have to listen. I just drowned."

At first, I'm baffled by her disinterest. Then I remember that I'm dead and she can't see me. If she could, she'd hug me and cry her eyes out, and she'd refuse to let me go.

Oscar, however, is another story. He's keenly aware of my presence. He gazes up at me intently, tail wagging, and runs to the basket where we keep his leash.

"Sorry, buddy, I can't take you."

He continues to stare, which is not surprising. Even when I was alive, he wouldn't take no for an answer.

"Where's Connor?" I ask Amanda.

Still no response from her.

I glance at the clock on the wall and remember that he had hockey practice this afternoon. I need to go to the rink, but I'm hesitant to leave. I don't want to say goodbye to Amanda.

She moves to the refrigerator, opens it, and reaches for a tub of yogurt. *Good, healthy choice,* I think as she peels back the plastic lid. She opens the cutlery drawer and digs around for a spoon.

Watching her, I feel strangely euphoric, which is shocking to me. Somehow, I know she's going to be okay. She's a beautiful soul. I've raised her well, and she's intelligent. Independent. A good person. My heart overflows with love for her and pride in the person she's become.

I don't want to leave her, and I regret that I won't be here for important events in the future, like her wedding day and the birth of her children. That will be difficult for her, but I hope she'll understand that we'll never be apart, and we'll see each other again. But right now, I have to go. I have no choice. I can't fight this.

Slowly, I withdraw from the kitchen. I treasure these last few seconds, watching her in this life. Then I zoom, at the speed of light, to the rink.

~

Connor is skating fast during a scrimmage. I hover over the centerline and watch him perform his magic.

I've never seen him skate from this angle before, and I'm captivated by his footwork and stick handling. Though I suppose this is nothing new. I've been captivated by my children since the day they were born.

Connor swerves around a defenseman and heads down center ice, straight to the net. He shoots and scores.

Under normal circumstances, I'd jump to my feet, cheer, and clap, but I'm already floating. Besides, it's just a scrimmage game. All the same, his teammates high-five him in their hockey gloves.

For a triumphant moment, I watch my son and feel his exhilaration as if it were my own. I'm a proud mother and also relieved. I'm confident that he'll live a good life. Whatever he does, he'll do it with gusto.

I wish I could stay longer to see his life unfold, but I feel a warmth that beckons, and I need to go to it. I'm compelled.

I fly straight up toward the rafters, and I don't look back.

CHAPTER SIXTEEN

Love

A marvelous aroma of freshly mowed grass fills me with ecstasy. The sky is endlessly clear, illuminated by a golden, ethereal light. There's a soft summer breeze on my face, untainted by pollution, and I'm weightless.

I've returned to the Annapolis Valley, where I was born and raised, and I feel at home in the lush green landscape of cornfields, graceful weeping willows, and towering, majestic maples. I'm not riding in a car, but I travel swiftly along familiar country roads. I pass by a white farmhouse. A black-and-white sheepdog frolics in the front yard. Is he chasing butterflies? A Frisbee? I can't guess, but it doesn't matter. He's happy, and his joy is contagious.

I close my eyes and savor the warmth of the sunshine and my sense of safety and well-being. How different it feels from my last few moments on earth, in those cold, churning waters that had taken my life, when I was terrorized by the violence of the stormy ocean.

Yet when I think of its salty fragrance, the fog and the mist, and the mesmerizing roar of those frothy, breaking waves, I harbor no animosity. I love the ocean devotedly. I'm a part of it now, a part of the force that took my life, along with the earth and the wind, the insects, plants, flowers, rocks, and minerals.

Here, in this place, the sky is a multifaceted shade of blue that astounds me. I've never seen that shade before. All the clouds have silver linings—a dazzling light that shines from beyond. The leaves on the trees are full of moisture, buzzing with life. The rational part of my brain—which continues to wield influence on my thinking—makes me wonder if I'm dreaming, because each individual leaf, among thousands, seems to regard me with love. We share a joy I can't even begin to comprehend.

What's happening here? I know I'm dead, but I'm surrounded by the miracle of life. Photosynthesis, metabolism, chemical energy. I'm enthralled by the world around me, though I know it's not real. How can it be? I've always imagined the hereafter to be a place beyond the clouds, but I've returned to the home I love.

Is this my own private, personal heaven, called forth just for me? Is that how this works?

~

I fly faster through the valley, over fields, forests, and winding roads. Colors everywhere are more vivid and harmonious than anything I've experienced on earth—blues, greens, pinks, and golds that blend together in perfect harmony. I pass over a tiny white chapel that shimmers with divine radiance. A bell is ringing in its steeple.

I keep moving and finally pause on a residential country lane, where I spot a tall concrete water fountain with a statue of an angel in someone's backyard. For some reason I can't explain, it speaks to me.

My feet are bare, and I set them on the cool, green grass. The physical sensation of my feet connecting with the earth is heady, but I feel wholly at ease as I approach the fountain, where three gorgeous red cardinals are splashing about.

I look up at the angel and realize it's just a baby, pure and innocent, with small rounded wings. Turning slowly, I take in the view of the house—a traditional Victorian, painted white with dark-green trim.

It's enormous, and again I feel safe, as if nothing unwelcome can touch me here. A thick hedge of pink roses lines the perimeter of the yard. It's blooming spectacularly, and its fragrance fills me with rapture.

Aside from the song of sparrows in the treetops, and the gentle whisper of wind through willow trees, it's blissfully quiet. But then the back door of the house swings open on squeaky hinges, and, to my utmost delight, Scooter rushes out. He runs past a man who has stepped onto the covered veranda. Scooter swerves around him and barrels down the wooden steps.

My heart swells with joy. "Scooter!"

I drop to my knees and open my arms. He tackles me, and I laugh. I topple backward as he licks my face. Flat on my back on the grass, I shut my eyes and mouth while his tongue laps at my cheeks. I breathe in his distinct doggy scent, which I've missed so much, and I hug him and kiss him over and over.

I could stay like this forever, rolling around in the grass with my beloved dog, but something appears in my peripheral vision. I turn my head to the side and take in a pair of bare feet in brown leather sandals. Slowly, my gaze travels up two muscular calves to a pair of well-worn khaki cargo shorts.

Remembering my manners, I gently push Scooter off me so that I can sit up and say hello. But the sun blinds me. I raise my hand to shade my eyes as I squint up at the tall man. He's a silhouette against dazzling sunbeams, and that's when I know who it is.

It's Jacob, my love.

In my disbelief, I become exultant, immersed in a state of eternal contentment, but oddly unsurprised to see him. Though I was flying over the valley with no known destination, I realize now that I felt the tug of my first love and the lure of the country house we would have shared together—for our entire lives—if we'd not gone hiking that fateful day.

"You're here," Jacob says.

The sound of his voice flows through me like a river.

"Finally." Impatient to hug him, I'm clumsy as I rise. I nearly knock him over with my embrace—just like Scooter did to me moments ago when he tackled me to the ground. I fling my arms around Jacob's neck and exclaim ecstatically, "I'm so happy to see you. I missed you so much."

But none of this feels real. It's like a dream.

"I missed you too." He draws back to hold me at arm's length. "But what are you doing here?"

I don't want to answer questions. I want only to look at him. He's older, like me. His hair is still thick and wavy, as it was in our youth, but it's partially gray. He's remained impressively fit, and his eyes still hold that beautiful unconditional love I'll never forget.

"I drowned," I tell him.

His eyebrows pull together with dismay. "How? Where?"

"At Peggy's Cove. I was swept off the rocks."

He shakes his head, not willing to accept it. "That wasn't supposed to happen."

"My thoughts exactly," I reply, feeling suddenly unsteady on my feet, lightheaded. "It was awful."

Jacob stands back and takes in my appearance. His gaze lingers on my face before it sweeps down the length of my body to my bare feet. Only then do I look down at myself and realize I'm wearing denim shorts and a plain white T-shirt, which is not what I was wearing at Peggy's Cove. But I suppose it's summer here, and this is comfortable and appropriate, except for the fact that I'm not wearing shoes.

"I'm not sure what's happening," I say, mystified.

"Are you *sure* you drowned?" he asks.

I glance down at Scooter at my side. He's sitting on the grass, panting heavily, looking up at me with wonder. I lay my hand on top of his head. "Yes. I sucked water into my lungs and lost consciousness, and I watched myself convulsing—from *outside* my body. Then I went still, and I sank."

Jacob nods, as if this is normal.

"No one could have rescued me in those waves," I continue to explain. "You know what it's like at Peggy's Cove after a storm. You can't get a boat around those rocks, and it was February. The water was close to freezing. Even if they could have gotten a rescue boat out, I wouldn't have survived more than a few minutes in those temperatures."

Jacob's breath hitches, and he exhales with gentle empathy. "I'm so sorry that happened to you." He pulls me into his arms again to offer comfort. "It must have been frightening."

I cling to him as I remember the panic and horror. "Yes, but you know all about that."

I'm referring, of course, to our fall from Cape Split.

"I do." He steps back. "But thankfully, after I died, I wasn't scared anymore. And I knew you were going to be okay."

"You held my hand on the beach," I say. "And you talked to me."

"I did."

"But how was that possible? I was told you'd died instantly."

He shrugs as if it's nothing. "I stuck around for a while because I didn't want you to be alone and scared."

I finally understand what truly happened that day, and I rest my cheek on his shoulder. "Thank you for not leaving me."

"I'll *never* leave you," he vows. "I'll always be there, watching over you, looking out for you, and loving you."

Another balmy breeze whispers through the branches of the weeping willows, and the chapel bell rings. I feel peace and love in these familiar arms and decide that if this is to be my eternity, I will accept it. I won't look back.

If I do, this sense of peace might be lost.

Jacob cups my face in his hands. "You're still beautiful."

A tear rolls down my cheek, and I smile. "So are you."

"Let's go inside." He takes hold of my hand. "I want to hear all about your amazing life—your success with your business, your husband and children. I'm so proud of you, Sienna. You did great. You really did it."

Scooter nuzzles my hip. I lay my hand on his head and stroke his smooth ivory coat. Love wafts all around me, and it's unfathomable, beyond my comprehension. This is where I belong, and the solace in my soul is perfect and true.

Hands clasped in warmth, Jacob and I cross the green lawn toward the back steps of the house. As we climb them, I take in the two white rocking chairs on the veranda, a vase of fresh wildflowers on the table between them.

Suddenly I tremble with anticipation. I hear music—the most triumphant, glorious chorus I've ever heard in my life. It fills me with awe, and I sense the presence of my parents beyond that door. I can feel their love, deep in my soul, and I can't wait to see them.

CHAPTER SEVENTEEN

Nate

Oh, God. She's in the water. What have I done?

Another explosive wave crashes onto the rocks, and I feel the vibrations in my chest, already burning with a terror I've never known.

My eyes sweep the raging ocean in a mad search for Sienna, but she's gone. I can't see her. Where is she? I look left . . . right . . . across the edge of the rock where we were standing.

"Help!"

No one hears me over the hellish thunder of the waves.

My brain stumbles in the wake of my panic, and I don't know what to do. Even if I spotted her, I couldn't save her. No one could survive those temperatures or swim through the power of those waves.

I need to ask for a boat. A helicopter.

After scanning the waves desperately one last time, I turn and run toward the restaurant. I leap over a dip in the granite and run like hell to the gravel path at the lighthouse. A young couple approaches. They catch my terrorized eyes and stop.

"I need help! My wife was swept off the rocks!"

The woman cries, "Oh, my God!" and the young man pulls his cell phone out of his pocket.

"I'll call 911."

"They'll take too long to get here," I reply, hating this sense of powerlessness as I leave them and continue running toward the restaurant, where there must be safety equipment or life preservers. I pull open the door and burst into the gift shop. My eyes dart everywhere, looking for someone. There are a few tourists browsing. I turn to the cashier.

"My wife was swept off the rocks."

She stares at me blankly, and I realize she's just a high school student.

I run into the restaurant and find an older man behind the counter. "My wife was just swept off the rocks. Is there a boat?"

He turns to his coworker. "Call 911." Then he hurries out from behind the counter. "Take me there."

I run outside, and he follows, but he stops briefly at a life preserver station I hadn't noticed before. He loops the orange doughnut over his shoulder.

I point toward the spot where Sienna fell in. The frothy surf is still crashing onto the rocks and erupting into the air.

She's dead, I think to myself. She has to be. There can't possibly be any hope.

~

There are moments in my life when I despise myself, when I know I've done everything wrong and I'm a complete and utter failure. In those moments, I'm overcome by a sense of dread. My bad decisions will surely turn on me, and I'll wish I'd acted differently. I'll wish I was smarter and possessed a better understanding about how certain situations might unfold.

The man from the restaurant is a faster runner. He's familiar with the crests and valleys of these sloping rocks, and he leaps like a gazelle over tidal pools.

I'm out of breath when I reach the high point where Sienna and I argued. I stop abruptly and watch the man hop from one outcropping to another. He then jumps into a small chasm, out of sight.

I follow. I run. I trip and fall, skin the heels of my hands on the rough surface of the granite. Quickly, I scramble to my feet and continue until I reach the edge of the rocks, halt, and look down.

I freeze.

There she is.

Sienna . . . lying on the rocks while two young men on their knees, on either side of her, perform CPR. One pumps her chest while the other bends to breathe into her mouth. The man from the restaurant stands over them with the life preserver on the ground at his feet. He's talking to someone on his cell phone.

All I can do is stare in shock at the scene before me. How did they get Sienna out of the water? Did one of them dive in after her? Did they swim and pull her to safety?

Again, I'm a failure, drowning in my inadequacy.

CHAPTER EIGHTEEN

Amanda

I'm sitting on my bed, working on an English essay, when my cell phone rings. It's Dad, and I'm half tempted to ignore the call because if I call *him* in the middle of the day and he's busy at work, I'm supposed to respect that.

In my opinion, schoolwork is, by definition, *work*, but I doubt the same rules apply when the roles are reversed.

The phone rings a third time, and Oscar, who has been trotting around the house anxiously for the past forty minutes, appears in my open doorway, tail wagging, as if this phone call is a side of beef.

"All right, all right, I'll answer it," I say as I reach for my cell phone and swipe right.

"Hello?"

"It's me," Dad says.

There's something strange in his voice. He sounds shaken, so I set my laptop aside, get off the bed, and rise to my feet.

"What's going on?"

"I need you and Connor to come to the hospital."

My stomach clenches into a sickening knot. "Why? What happened?"

"Mom was swept off the rocks at Peggy's Cove."

Suddenly I can't breathe. I can't even feel my legs. "Is she okay?"

"I don't know. They did CPR, and right now she's in the trauma unit at the Halifax Infirmary. I'm still waiting for someone to come out and tell me something."

I grab my jacket and hurry down the stairs. "You're at the hospital now?"

"Yes. Can you bring Connor?"

"He's at hockey practice," I tell him.

"Where? Is it far? Can you get him on the way?"

"He's at the Centennial Arena," I explain, annoyed by the fact that Dad never knows what's going on with us. "I'll call Becky and tell her what happened, and she can pick him up." Thank God for Becky. She's always there for us. "I'll get in the car now and come straight to the hospital. I'll be there in ten minutes."

"Okay. See you soon," Dad replies.

He ends the call before I even think to ask what happened and how Mom could have been standing so close to the waves at Peggy's Cove. She's always warned us about the dangers, and she's told us hair-raising tales of tourists who perished because they didn't know any better. But those of us who grew up in Nova Scotia have always understood the merciless power of the ocean. We know better than to risk getting too close to those treacherous black rocks.

~

It's far worse than I could have imagined. I honestly thought my mother would be okay. When I drove to the hospital, I expected her to be hurt, but now I'm sitting next to her bed in the ICU while she lies unconscious. She's surrounded by medical equipment, and there's a huge plastic tube down her throat so she can breathe with a ventilator. A heart monitor beeps, and IV lines run into her arms, delivering fluids and medication.

Her arm is in a cast because her humerus snapped in two when she hit the rocks. Someone told me she was dead by that point—drowned in near-freezing water before the ocean decided to spit her out. The waves tossed her ashore, and that's when two young men grabbed hold of her and dragged her to safety, where they performed CPR.

Worst of all, she's in a coma because she had no pulse when she was rescued, and it took about twelve minutes to revive her.

So here we are, in the ICU, hanging on to hope because my mother defied the odds and came back from the dead.

I want to believe it's because she's a fighter. I've always known that about her. She's the center of our family, the sturdy post we all cling to. I'm still clinging to her now, even though she's unconscious.

I wish I could stop crying, but I can't.

~

Becky brings Connor, but she's not allowed into Mom's room yet because there's a limit of three visitors at a time in the ICU.

Connor walks in, takes one look at Mom, and breaks down. Dad tries to hug him, but Connor pushes him away and bends over Mom, sobbing. It breaks my heart to see him like this because he's learned how to tough it out on the ice, to take hits and shake them off. But this is a different kind of pain, and I don't know how to help him. I'm his older sister, and I want to be strong for him, but I'm terrified that Mom's not going to come out of this.

How will we survive if we're left alone in the world without her? No one knows me like she does. Certainly not Dad, whose fault this is.

There. I've said it. Only to myself, but I can't be the only one who's thinking it.

I shift my watery gaze from Connor to my father, who looks half comatose himself. Shell shocked.

God, he could never be what Mom is to us. He's never home, and I honestly don't think he even cares about us. He's a complete stranger to me, and I don't understand why he took Mom to Peggy's Cove in the first place, especially during the day, when he's always at work.

I hate him right now!

But it wasn't always like this. When I was little, he seemed more like a real dad. I have fond memories of my childhood—like when he'd come home from work and toss me onto his shoulders, run around the house hee-hawing like a donkey. I also remember him playing with Connor and me on Christmas mornings, assembling our toys and taking us sledding.

I'm not sure when he stopped being a good dad. It was such a gradual thing.

Oh, God, I can't stop crying. I could really use a father right now.

~

It's almost ten o'clock. Becky has been in the waiting room for hours, though we've taken turns coming in to see Mom, which has given us each a chance to take a break—to use the washroom or get food in the cafeteria. Though I haven't been able to eat much of anything besides a bag of chips.

Right now, it's just me, Connor, and Dad.

It's surprising that we can all sit together in this room, barely talking to each other, while nurses come and go. If we do speak, it's in hushed tones. We're either holding Mom's hand, rubbing her forehead, or retreating to our individual chairs against the wall to watch her. We stare at the machines that beep, and we listen to the ventilator—that eerie click, followed by the sound of the exhalation valve.

I check my phone and answer texts from friends and family who've been sending thoughts and prayers.

I've been communicating mostly with Jeff, who has offered to come to the hospital and sit with me. He's been wonderful through all this, and I'm grateful that he had the chance to meet Mom. I feel like he understands everything I'm going through.

Eventually, I set my phone down on my lap and look up. Connor catches my eye and gestures with a toss of his head to meet him outside the ICU. I nod and rise to my feet.

"We're gonna take a walk," I say to Dad.

"Sure," he replies.

I kiss Mom on the forehead and whisper close in her ear, "Connor and I will be right back. Hang in there, okay?"

I straighten and look down at her for a few seconds. Her long dark hair is unkempt, splayed in all directions on the pillow, and the breathing tube in her mouth is doing all the work, keeping her alive. She seems so far away.

Where is she?

I'm afraid to leave her, but Connor is waiting, so I remind myself that Mom is stable. Nothing has changed for the past seven hours.

I walk out of the room, leave the ICU, and find Connor in the outer hall, texting. "What's going on?" I ask.

He holds up his screen. "You haven't seen this?"

I move close, and he restarts a video. It's a spot from the local evening news, a piece about Mom's accident and an interview with the two guys who saved her. They're standing on the viewing platform at Peggy's Cove, and the ocean is raging in the background. One guy is tall with a buzz cut, and the other is short and stocky and wears glasses with a gray wool beanie.

"We saw her in the water," the tall one says. "Then she went under, and we just kept watching, hoping to see her surface. Then a huge wave crashed on the rocks, and she came flying out!" He gestures wildly with his hands and points toward the lighthouse. "She landed right over there. When the wave receded, we had time to jump down and drag her to the dry rocks. We checked her pulse, but she wasn't breathing, so we started CPR."

"Where did you learn how to do that?"

"We're both in training to be firefighters."

"That's fortunate for the woman today," the reporter replies.

"For sure. And the man from the Sou'Wester was a retired marine, so I guess her lucky star was shining."

Another wave explodes behind them. "What about her husband?" the reporter asks. "He must've been incredibly grateful to you."

The shorter guy in the hat shrugs. "He was in shock, I think. He wasn't there when we pulled her out. I'm not sure where he went, but he stood back and let us do our thing."

The reporter nods. "I appreciate you talking to me. You're a couple of heroes. I hope you know that."

"We just did what anyone else would've done," the tall one replies.

Connor swipes at his phone to clear the video and gives me a look. "Except for our dad. All *he* did was stand back and watch."

I'm starting to feel sick to my stomach, so I move to a chair and sit down. "They made him sound like a coward, but he went for help."

Connor sits in the chair beside me. "Yeah. *We* know that, but TikTok has been blowing up." He starts scrolling. "Look at this. People know him as a celebrity chef, so they're all over it, saying he might have pushed her."

I wrench back in shock. *"What?"*

Connor keeps reading. "One person posted about the electrical fire at the restaurant, and now everyone's talking about how he must have done it for the publicity, and that he wants Mom's life insurance."

I pull a face in disbelief and lean close to look at his phone. "You're joking."

"No, look, it's everywhere."

He hands me his phone, and I scroll through a long thread on X with the hashtag PeggysCoveMurder.

"This isn't happening." I rake my fingers through my hair.

"It is," Connor replies. "And Dad has no idea."

I slide him a look. "Don't be so sure about that. He's been on his phone constantly for the past hour. He's barely looked up."

Connor's eyes are bloodshot, his expression fraught with apprehension. "But there's no way he did that, right? You don't believe it. Do you?"

"Of course not! He hasn't been the best dad lately, but that doesn't mean he tried to murder Mom. That's insane!"

"But what happened?" Connor asks. "Why did she get swept off the rocks? She was always so careful. And why would he take her there after a storm, when the waves are so dangerous? He never takes time off work. Not even for my games!"

Connor is angry, and so am I. Mom is bruised and bloodied and in a coma. We almost lost her today. We might still lose her.

My emotions spiral, and I burst into tears. Connor wraps his arm around me, and I cling fast to him.

~

Back in Mom's room, I'm conscious of the heart monitor beeping and the sound of the ventilator machine pushing air into Mom's lungs.

I text Becky: Have you seen the news?

She replies instantly: Yes.

People are saying terrible things about Dad. #PeggysCoveMurder.

Becky responds: I saw that too, but don't let it get to you. People have too much time on their hands. They're just looking for entertainment. It'll blow over.

I hope so.

I watch three dots floating, and then Becky texts again.

Chin up, okay? I'm here for you and Connor. We have to stay strong for your mom.

I'll do my best.

I put my phone away and look up when the nurse walks in. She's a slender woman in navy scrubs, about Mom's age.

"Maybe you should all think about going home to get some sleep," she suggests. "It's important that you get your rest. We'll take good care of her and call you if there's any change."

"But what if she wakes up?" I ask. "We want to be here for that."

The nurse speaks to all of us reassuringly. "We'll be watching her closely all night, and I promise, if there's any change in her condition—any improvement at all—we'll call you right away."

Wondering what Dad thinks, I turn to him.

"She's probably right," he says. "We should get some rest because we'll be no good to Mom over the next few days if we're all exhausted."

I stare at him in disbelief. "Dad, are you serious? She almost drowned today." Out of the corner of my eye, I notice the nurse leave the room. "You don't want to stay with her?"

He scratches the back of his head. "Of course I do, but we all need to sleep at some point. We can't function otherwise, and if Mom wakes up, she's going to need us to be strong." He gestures toward the door. "And the nurse said she'd call if anything happens."

I wonder if he cares at all, or if it's all just fake, because he certainly didn't care last week when Mom and I were at the police station, or when Connor was scoring goals in the tournament.

Dad reaches for his jacket draped over the back of the chair. "Let's go home. We'll come back first thing in the morning."

While he moves to kiss Mom on the forehead, Connor and I exchange a look and gather our things.

A moment later, we're following him out of the ICU. The door swings shut behind him, and he uses the wall dispenser to sanitize his hands. "You guys okay?"

"As good as can be expected," I reply, feeling bitter inside.

"Are you hungry?" he asks.

"Always," Connor says.

Dad wraps his arm around Connor's shoulders. "Me too. Let's stop for some takeout on the way home."

"Five Guys?" Connor asks.

It's an understatement to say that Dad is not a fan of fast food, but tonight he passes no judgment. "Sure."

We walk to the elevator, and he presses the down button. While we wait, I try not to stare too closely at him, but it's not easy. I'm still so angry with him for taking Mom to Peggy's Cove. He may not have pushed her, like people are saying, but what happened to her is still his fault, and if she doesn't make it, I'm not sure I'll ever be able to forgive him.

~

Dad is behind the wheel, driving, while I sit in the front seat with him. Connor sits in the back, devouring his burger and fries. I still have no appetite, so I opted out of the takeout order, but surprisingly Dad got a burger and fries for himself. I suppose everyone has to eat.

"Did they miss you at the restaurant tonight?" I ask him.

He keeps his eyes on the road. "I'm sure they did."

I stare at him intensely and can't resist a spiteful dig. "Martina must have been in a state without you. How will she ever manage?"

He glances at me and frowns. "She'll manage just fine. And everyone knows what's going on. They understand why I can't be there."

Great comeback, I think to myself. *A perfect deflection.*

Exhausted, I rest my head against the window and stare at the houses as we pass. There are so many hateful things I could say about Martina right now—pretty Martina with the Italian accent, who sends him texts with little heart emojis. I wonder if Mom ever noticed that.

But then I find myself thinking about all the haters on social media who, at this very moment, are accusing Dad of cowardice and murder. He's been slammed with enough vitriol tonight, so I decide to bite my tongue.

And I still don't believe he would ever try to hurt Mom.

Or maybe I just don't want to talk to him anymore or open up to him about my feelings. I certainly don't want to talk about Martina. I just want to be quiet and stay mad.

~

As soon as we arrive home, Oscar greets us with enthusiasm at the door, his tail swinging, his nose nuzzling. He rises up on his hind legs and paws our thighs, desperately seeking affection. Connor and I kneel and make a huge fuss over him. We stroke his back and scratch behind his ears.

It's exactly what we both need—this little bundle of merriment that lets us escape our hardships for a few brief seconds.

"Do you want to go outside to pee?" I ask, and Oscar bounds toward the back door. He skids to a halt on the family room carpet, spins in a circle, and prances around while I remove my backpack.

"I'm coming, I'm coming," I say as I lead him across the room.

~

A short while later, I come back inside with Oscar. Dad sits at the kitchen island with his burger and fries, scrolling through his phone.

I don't have the emotional energy to talk to him about the day or what horrors he might be reading online, so I simply say good night and retreat to my room.

Oscar follows. As soon as he trots into the room, I shut the door behind us. "What an awful day."

He jumps onto my bed.

I watch him for a few seconds, then move to sit down on the edge of the mattress. He lays his furry little chin on my thigh and blinks up at me with sweet brown puppy dog eyes that melt my heart. But as I pat his soft head, I start to feel sick at the thought of Mom in the ICU, alone, with a plastic tube down her throat and a breathing machine keeping her alive.

What if she never comes back? No one loves me like she does. Who will I depend on?

Becky, I suppose. She's like an aunt.

But it's not the same.

I wonder suddenly if Mom named Becky as our guardian in her will. If she did, could Becky take care of us, even if Dad was still alive?

Does Mom even *have* a will?

I glance at the clock. It's late. I shouldn't text Becky now, but I decide to text her in the morning and ask if she and Mom ever discussed anything like that.

What a horrible conversation. Why am I even thinking about this? I need to stop imagining the worst.

~

At four in the morning, I wake, heart hammering in my chest because a ghost is moaning in the house. I sit straight up in bed.

Oscar is awake, on the carpet, sniffing under the door. He's pacing, desperate to be released into the hall, which fills me with fear.

It takes a few seconds for me to gather my senses before I realize it's not a ghost. Someone is crying. It's Connor.

I toss the covers aside, leap out of bed, and pull my door open. Oscar dashes out, and I hurry to help my brother through this horrific experience. But when I reach his room and open the door, the lights are out. He's sleeping soundly.

Confused, I back out of the room, careful not to wake him, and close the door softly behind me. Then I spot Oscar sitting outside my parents' bedroom, sniffing again under the closed door.

Does he think Mom's in there? Is he missing her?

Then I remember what woke me, the moaning ghost, and I realize it was my father, weeping.

The house is quiet now, so I'm not sure what to do. Should I leave him be? Allow him his privacy?

He's a grown man, and we're not exactly close. Would it be weird if I knocked and checked on him? I wonder if he even knows that I'm awake. At the very least, he must hear Oscar's loud sniffing under his door.

Without warning, the door slowly creaks open. Oscar's tail wags, and he looks up.

Dad whispers, "What are you doing here, buddy? You're supposed to sleep in Amanda's room." Then he peers out and sees me standing in the hall. My cheeks flush with heat.

"You're up," Dad says.

"Yeah."

"Are you okay?"

"Not really." I'm shaken by what I thought was a spirit howling in the night. "How about you?"

"Not so good. I can't sleep. Fancy some cinnamon toast?"

My heart squeezes at the mention of the snack I loved most when I was a preschooler. It's something I grew out of a long time ago, but in this moment, it's the ultimate comfort food, and suddenly I'm craving it.

"That would be perfect."

Dad leads the way to the stairs, and Oscar pushes ahead of us to run down first.

"Did anyone give him his supper?" Dad asks, and I realize I forgot.

"I don't think so. He must be starving."

We reach the kitchen. "Do you know where Mom keeps his food?" Dad asks.

"Of course. Don't *you*?" It's another dig that I can't bring myself to regret as I open the pantry door and reach for the bag of kibble.

"I suppose I deserve that," Dad says. "I haven't been around much lately."

There are a dozen acerbic ways I could respond, and though I'm tempted to lash out, I resist the urge. We're all going through hell right now, and I don't want to fight, especially when he's creating the perfect mix of cinnamon and sugar for my favorite kind of toast.

While I pour Oscar's kibble into his bowl, Dad drops two slices of bread into the toaster and pushes the lever down. He then retrieves the milk from the refrigerator.

"I've known for a long time that your mom's been doing everything around here to take care of you guys," he says. "And I've been about as helpful as a bag of rocks."

I slide onto a stool at the kitchen island and say nothing.

"It's my fault this happened," Dad says, his voice breaking. "I'm responsible."

After everything I've read online, this confession from him cuts into me. I wince with discomfort, especially when his chin trembles. I've never seen my father cry before, and I don't know what to say or do. So I sit there like a lump, speechless.

Dad fights to regain his composure and pours the milk, but I can't forget the baleful sound of his grief that woke me earlier. It was the sound of deep, pure agony.

He moves to the cupboard and brings down the butter dish and two plates. The toast pops up, and I watch him butter both slices generously and use a teaspoon to carefully sprinkle the cinnamon and sugar. It melts into the hot butter, and my mouth waters. Then he cuts each slice into triangles.

He sits on the stool beside me, but we don't speak. We pick up our toast and bite into it at the same time.

Despite the menace of this horrible day, the flavor on my tongue takes me back to my happy childhood, when I felt safe and loved and knew nothing about grief or loss. My mother was my sunshine, and my father was the steady ground beneath my feet.

But those days are long gone. I finish my toast and look at him. His elbows are perched on the island countertop, his hands clasped together, and his eyes are closed.

"Are you praying?" I ask with surprise.

"Yes. Praying for your mom. And for myself."

I'm perplexed. "Why for yourself?"

"I'm asking for forgiveness."

I'm jolted by his response, and all my extremities go numb. What, exactly, does he need to be forgiven for? Being a bad father? Or hurting Mom?

Dad pinches the bridge of his nose. "Have you read what people are posting on social media?"

"Yes."

"And what do you think your mom would say about it if she were sitting here right now?"

I consider that thoughtfully for a few seconds. "She'd tell you to ignore the haters. Then, if anyone crossed a line, she'd take you to the police station to file a report."

He acknowledges this with a nod. "You're right. That's exactly what she would do." He sips his milk and sets the glass back down. "Sorry I wasn't around to help you through that bullying situation."

I shrug a shoulder. "It's fine. Mom took care of things, and it all worked out." I glance down at Oscar, who's curled up on the floor at my feet.

Dad makes an effort to keep the conversation going. "She said Jeff's a nice guy. I'd like to meet him at some point, size him up for myself. See if he's good enough for my favorite daughter."

He's trying way too hard to get on my good side, but I don't fall for the flattery. I rub my finger across the cinnamon and sugar left on my plate and lick it. "You can give me your opinion, and I'll consider it."

Dad watches my profile for a moment. "I always knew you'd turn out to be a strong woman. Even as a toddler, you had a will of your own. We used to call you the Iron Lady."

I glance up. "You did? I never knew that."

He sits back and folds his arms. "It wasn't something we ever said in front of you."

"Oh, I see. It sounds like a compliment now, but at the time it was probably an insult because you hated it when I wouldn't let up about getting a cell phone."

"You wouldn't take no for an answer," he agrees, "until you finally got your way."

I reach for my milk. "Maybe I should have listened to you, because sometimes that phone has been a curse. It must've been nice to grow up in the nineties, when there was no such thing as Instagram and 'likes' and stupid algorithms." I sip my milk.

"This has been a hellish day," he says, "but at least it feels good to talk to you."

He holds out his arms, and I let him hug me like he used to do, but it's awkward and uncomfortable. I can't let go of what happened to Mom today, and I don't trust Dad to ever put me and Connor ahead of his stupid restaurant.

I sit back and look down at Oscar still curled up under my stool. "We should probably get some sleep," I say.

Dad rises and collects the plates, carries them to the dishwasher, and loads them onto the bottom rack.

"Come on, Oscar," I say. "Let's go back to bed."

He sits up, stretches, and follows as I head for the stairs. I pause at the bottom and turn back to Dad. "What time should we go to the hospital in the morning?"

"As soon as we're up," he replies.

It's a vague answer, and it won't do. Clearly Dad has no idea that Connor will sleep until noon if we let him.

"I'll set my alarm for eight and wake Connor."

It irks me that Dad doesn't know much about anything around here.

~

When my alarm goes off, it feels like I just laid my head on the pillow. I wake up exhausted and press the snooze button, but I can't fall back to sleep because yesterday's events descend on me like a hammer.

Mom . . . swept off the rocks at Peggy's Cove. She's in the hospital, in a coma, and everyone seems to think my dad pushed her.

I wish it were all just a bad dream, but it's real, and today is the first full day of this waking nightmare.

At least the nurse didn't call during the night. No news is good news, I tell myself.

I roll over, reach for my phone, and discover that Becky texted me at 7:40 a.m.

> Good morning, sweetie. I hope you got some sleep. I'm going to cook a pot of your favorite chicken chili and put it in your fridge while you're at the hospital. I can let myself in through the garage. Heat it up when you get home.
>
> I'd also like to come to the hospital to visit your mom. Just between you and me, I'm struggling because this whole situation reminds me of the day I lost my brother and almost my best friend too. Your mom was in the hospital for a long time back then, but she survived, and that's what I'm trying to remember—what a fighter she was, and still is. <3 I can come to the ICU at lunchtime, if that's okay, to give you guys a break.
>
> And I hope things were okay at home last night. I've been reading all the comments on social media, and that can't be easy for any of you. Call me if you want to talk. I'm always here for you. <3

Becky sent the messages only twenty minutes ago, so I decide to call her instead of text, because I do want to talk. I want to tell her about how I woke up in the middle of the night and heard my dad crying.

I press the call button, and Becky answers before the second ring.

"Hello?"

"Hey," I reply. "I just woke up. I read your message about your brother, and I didn't think of that. I'm sorry."

"It's okay, kiddo. This is rough on all of us."

"Yeah. A pot of chili would be great," I add. "That's so kind of you."

She lets out a sigh. "It's not kindness. I need to stay busy, or I'll lose my mind. I assume you haven't heard anything from the hospital?"

"Nothing." I sit forward and pat Oscar, who's stretched out on the bed at my feet.

"And how are things this morning?" Becky asks. "After a fresh social media explosion?"

"Oh, God." I cup my forehead in my hand. "Please don't tell me it's gotten worse."

"Not worse. There's just more of it. Has your father seen it?"

"Yes." I rise from bed. "And I don't think he's taking it well. I woke up in the middle of the night to the sound of . . ." I pause because I'm not sure how to describe it to Becky. It feels like a betrayal of Dad's privacy, but I really do need someone to talk to, and Mom—my usual confidante—isn't here. "He let out a terrible moan," I tell her. "It was awful . . . like someone cut him in half."

She pauses. "I'm so sorry. Does he know you heard him?"

"Yes, I think so. Oscar was at his door sniffing, so Dad came out and saw me standing in the hall. We went downstairs and talked. Dad made cinnamon toast for us."

"Really." She sounds skeptical. "He still remembers that."

"Yeah. It was kind of nice, actually. It felt like I had my old dad back, but still . . ." I stop talking because I'm not even sure what, exactly, I want to say.

"Can you finish that thought?" Becky asks gently.

I move to my closet to choose what to wear to the hospital. "I'm just so freaking angry with him. More than angry, and not just for being an absentee father since he opened the restaurant. I'm mad at him for making Mom handle everything on her own. And the cherry on top is him taking her to Peggy's Cove after a storm and letting her get too close to the waves. It's his fault this happened to her. She should never have been there."

Becky gives me a moment, then speaks calmly. "Did you communicate that to him?"

I find my black turtleneck sweater, pull it from the top shelf in the closet, and reach for my most comfortable blue jeans. "Yes, and he said he felt bad about everything, and that he knows he hasn't been a great dad."

"Well, that's progress, isn't it?"

"I suppose. But it's hard to look past what happened to Mom. He even admitted to me that he was responsible."

Becky takes a long time to respond. "I beg your pardon?"

I pull off my pajama top and toss it onto the bed. "He said it was his fault this happened. He obviously feels guilty, but I'm glad. He deserves to feel that way." I pull my sweater on over my head. "Then he just sat there and said he was praying for forgiveness. Maybe God can forgive him, but if anything happens to Mom—if she doesn't wake up—I don't think I could." I take a few seconds to recall our conversation last night. "But he is my dad. Connor and I would be orphans without him. He'll be responsible for looking after us." The next words out of my mouth are infected with hostility. "We'll see how he does without Mom around. He should've appreciated her more."

"Don't talk like that," Becky firmly says. "She's going to wake up."

I button my jeans and move to my dresser to find a clean pair of socks. "I hope so."

The sound of the shower lets me know that Dad is awake, so I tell Becky I have to go.

"Text me when you get to the hospital," she says, "and let me know how she's doing."

"I will."

We end the call, and I return to the bed to snuggle with Oscar for a moment and gather strength to face this horrible day.

~

In the car on the way to the hospital, I'm influenced by my brother's anxieties at breakfast and succumb to the temptation of social media—in particular the hundreds of comments on Oblique's Facebook page.

It's shocking to me that my mother's ordeal at Peggy's Cove has gone viral. As of this morning, a whole new group called *The Peggy's Cove Murder* has been established. So far, there are 350 comments, and some are from people who were there and saw my parents arguing.

The way they describe it makes it sound heated, like Dad was going to beat her up or something. I'm trying not to believe everything I read, especially stuff like this, because that's not the dad I know. But it still scares me because . . . what if I *don't* really know my dad?

Other comments leave condolences, thoughts, and prayers.

By the time I skim through everything, it appears to have become a battle of yes or no. Did he do it or not? Half the commenters think he's guilty, while the other half believes this is a ridiculous conspiracy theory and our family deserves privacy.

With all these comments to read, the drive to the hospital passes in a millisecond. When I glance up from my phone, I discover that we've arrived and Dad is pulling into a parking spot.

I quickly put my phone away, but my stomach keeps burning with anxiety. It's physically painful, like acid churning. This is all too much to take. I need yogurt or something.

Dad shuts off the car and unbuckles his seat belt. My eyes are wide open, like a couple of Ping-Pong balls, as I watch him and think about some of what I just read on that awful Facebook page.

~

At the ICU, we learn that Mom's condition is still critical, and her blood pressure dropped this morning. They took her for a CT scan, which revealed some bleeding with swelling around her brain. The doctor explains that it's not because of drowning and being deprived of oxygen but a result of the skull fracture she received when she hit the rocks.

The news breaks me. I burst into tears and turn to Connor, who gathers me into his arms.

"Everything's going to be okay," Dad says, rubbing my back. "She's getting the best care."

"It's not a lost cause," Dr. Malik adds.

At this, I wipe my eyes and face him.

"We'll be taking her to the OR this morning to relieve that pressure and will see how she responds."

"Is there a chance she might wake up after you do that?" I ask.

"I can't say anything for sure. Just know that she's in good hands. The whole team will do everything we can for her."

"Thank you," Dad says.

He tries to wrap his arm around my shoulders, but I shrug away from him and start walking to Mom's room.

~

Moments after Mom is taken to the OR to prep for surgery, we gather our belongings to go down to the cafeteria and wait, but a nurse walks into the room. She isn't one of Mom's regular nurses, and she has a commanding air about her.

"Mr. Palmer?"

Dad looks up. "Yes?"

"You're wanted outside the unit."

"What for?"

She clears her throat with authority. "There are some people here who would like to talk to you."

Dad pulls on his jacket. Watching him, I sense that he's unnerved.

After everything that's happened to Mom, followed by the vitriol on social media directed at our entire family, I feel the same. It's as if the universe has it out for us. What's next? I'm terrified to imagine. They say bad things happen in threes.

We walk out of Mom's room, which feels hauntingly empty since they've rolled her hospital bed out and wheeled her to the surgery floor.

As we pass the nurses' station and walk by a cleaner pushing a mop, I feel everyone's eyes on us. I don't think I'm paranoid. I suspect they have all been glued to their phones and are whispering about my father's guilt or innocence.

Dad, Connor, and I walk uncomfortably in silence to the double doors out of the ICU, push through them, and find ourselves face-to-face with two men. One is over six feet tall with gray hair. The other looks younger. They're dressed in black winter jackets, dress pants, and boots with white salt stains on the toes, but they flash badges before the ICU doors have a chance to swing shut behind us.

"Mr. Palmer," the man with the gray hair says in a friendly voice, which calms me a little. But it's not a question. They already know who Dad is. It doesn't come as a surprise because Dad's a bit of a celebrity in town. His restaurant has been featured in most of the local lifestyle magazines, and his image, in chef attire, tops the website's home page.

"I'm Inspector Lawson, and this is Sergeant Major LaPierre. We're with the Criminal Investigation Division of the RCMP. Sorry to bother you here . . ." He looks me straight in the eye, then at Connor. "We know this is a difficult time for you all." He returns his attention to Dad. "But we're looking into what happened to your wife, and we'd like to ask you some questions."

Dad is frozen on the spot, and his face has gone pale. He won't speak.

It's not a good look, so I nudge him. "Dad?"

He meets my gaze. I see fear in his eyes, but he quickly recovers. "I'll answer any questions you have. But I hope this doesn't have anything to do with what's been posted on social media."

Inspector Lawson inclines his head. "Well—"

Dad interrupts him. "It's a bunch of nonsense because people are looking for dopamine hits from their phones. They don't know anything about what happened yesterday. They weren't there. They didn't see the waves, and it's pissing me off."

LaPierre nods. "I understand, and we get it. We've seen this before. People can go crazy about crimes on the internet, which is why we want to talk to you—to eliminate any cause for suspicion. Then we can all get on with our lives."

I let out a breath of relief, because deep down I don't want to believe Dad pushed Mom off the rocks, and I don't want him to go to jail. Sure, I'm angry with him about the situation, but like Sergeant Major LaPierre says, people can go crazy posting online. I don't want to follow them down a rabbit hole.

"Would you come to the station with us?" LaPierre asks. "Your children can remain here. We'll bring you back afterward."

Dad frowns. "You can't talk to me here? Now?"

"It's best if we do it at the station. We just need to make sure we get everything down."

I'm not exactly sure what he means by *down*, and the whole situation is making my stomach turn somersaults. What if they believe everything they're reading online? What if they already think he's guilty, that he took Mom to Peggy's Cove to murder her for her money?

Dad turns to me and Connor. "I might as well go with them and get it over with. You guys stay here and wait for Mom to get out of surgery. Becky's supposed to come by, right?"

I quickly nod. "Yes. She was going to take some chili to our house this morning. I'll text her."

The officers start walking, and Dad winks at me as he goes. He wants to reassure us, but I'm not entirely reassured. In this moment, both my parents have just been taken away. One has been wheeled to an operating room to have brain surgery, while the other will be questioned for attempted murder.

Emotionally, I'm paralyzed. But I need to keep it together for Connor, who is looking at me expectantly, waiting for me to take the lead.

"Let's get some food," I say, trying to make light of what just happened. Wordlessly, he follows me to the elevator.

~

Connor and I have just finished grilled cheese sandwiches and fries when I receive a text from Becky.

I just arrived at the hospital. Is your mom still in surgery?

I thumb a reply: Yes. We're in the cafeteria waiting. No word from Dad yet.

I'm just getting out of my car. Stay put. I'll find you.

I respond with an "okay" emoji.

~

Becky enters the cafeteria, and I'm relieved to see her face. I get up from the booth and meet her halfway, where we hug. Then I start to cry again. She holds me tight and doesn't let go.

When I get the tears out of my system, I wipe my cheeks and lead her back to the booth. Connor gets up and hugs her.

"This sucks," he says.

"I agree. It's brutal." Becky tosses her purse onto the vinyl seat, removes her coat, and hangs it on the hook. "How are you guys holding up?"

"Not great," I reply.

"Still no word from your dad?"

I shake my head, and Becky reaches for a cold french fry on my plate. "The most important thing is to stay focused on your mom," she says. "Your dad can take care of himself."

"I hope so," Connor says, "because the internet has no mercy. Have you looked lately?"

"No, I couldn't take it anymore, so I stopped reading. You should do the same. Both of you. Put your phones away." She gives Connor a stern look, and he slides it into his back pocket. "What did the cops say, exactly?" Becky asks me with concern.

"Just that they wanted to get everything down, whatever that means. And Dad got a bit testy about social media. I'm not sure if that was a good or bad thing."

"It's understandable that he'd be angry," Becky says. "He should see what he can do to get that group shut down."

"I hope the cops see it that way." I check my watch. "We should probably head back up to the ICU. Mom might be out of surgery by now."

We gather our belongings and leave the cafeteria.

As we walk down the corridor to the elevators, Becky nudges me to look at my phone.

I need to talk to you, but not in front of Connor.

A chill grips my heart. I glance at her, and she puts her finger to her lips to say, "Shh."

We reach the elevator, and Connor presses the button. When the doors slide open, we step inside and ride up in silence until we get off on the ICU floor. We walk to the waiting area, and I pick up the wall phone to call the nurses' station. They tell me that Mom is still in surgery, so I relay that information to Becky and Connor.

"I need to use the washroom," I say to Becky. "Want to come?"

"Sure." She turns to Connor. "Have a seat. We'll be back in a bit."

Without looking up from his phone, he nods, and Becky and I start off down the hall.

"Why do I feel like you have something terrible to tell me?" I ask. "I'm not sure if I can handle any more bad news."

She wraps her arm around my shoulders. "Sorry, but I need to come clean."

I frown. "What are you talking about?"

We reach the bathroom but decide to keep walking because neither of us really has to go.

"I might have said something to the police that made them suspicious," Becky finally confesses. "When I was dropping the chili off at your house this morning, two RCMP officers came to the door looking for your dad. I told them he was at the hospital, but they asked who I was. I said I was your mom's best friend, and they had questions."

"Like what?"

She hesitates. "Well . . . they asked about your parents' relationship, and I couldn't lie. Not to law enforcement."

Becky hesitates again, and I have to prompt her. "Please, go on."

"I told them something you don't know, and now I'm afraid that they're going to ask you about it, and I want you to hear it from me, not them."

My heart starts to race, and I stop at the end of the hall. "What is it?"

Becky presses her fingers to the space between her eyebrows. "A few weeks ago, your mom talked to a lawyer about the possibility of a legal separation, maybe even divorce."

I draw back slightly, as if Becky just swung a punch at me.

"She hadn't made any firm decisions," Becky explains, "but you know that she was tired of your father's promises about spending less time at the restaurant. He kept saying he'd do better, be more attentive, but nothing ever changed. On top of that, the restaurant was struggling financially, and he was asking her for money, but she didn't want him to touch the trust fund that was intended for your education. That's why she talked to a lawyer. She wanted to know what would happen to her savings if she . . ."

"Got a divorce," I finish for her.

I realize my heart is pummeling my rib cage, and I'm starting to feel sick to my stomach.

"I think," Becky says, "at the end of the day, what she really wanted was to give him a wake-up call."

"And what did he say when she told him?" I ask with bated breath.

"I don't know," she replies. "Only your mom knows the answer to that."

I back up against the wall and slide down to a squat, where I gather my hair in my fists and squeeze. "So they *were* arguing on the rocks."

"Probably," she replies.

"And there were witnesses."

"Yes, and I suspect the police are contacting those people as well, to confirm what they saw."

My eyes sting with tears as I look up at her. "Do you think he pushed her? And that someone actually saw him do it?"

Becky shakes her head and speaks with desperation. "Honestly . . . I have no idea what happened."

My throat constricts, and I swallow hard. This isn't real. There's no way Dad would push Mom off the rocks. They love each other. And Dad loves Connor and me. We were a close family once, and I genuinely, deep down in my bones, believe that he wants us to be close again. I heard him crying in his room last night, and he remembered the cinnamon toast. He apologized for not being around more. And he hasn't been to the restaurant since any of this started. Although maybe he's been texting Martina all this time. God knows what's going on there.

Slowly I try to rise, but I'm unsteady. Becky offers her hand and pulls me to my feet.

"You don't think they're going to arrest him, do you?" I ask. "Will they put him in jail?"

"I don't know. It depends on what happened, what he says about it, and what the witnesses say."

Feeling dazed, I walk slowly back to the ICU. A fog rolls into my head. It's cold and numbing, but I fear hysteria is just beyond it.

"Amanda!" It's Connor, calling to me from the end of the corridor. "Mom's out of surgery! She's back in her room, and we can see her!"

With relief, I exhale. "Maybe she'll wake up." I turn expectantly to Becky. "Then she can tell the police it's not true."

"That would be wonderful," Becky replies, but I sense a pessimism in her.

I understand it, but I don't want to be infected by it. I want to manifest a positive outcome, so I shake off the fog and run down the hall.

CHAPTER NINETEEN

Nate

The drive to the police station feels like a slow ride to hell.

All the comments on social media have pushed me over the edge, into a dark pit of terror. I shouldn't have stayed up so late scrolling. Every comment was like a knife blade against my throat. I felt sick reading it, but I couldn't stop. I kept scrolling and scrolling . . .

Now I'm convinced that the entire world has turned against me. My wife is in a coma, and there's no one to blame but me.

> It's always the husband.
>
> He's one of those heartless celebrity chefs. Too ambitious, probably a sociopath.
>
> My cousin knows one of the servers at his restaurant. Apparently, they've been struggling financially so he was probably after the insurance money.

I start to have heart palpitations. How would one of my servers know about our money troubles? Nobody ever went without a paycheck.

In the back seat of the officers' car, I'm sweating profusely. I wipe the pads of my fingers across my forehead and try to breathe calmly. The last thing I need is for them to look over their shoulders and see me in a panic. I need to be cool. I did nothing wrong. I love my wife. I'd never do such a thing. I'm a good person. My family means more to me than my restaurant. I'd give it up in a heartbeat to have Sienna wake up and be okay.

I repeat those words over and over in my head, because that's what they're going to ask when we get to the station. And this is what they'll need to hear from me.

We pull into the parking lot, and LaPierre makes small talk about the weather and how the storm blew the shingles off the station roof.

"If they don't replace that roof soon, we'll need buckets next time it rains."

"It was a bad storm," I reply, like an idiot, because I'm flustered.

Inspector Lawson leads the way up the steps and says nothing. He looks cranky, and I wonder if this is the start of a good-cop-bad-cop interview. I'm not stupid. I come from a long line of legal professionals, and I attended law school myself, however briefly.

LaPierre holds the door open, and I'm escorted to an interrogation room with double-sided mirrors and a table with two chairs on opposite sides. I stop just inside the doorway.

"Do I need a lawyer for this?"

"That's totally up to you," LaPierre replies in a friendly manner, "if you think you need one."

He's challenging me. He wants to see if I'm worried about what might come out when I start talking about the tragedy on the rocks.

"We just want to hear what happened from you," LaPierre adds, "because most of those internet trolls weren't there. They're just speculating, and to them, this might as well be another true crime Netflix show." He gestures for me to take a seat at the table. "I want you to know that we recognize that, and we're here to help you."

That's bull crap, and he knows that I know it. Nevertheless, I remain calm and cool on the outside while my mind screams in terror.

"I appreciate that." I take a seat.

LaPierre points at a camera in the corner of the room and lets me know that this discussion is being recorded. He then asks me what happened at Peggy's Cove. I tell him everything, from the moment Sienna and I left the house to when we argued on the rocks and a wave came out of nowhere and swept Sienna into the ocean.

"That must've been frightening."

"It was," I reply. "I didn't know what to do. Have you ever been to Peggy's Cove? Have you seen the power of those waves when they hit the rocks?"

"I have," LaPierre replies. "There's no way I would jump in to rescue anyone. We'd both end up dead."

I stare at him for a few seconds. Grateful. Frozen. "Thanks for saying that. I know, rationally . . . that it wasn't possible to rescue her, but I still feel guilty about it. For not saving her."

He nods and writes something in his notebook. My sense of relief evaporates.

"What did you do after you saw her fall into the water?"

"She didn't fall," I correct him. "A wave knocked her off her feet."

I clear my throat as I recount every horrendous second—my frantic searching of the waves, how I ran for help. The young couple I encountered, and the guy performing chest compressions, the other pinching her nose and blowing in her mouth. The ambulance finally arriving.

I wipe sweat from my brow while LaPierre writes certain things down.

After all that, I'm in a fragile state. He gives me a moment to recover. We sit in silence for what feels like an eternity. I can't be sure how long because I'm shredded.

"Let's move on," he says. "There's been talk about your restaurant having financial troubles. Is this true?"

I'm hit with a sudden wave of nausea. Serious queasiness. I glance around for a trash can in case I need to throw up.

"Are you okay?" LaPierre asks.

"Yes." I swallow hard to keep the bile from coming up. "I just hate people knowing about that."

"Really? It's worse than people thinking you tried to murder your wife?"

It's a gut punch but also a fair question that fills me with self-loathing. "I'm not feeling so well. I haven't eaten since seven a.m.," I explain.

"Want a cookie or something? We have food in the lunchroom."

I consider it, but the thought of chewing and swallowing makes my insides curdle. "I'll just stick with water."

LaPierre looks down at his notes. "Let's continue. I want to get through this so you can get back to your family." He flips a page. "So . . . you didn't answer the question about your restaurant. Have you had money troubles? And was your wife aware?"

"Of course she was aware. We had good communication about the business."

"And how did she feel about it?"

"Not great. She thought I worked too much."

His eyes lift from his notes. "Was she worried that you might bankrupt the family?"

The question sets me on edge because that's exactly how Sienna had phrased it. "Yes, she was worried."

"Did you ever ask her for money?"

My heart races faster. "Yes."

"But she didn't want to give you any more money. Correct?"

I feel impaled by his accusing stare, and I wonder where he's gleaned this information. Not from Facebook. No one knew anything about my private conversations with Sienna, so it must have been Becky. She and Sienna told each other everything.

Now that I think about it, Becky was probably the one who convinced Sienna to talk to a lawyer in the first place. Those two were like peas in a pod after Jacob died. I've witnessed it. They have a bond I could never quite compete with.

I wish suddenly that I'd insisted on having a lawyer present for this.

"It sounds like you've already done some investigating," I say.

LaPierre sits back. "Just answer the question."

I slowly exhale. "She didn't want to pour any more money into the restaurant."

"And how did you feel about that?"

My fingers drum against my thigh, quick and restless. "I think this is the moment when I ask to call my lawyer, because it's starting to sound like I'm being treated as a suspect."

LaPierre tosses his pen onto the file in front of him. "Fine. Who's your lawyer? I'll give him or her a call. In the meantime, I'll get you some food from Tim Hortons. What would you like?"

I still don't feel like eating, but I don't want to pass out. "Coffee and a bagel."

"What do you take in your coffee?"

"Just black."

He picks up his pen. "The name of your lawyer?"

God help me. My lawyer is a tax attorney who handles my business and personal real estate issues. He's not the sort of lawyer I need today. What I need is a courtroom bulldog. My father would be perfect, but there's no way I'm calling him. So I'll take the next best thing.

"Arthur Palmer at Palmer and Associates."

LaPierre's eyes lift. "I've dealt with the Palmers. Are you related?"

"Arthur's my brother."

LaPierre's forehead creases over drawn brows. "That must make Bill Palmer your father."

"It does."

LaPierre shakes his head and laughs softly as he writes that down in the file. "Perfect. Just my luck."

~

It's been years since I've spoken to my father. The last time we stood face-to-face was at my twenty-fifth birthday party, when I announced I was quitting law school.

My mother has secretly kept in touch. Her visits began when she came to the hospital after Amanda was born, and she started popping by the house regularly from that day forward. The children came to know and love her, but a few years back, she was diagnosed with Alzheimer's. Around the same time, Dad filed for divorce, but he came out smelling like roses when he milked the sympathy from his colleagues and set her up in a posh nursing home. He then sold the house in St. Margaret's Bay and bought another in the city, overlooking the yacht club on the Northwest Arm. Within a year, his young and beautiful fiancée moved in.

I'm not sure if he ever visits my mother in the home. I highly doubt it because he has a low tolerance for anything less than perfection. Everything around him must serve to impress. Mom succeeded in that department for many years, until she didn't. Then she, like me, was dispensed with, and along came wife number two.

I'm on my feet and pacing when LaPierre walks into the interrogation room with a large Tim Hortons coffee cup and a brown paper bag. "Here you go." He leaves my lunch on the table. "I'll be back shortly."

By this time, I'm famished, so I sit down to eat and try to be grateful for this moment alone, which gives me time to think about Sienna in surgery. I've been praying that she'll come out of it okay. I've also prayed for Amanda and Connor—that they'll find the strength they need to get through this ordeal, especially if I get charged with attempted murder.

I wonder if anyone is praying for *me* today. Probably not. As far as the outside world is concerned, I should rot in jail for the rest of my life, because that's what killers deserve.

For those who aren't convinced that I tried to push my wife to her death, I am, at the very least, a failure as a husband, a father, and an entrepreneur.

With that thought, I bite into the toasted bagel and imagine my father following all this on the local news. I wonder how he's taking it. He's probably saying "I told you so" to his new wife.

The image of him gloating about being right makes me want to ram my fist into a wall.

But I can't do that. Not here. There's a camera recording my every move, and I know how this works. I have to look like an innocent man without any violent tendencies.

The door opens again. I set down my coffee and look up.

It's Arthur. My brother. The door closes behind him, and we stare at each other. I can't speak or move because I'm in such a volatile emotional state. I'm afraid I'll fall to pieces and cry like a baby. Maybe I should. Maybe that would look good on the recording. I'd be perceived as a man who is distraught after the near death of his wife. Which is what I am. Distraught.

Why can't I just let it show? Why must I overthink it?

I suppose I know the answer. I don't want to cry in front of Arthur because he's too much like Dad.

CHAPTER TWENTY

Amanda

"She's stable now," Dr. Malik tells us. "But she had a depressed skull fracture near her temple, which caused damage to the superficial temporal artery. There was also a tear in the dura mater, the tough membrane that encases the brain. We were able to repair the tear and drain the pooled blood, and we're hopeful that will help."

This is all Greek to me.

"Will she be okay?" Connor asks.

"I wish I could answer that," Dr. Malik replies, "but I don't know yet. We need to wait and see how she does over the next twenty-four hours."

I hate hearing this, but I'm glad he isn't sugarcoating anything, as adults often do with teenagers.

"Will she have brain damage?" Connor asks. "Or never come out of the coma?"

I recognize sympathy in Dr. Malik's eyes as he speaks. "It's possible that she could never regain consciousness, and if she does, she could have some long-term disabilities like lost motor skills or speech impediments. But it's also possible that she could wake up in the next hour and make a full recovery. We just don't know."

Tears well up in my eyes, and Becky squeezes my hand.

"Right now," the doctor continues, "the best thing you can do for her is let her know that you're here and you want her to keep fighting. Talk to her."

"We can do that," I say, relieved to be given a specific, concrete task. For me, the worst has been feeling as if there's nothing I can do to help Mom wake up.

Needing to move on to his next patient, Dr. Malik backs away. "We'll keep a close eye on her and do everything we can."

"Thank you." I watch him go. Then I thank God for giving us the miracle of modern medicine. A hundred years ago, my mother would be dead.

~

Though I'm shaken by the sight of the bloody bandage around Mom's shaved head, I try to sound positive when I say hello to her. I bend and kiss her on the cheek, but a tear spills from my eye as I take in all the bruises and lacerations.

"You're doing great, Mom," I say shakily. "I love you so much. Please come back to us, because we need you. You're everything."

Connor, on the other side of the bed, grasps her hand. "Hi, Mom. I'm here too. We're both here. And Becky."

Becky approaches and gives Mom a kiss on the cheek. She speaks loving words in her ear.

I remain at Mom's side and stroke her arm. She's deathly pale, and if it weren't for the respirator and the IV fluids pumping medications into her system, she wouldn't be alive. Her body is so badly damaged she's not strong enough to survive on her own.

"Mom, we love you. Please keep fighting. We need you to wake up. We'll be here for you, no matter what."

I can scarcely stomach the smells of antiseptic and blood, and tears start pouring down my cheeks. I become aware of Connor's hand on my back, rubbing in slow circles because I'm crying again.

At least I have my brother. I'm grateful for his strength, even though he's only thirteen, and I'm thankful we have each other.

"She made it this far," he says. "She'll make it the rest of the way."

His optimism refills me with hope. I turn in my chair and hug him tight.

~

Later in the day, Becky returns to our house to pick up Oscar and take him to her house for the night. Connor leaves the hospital to get some food on Spring Garden Road. I stay in the ICU because I want some time alone with Mom. I have so many questions, and part of me believes that if she hears me asking them, she might fight harder to wake up and tell me the truth.

"Mom, they're saying terrible things about Dad." I sit forward in the stiff chair and clasp her hand. It feels cold and bony, not like normal. I'm distracted by this, but I focus my thinking and push on. "Becky told me that you talked to a lawyer about a divorce, and that you and Dad were arguing about money for the restaurant. Is it true? Were you arguing before you were swept off the rocks? Or did he push you?" I fight to keep my voice from breaking. "I think he might be in trouble. The police took him to the station. They said they'd bring him back, but it's been hours, and he hasn't answered my texts."

I stare at Mom, but in her coma, there's no life in her, no response whatsoever. I feel alone and abandoned, but I don't want to give up hope that she can hear me. I need to believe that she can. I want to have some effect, so I keep talking.

"Is it true?" I ask again. "Did he push you? I don't want to believe it, I really don't, but after what Becky told me, I'm confused. I feel like I don't know either of you, because I had no idea any of this was happening—that you were arguing about money and talking to a lawyer about a divorce. So please, Mom, wake up so you can tell me what's happening and take care of us if Dad goes to jail."

I sound desperate, and I know it. I'm begging and pleading. I'm borderline hysterical, but it makes no difference because she isn't listening. I don't even know if her soul is still in there. Maybe she's just a shell of the mother I love, and it's only the machines keeping her alive. *Where are you, Mom? Where did you go?*

I can't take it. Even though she's lying right here in front of me, I miss her terribly, and I can't imagine my life without her.

I break down again, and hot, stinging tears stream down my face.

CHAPTER TWENTY-ONE

NATE

"Thanks for getting me out of there," I say to Arthur as we descend the police station steps.

My relief is off the charts. There were moments when I expected to be cuffed, dragged to jail, and locked up. I can't even fathom how I'll endure it if that happens. I'll never be able to live with the shame.

"They couldn't hold you indefinitely," Arthur replies.

We reach his car—a silver Mercedes-AMG GT Coupe—and I pause on the sidewalk. "Is this new?"

"Not really," he replies. "I got it a year ago. Get in."

I open the car door and slide into the black leather-upholstered passenger seat. Arthur buckles his seat belt and starts the engine.

"How's Sienna doing?" he asks. "Any improvement?" He checks his rearview mirror and pulls onto the road.

"No. She had surgery this morning, and the kids are terrified that she won't wake up."

He speaks with genuine sympathy. "I'm sorry. If there's anything I can do, say the word."

"Thank you. I appreciate it."

We drive in silence for a few minutes, and it's awkward because we haven't spoken since the kids were little. I'm to blame for that because I've been so busy with the restaurant. I turned down a lot of invitations to his house. I'm pretty sure the last time he called, I never called him back. He must have given up on me, because he stopped calling.

At least the kids have kept in touch with their cousins through social media, and Sienna occasionally runs into Alex at the grocery store, though not often.

Arthur glances at me repeatedly. "Can we talk frankly?"

"Of course."

He wastes no time. "Did you do it?"

I'm dumbfounded and appalled. "Do *what*?"

"Push her."

I scoff because the question is ridiculous. "I can't believe you're asking me that."

"I have to," he replies, "because if I'm going to defend you, I need to know the truth. You have to tell me everything—every little, insignificant detail about what happened that day and every argument you and Sienna have had for the past ten years."

Part of me wants to tell him to shove those questions up his ass, but I can't because the whole world is against me, and I need someone in my corner, and my brother is someone who doesn't like to lose.

I tip my head back and let out a sigh of frustration. "I swear on our mother's life that I didn't push her. But we were arguing. Apparently, people noticed, and it's that goddamn Facebook page that created all these suspicions."

Arthur remains focused. "What about your financial situation? Is the restaurant struggling? And did you ask Sienna for money?"

"Yes, to all of it," I reply. "And I've been a total dick about it."

Arthur makes a left turn, which is not the way to my house.

"Where are we going?"

"Not to your place, because reporters are camped out on the sidewalk."

"Seriously?" I reach for my phone in my coat pocket. "I need to call the kids."

Arthur keeps driving and says nothing while I notice all the texts from Amanda. I call her, and she answers after one ring.

"Hello. Dad?" She sounds panicked.

"Yeah, it's me. Are you okay? How's Mom?"

"I'm fine. We're both fine. What's going on? Why haven't you been answering my texts?"

My daughter is in a heightened emotional state, and I hate that this is happening. I squeeze my eyes shut and run my hand down my face. "I'm so sorry. They were grilling me, and I had to put my phone away. How's Mom?"

Amanda speaks in a more measured tone, and I'm glad that she sounds calmer. "She's out of surgery but still the same. I've been sitting with her."

"Good. And how's Connor doing?"

"Not great," she replies, "but he went out to get McDonald's. He just texted, and he's on his way back now."

Feeling exhausted and defeated, I rest my elbow on the car door and prop my head in my hand. "I'll come to the hospital soon."

"Are you still at the police station? Are they going to arrest you?"

"No, that's not happening." I speak firmly because I don't want her to worry. "Your uncle Arthur just picked me up, and we need to talk for a bit, okay?"

"He's a lawyer, right?"

She hasn't seen him in years, and the fact that she has to ask this question piles on more guilt and regret. As soon as we end the call, I accept that my life has gone to shit. Sienna was right. I became obsessed with my career and viewed everything else in life as a bothersome interruption. My family included.

The car slows, and I realize Arthur is taking me to his house in the South End. We turn onto his street, and I gaze at all the mansions on wide landscaped lots. They must all have gardeners, handymen, and house cleaners. The house that Sienna and I share is far more modest. She's the one who looks after the gardens. But *this* . . . this is what my father wanted for me.

I don't regret my choices, but I hate that my father probably revels in my lack of wealth, because in his mind, it proves him right. By his standards anyway.

Arthur pulls onto his sloping driveway and shuts off the engine.

"Will Alex or the kids be home?" I ask, fighting shame as I imagine them reading about their uncle's run-in with the law, which is a far worse scandal than my Birthday Brunch rebellion at their grandparents' house.

"No, they're all at school," Arthur replies, "and Alex is with her mom."

I realize I don't even know what his children are doing, what schools they're attending. "You'll have to catch me up on everything," I say.

"Sure," he coolly replies as he gets out of the car. "Come on in. I'll fix you a drink, and we can talk."

I slide out of the passenger seat and follow him up the steps to the impressive oak door.

~

Arthur hands me a glass of top-shelf Scotch whisky, which goes down as smooth as calm water. It's exactly what I need. I sit back in the leather armchair in his office and wait for the alcohol to drown my regret.

"I'm glad you asked for me," Arthur says. He takes a seat in the opposite leather chair. They're a matched set in front of floor-to-ceiling bookcases staged with framed family photographs.

"I knew I had to." I toss back the rest of the Scotch in a single gulp.

Arthur gets up, fetches the bottle from the corner of his desk, and pours me another. He sits back down and gives me a moment to relax before he clobbers me with a question.

"Can you tell me about the restaurant? And for the record, I've been there. Incognito. The food was fantastic. Best in the city."

I blink a few times in surprise. "When?"

"I don't know. A few times over the past year."

A few times. With whom? What was the menu that night? What did you order?

"Why didn't you let me know?" I ask. "I would have come out to say hello."

"I didn't want to get in your head," he replies with insight. "I just wanted to check it out because everyone at work was talking about how great it was."

It's not the correct moment for me to feel flattered, but I appreciate the compliment, more than he can ever know. I only wish I could enjoy it more, but my head is elsewhere.

"In case you're wondering," he says, "Dad has been there too."

And there it is—the answer to the burning question I couldn't bring myself to ask. I didn't even want to admit to myself that it mattered.

I swirl my whisky around in the glass. "I hope the food was good that night."

"It was phenomenal," Arthur tells me. "The wine pairings were spectacular, and I know because I was with him." Arthur sips his Scotch. "He finally booked a table because his colleagues kept congratulating him. I actually enjoyed watching dear old Dad stumble and try to act like he knew what they were talking about or pretend that he had some hand in your success."

It's a surprise to hear my brother make fun of our father. He's always danced to Dad's tune, and he never once stood up for me.

"Next time you make a reservation," I say, "let me know. I'll come out and say hello and make sure you're treated right." Arthur nods, and I take another sip of my Scotch. "If there is a next time, because if anything happens to Sienna . . ." My voice breaks. "I don't know how I'll manage anything."

Arthur watches me intently. Then his expression grows hard and grim. "I was serious in the car when I told you that I need to know everything. You have to tell me every possible detail that the prosecutor could use against you if they start digging."

Maybe it's the Scotch, but I'm feeling more willing to open up to him. "What else do you want to know?"

"Are you seeing anyone?" he asks. "Having an affair?"

I flinch in my chair. "God, no!" But then I think of Martina. Sienna always felt threatened by her, and even Amanda grilled me about Martina in the car just last night. "I love my wife," I insist. "And when would I have time for an affair? I barely have time for my kids."

"That's not for me to say," Arthur replies. "So what else? Anything damaging that you can think of?"

Unfortunately, there's plenty. "We went to Peggy's Cove to spend time together because we have been having some relationship problems," I confess, "and Sienna went to see a lawyer about a legal separation. But she didn't follow through with anything."

Arthur stares at me. "That's definitely something I would consider damaging. Next question: Any new life insurance policies? And what's in her will? I assume you get everything? As I recall, she sold her company for a nice chunk of change."

"She did, and the life insurance would be enough to bail me out of all my problems with the restaurant. Don't flip out, but we renewed it about six months ago and tripled the value."

Arthur slowly blinks.

"I'm not stupid," I say. "I know that looks bad, but we talked about it and wanted to make sure the debts would be covered if anything happened to either one of us."

He tips his glass back, empties it, and sets it down. "Okay. Well. At least there's no evidence of foul play—it's all circumstantial—unless there are witnesses. It sounds like people saw you arguing, but no one saw you push her."

"Because I didn't," I insist. My voice breaks, and I hang my head. "I don't want her to die. And I don't want to lose my family."

I fight hard to choke back a sob because Arthur and I were taught to never show weakness. It was beaten into us. We were raised to be warriors, tough as nails, which is why Arthur is such a damn good defense attorney.

He gets up, moves to his desk, sits down, and opens his laptop. While he types something, I stare down at my Scotch and hunger to get back to the hospital. I want to hold Sienna's hand and tell her how sorry I am and how much I love her. I need her to wake up so that I can start over, be a better man, and prove myself to her instead of my father.

Arthur's cell phone rings, and he answers it. "Hello?" He glances at me briefly, then rises from his chair. "When? Okay, thanks for letting me know."

He ends the call, and his expression tightens with displeasure. "LaPierre got a search warrant. They're heading to your house now."

A trembling begins in my limbs, followed by convulsions of panic. "Based on what evidence? You said it was all circumstantial."

"They could have information from a witness, or maybe you said something to give them cause?"

"I don't think so."

Arthur considers that. "They're looking for digital and print records. Should we be worried?"

"I don't know," I reply. "But Sienna wasn't happy. They might find evidence of that. God knows what she texted about me to Becky."

"They need more than feelings to use as evidence in court."

My hands turn clammy, slick with nervous sweat. "I just want to get back to Sienna."

"Give me the key to your house," Arthur says, "so I can let them in. I'll drop you off at the hospital on the way."

I'm grateful for his decisiveness. And the hospital is the only place I want to be right now.

I drain my glass of Scotch and get up.

"Thanks for helping me," I say.

"It's what families do," he replies and holds out his hand.

I stare at it and feel undeserving of his kindness. He's not my father, and I should have been a better brother to him, a better uncle to his children.

"I need the key to your house," he says flatly, which pulls me back to reality. I'm being investigated for attempted murder. I need to keep my emotions in check.

CHAPTER TWENTY-TWO

AMANDA

I startle awake and don't know where I am. Then I sit up and stare groggily at my father, who has just touched my shoulder. My eyes dart to Mom. She's still the same. Her face is bruised and marked with scabs and stitches. A bandage covers the area where her head has been shaved, and she's still in a deep coma, eyes closed.

"How are you doing?" Dad asks.

Arching my back in the uncomfortable chair, I stretch my stiff muscles and bend from side to side. "I'm okay."

"Where's Connor?" he asks.

"Probably went to the snack machine. He can only sit in here for so long before he gets restless."

Dad moves to bend over Mom in the bed. He kisses her forehead, on a spot that's unmarked by wounds. Then he whispers something I can't make out.

Eventually, he turns to me and removes his jacket, which he hangs on the back of a chair.

"What happened with the cops?" I ask as he sits down beside me.

"Exactly what you'd expect. They asked me a lot of questions, so I called my brother when I started to feel like a suspect."

Silence rises between us while I struggle to consider what this might mean. "Is he going to help you?"

"Of course. He's looking after things today because . . ." Dad pauses and lays a hand on my knee. "I don't want to worry you, but the detectives got a search warrant for our house."

My pulse skitters. "What?"

"Arthur's there now," he assures me, as if that makes this news less terrifying. "Everything's going to be fine because I didn't do anything wrong."

"Then why is everyone accusing you?" I ask desperately.

"Because some people crave drama," he explains. "That's the *only* reason. I swear it. And when the detectives finish their investigation, they'll come to that same conclusion because it's the truth. Yes, Mom and I argued, but it was bad luck that made the wave come over the rocks when it did." He turns to look at her in the bed. "I wish we'd never gone there. I should have just taken her to lunch."

I look at Mom as well and can't shake the anger I feel, which is still directed at my father.

~

At 8:30 p.m., I'm scrolling mindlessly through TikTok videos on my phone when a nurse enters the room.

"You three should go home and get some rest," she says. "Your mom's stable, but we'll call you if we need to."

"Thank you," Dad says politely.

She leaves, and I turn to Dad for a decision. He checks his watch, and I suspect he's worried that the police might still be at our house.

"Do you think it's safe for us to go home?" I ask.

"Arthur texted an hour ago and said they're finished, but they left a mess. And there are still reporters on our street."

Connor shrugs. "I don't care."

"We could go to a hotel," Dad suggests.

I shake my head. "No, I want to sleep in my own bed and change my clothes. And maybe Becky could bring Oscar back," I suggest.

Dad reaches for his coat. "Why don't you text her and ask. I'll tell the nurse that we'll be back in the morning. Grab your stuff, and we'll head home."

He moves to bend over Mom, whispers in her ear, and nuzzles her cheek. I truly hope his affection for her is genuine.

~

Twenty minutes later, we pull into the driveway. The house looks unfamiliar with all the lights off, because Mom always leaves a lamp on in the front room.

Dad shuts off the engine and unbuckles his seat belt. "We should prepare ourselves for the worst because the investigators had no obligation to put anything back in place after they disturbed it."

"Do you think they went in my room?" Connor asks, disconcerted.

"I don't know," Dad replies.

"My Xbox better not be missing," Connor says with ire as he gets out of the car.

We make our way up the steps, and Dad unlocks the front door. He pushes it open, and we all enter. He turns on the light, and the front hall, at least, is undisturbed.

I walk to the kitchen and family room. We turn on more lights and discover that half the books from the bookcase are spilled out, and papers are scattered on the table, which the police must have used as a surface to sort through our stuff.

None of us says a word. Connor looks around in a daze, then dashes to check his room in the basement. Heart racing, I run upstairs.

I push through my bedroom door, which has been left ajar, and lose my breath because all my dresser drawers have been yanked open. I'm sickened to imagine policemen rummaging through my socks and underwear. I don't know what they thought they were looking for, until I remember my diary in my bedside table. I move quickly to retrieve it, but it's gone.

I stifle a cry. How could they have taken my diary? It's private!

I scramble to remember what I've written lately. Mostly stuff about Jeff, which I wouldn't want my parents to read. But if the cops go back a few weeks, they'll find things I wrote when I was angry at Dad for ignoring my texts about Marissa, my stalker, and not being here when I needed him.

What if they use that to judge and convict him?

Why did I write those things? I don't want to get him in trouble!

At least I didn't write anything about what happened to Mom and how I've blamed Dad. I haven't written in my diary since before the accident.

A shadow appears in the doorway, and I turn.

It's Dad. He looks stricken. "You okay?"

"Not really," I reply. "They took my diary."

He nods with understanding. "They took my laptop and papers from our filing cabinet."

I don't know what Dad was keeping in those files, but it sounds like the police will know everything about us as a family.

"It's not fair," I say, fighting tears. "Mom's in the hospital. Isn't that enough? Why is this happening to us?"

He strides quickly toward me and pulls me into his arms. "Everything's going to be okay."

"No, it won't. What if I wrote something bad about you?" I bury my face in his shoulder.

"Is that a possibility?" he asks.

"I don't know. Maybe. I was upset when you didn't call me the night when we went to the police station to report that girl."

He rubs his hand in circles over my shoulder blade. "I'm sorry about that. I wish I could've trusted my staff to look after things at the restaurant that night."

I take a step back and wipe at my tears. "Are they not good workers?"

"They're fine," he tells me. "But I'm a control freak because I don't want to fail. I've wanted the restaurant to be the best in the city, and it's become an obsession for me."

I look at him through the blur of my tear-streaked lashes. "But how can that matter to you more than we do?"

"Because I'm an idiot. Mom thinks I should go to therapy. That was the last thing she said to me, actually, and I'm never going to forget that."

It takes a moment for me to digest this, because my brain isn't working like it should.

In that moment, my phone chimes, and I dig it out of my back pocket. "It's Becky. She's here, and she brought Oscar."

I can't wait to see him. I turn and dash downstairs to greet them at the front door. At the same time, Connor runs upstairs from the basement.

"They didn't take any of my stuff," he tells me, "but they made a mess of my closet."

"It was already a mess, you dork," I reply as I grab hold of his arm and drag him with me. "Becky's here with Oscar."

We go outside to the veranda, where the winter wind hits me like a smack in the face. I hug myself and shiver as I watch Becky get out of her car. Oscar leaps out. He runs and tugs at his leash to reach us.

"He really missed you guys," Becky says, jogging to keep up. "He was sitting at my front door all day with his chin on his paws, looking depressed."

Connor and I squat to greet him. Oscar bolts up the steps, and I laugh as he nuzzles my face and spins around in circles.

"My sweet boy!" I try to hug him, but he can't sit still. His tail wags so fast his whole bottom wiggles. "Let's go inside and get a treat!"

Becky follows and unhooks Oscar's leash from his collar. He immediately darts to the kitchen and living room, where he stops, looks all around, and runs up the stairs.

"Where are you going?" Connor shouts after him.

We listen to the sound of his paws padding down the hall and into each room.

"He's looking for your mom," Becky explains somberly.

His toenails click all around the hardwood floor in her bedroom.

Connor moves to the bottom of the stairs and looks up. "We could try and smuggle him into the hospital."

"Great idea, genius. Then we'd end up in jail too."

Oscar trots down the stairs and tries the basement next, ignoring us as he passes. Connor follows. Only then do I notice that Becky has wandered into the family room. She inspects the piles of books on the floor and my mom's empty desk, where her laptop used to be.

"How are you holding up?" Becky asks.

"Not great," I reply. "All I want is for Mom to come home."

"That's what I want too." She turns to me, and we embrace.

I'm not sure how long Becky holds me, or how many tears spill from my eyes, but when I step back, Oscar is at my feet, staring up at me. He looks worried, so I scratch behind his ears and drop to one knee.

"Everything'll be okay," I tell him. He starts to pant, maybe because he knows I'm lying. I have no idea if things will get better, and frankly, I've spent a lot of time imagining the worst. "I promised you a treat, didn't I?"

He bounces on his back legs, so I rise and get the bag of freeze-dried liver treats from the pantry.

"Sit, Oscar! Good boy." I set the treat on the floor, and he gobbles it up in a millisecond.

When I turn back around to face Becky, I see Dad standing at the far end of the kitchen island, staring at her.

"Hey," he coolly says.

She averts her gaze, and I'm not sure if she's angry with him for what happened to Mom or if she's feeling guilty about what she told the police.

"Thanks for bringing Oscar back," Dad says.

"You're welcome." After an awkward silence, she meets his gaze. "I should probably get going."

My stomach pulls tight with dismay as I watch her head for the door. Dad steps aside and lets her pass, and I have no doubt that he blames her for the search warrant. He must know that she talked to them.

Becky hurries to pull on her overcoat while Dad remains in the kitchen without seeing her out. I'm not sure what to say. All I know is that this feels wrong. Becky has been good to us. She's been an honorary aunt, while Dad has been absent for everything that has ever mattered in my life.

I can't let Becky leave like this, so I follow her to the door. "Thanks for looking after Oscar."

"It was no problem, sweetheart." She pulls me fast into her arms again and whispers in my ear. "Don't blame him. I should've kept my mouth shut."

She steps back, and again, I don't know what to say. I don't want her to feel bad about what happened. The truth is the truth. I understand that she didn't want to lie to the police. I wouldn't want to do that either. I'm only sixteen, but I've watched enough true crime documentaries to know that the truth always comes out in the end.

CHAPTER TWENTY-THREE

Nate

I wake at dawn, before the kids stir, and stand with a cup of hot coffee at the window in my den. Snow has fallen. The pinkish glow of sunrise casts an ethereal light on the street. Ice crystals sparkle like gemstones, and I wish Sienna were here to see it. She's always appreciated the color variations and patterns of the natural world. From it, she drew inspiration for her decor.

I, in turn, drew inspiration from *her*. Without knowing Sienna, I never would have made it as a chef. I owe her everything, which is why I'm steeped in regret over the choices I've made. Whenever I think of her last words to me, I feel myself eroding into a pit of disgrace.

Turning from the snowy view outside the window, I scold myself for thinking that I can't come back from this. Sienna's not gone. She's still in the hospital, fighting to live. Amanda seems to think she can hear us when we talk to her. I'm not sure if that's true. Maybe it's just something we humans like to believe because it brings us comfort or a sense of purpose, as if we're doing something to bring loved ones back from the brink, whatever that means.

Either way, I'm feeling desperate. I want to return to the hospital and turn things around. I can't wait for the children to rise. I'm too restless.

Twenty minutes later, I pass through sliding glass doors and head for the elevators. I'm still cold from the morning chill, so I keep my jacket zipped until I step off the elevator and reach the doors to the ICU, where I stop and pause.

I picture Sienna in her hospital bed with tubes coming out of her and the ventilator breathing for her. I see the cuts and bruises on her face, the bandage around her fractured skull.

I swallow heavily and prepare myself to walk in and see her that way again. It's not an easy sight to behold, especially when I'm the one responsible.

Amanda was right. Life isn't fair. Sienna is a good person, a loving wife, but all I ever thought about was my own success and getting my hands on her money. I'm a horrible person, and I hate myself.

It should have been me. I'm the one who should have drowned.

~

After a brief conversation with the nurse who is just coming off the night shift, I enter Sienna's room. I stop at the foot of her bed and take in the disturbing picture before me: my beautiful wife, bruised, cut, and battered. Her eyes are closed, her lids heavy. The room is quiet, the air tense with the uncertainty of her condition.

Where is her soul right now? Aside from the ventilator machine, it's deathly quiet. Until another monitor beeps noisily.

I jump because I'm skittish. I feel like God is standing over my shoulder, judging me and finding me selfish and prideful because of how I took my wife for granted. I thought only about what she could do for me, how she could lift me up. That's not love. It's greed. My stomach squeezes like a fist. I don't deserve her.

If she survives this horror, I swear on my life that I will turn over a new leaf. I'll stop thinking about myself, and I'll spend the rest of my days giving her everything she wants and needs.

Then I realize that the time to start giving is now because I'm in no position to bargain or negotiate. The doctor said we should talk to her, so I move to the chair, sit down, and take hold of her hand.

I sit in silence at first and stare at her face. I study every bruise and laceration, and I torture myself by imagining her in the water, panicked and terrified when she was dragged by a fast and powerful current toward the hard rocks, then catapulted into the air on a breaking wave.

My heart is on its knees. "I'm so sorry. I never wanted to hurt you."

My soul begs for her forgiveness.

Does she feel my presence? My remorse?

"I wish I had a time machine," I say shakily. "Do you remember how happy we used to be? Do you remember walking the dogs every night after supper? Scooter and Dolly. What a pair they were."

I close my eyes and think of it. The crickets in the grass. Chatting with neighbors who were also out walking their dogs. Riding the elevator back up to our apartment and smiling at each other.

I sit back in the stiff chair in the ICU and watch Sienna's eyelids. I search for a flutter, but there's no sign of life. Her hands are limp as I clasp and kiss them.

"Where are you right now?" I ask, feeling desperate, as if time is running out and this is my last chance. "Can you hear me? If you can, please know that I'd be nothing and nowhere without you. Please come back. I need you, and the children need you."

I become aware of another presence in the room. It feels dark, not what I want. I turn in the chair and look toward the door.

The morning nurse, the same woman from yesterday, speaks in a disturbingly loud voice. "Mr. Palmer. You have to talk to the police again."

My insides coil with panic. "They're back?"

"Yes, outside the unit." Her eyes are dark with judgment, and I feel her disdain, as if she's shooting it straight at my head. I wonder what the Facebook trolls have been posting overnight.

After rising from my chair, I bend over Sienna and kiss her forehead. "I'll be back, I promise."

The next moments are a blur, as if I'm shrouded in a fog. The nurse leads me to the main ICU doors and pushes the button. The doors open, and I walk out.

LaPierre and Lawson approach.

"Mr. Palmer," Lawson says. "You're under arrest for the attempted murder of your wife, Sienna Palmer."

Oh, God. What did they find?

LaPierre takes hold of my arms and cuffs my wrists behind my back.

I know better than to argue or resist, so I cooperate and walk willingly. "Call my brother, Arthur," I say to LaPierre.

"We'll do that from the station," he replies. "And just so you know, the press is out front."

"Great." My perp walk will be on the midday news, and my family will see my shame.

CHAPTER TWENTY-FOUR

Look Up, Sienna

As I enter Jacob's house, I feel a persistent tug back to my old life, but the sensation retreats when I behold his cozy kitchen. There's an enormous wood-burning oven on the far wall, and the smell of bread baking fills me with comfort and belonging.

At the same time, I'm conscious that if I'm truly dead, this kitchen is not my final destination. It must be a vestibule, one channel that connects to another, because I feel a presence, just beyond these walls, of divine beings and loved ones. I long to go to them.

Then I hear music. I can't define it. It sounds like celestial choirs and heavenly instruments in gentle harmony, and it resonates in my soul. I raise my face and look up. "Where's that coming from?"

Jacob offers no explanation, so I turn my attention to the room before me. Not far from the woodstove, Scooter's familiar red cushion is laid out for him. It's crisp and clean, like new. He steps onto it, turns a few circles, lies down, and curls up comfortably.

"Would you like a cup of tea?" Jacob asks.

"Yes. Thank you."

I pull out a chair to sit at the table, and Jacob fills a kettle at the sink. He sets it on a burner, opens the door to the firebox, and inserts a fresh piece of wood. He adjusts the damper and joins me at the table.

"That oven looks like something out of the pioneer days," I say.

He regards it with fondness. "I enjoy chopping wood for it, and it gives off a nice heat."

"Scooter seems to like it."

With affection, we watch our sleeping dog. Then Jacob turns to me. "I'm still surprised to see you."

"*Pleasantly* surprised, I hope? I'm certainly happy to see *you*."

"Yes, of course, but . . . honestly, I'm confused. I didn't expect you so soon. It feels like a mistake."

I'm not sure how to take that. Now that I'm here, I'm in a state of perfect tranquility. Time doesn't exist, and there's a fulfillment growing in me, as if all the mysteries of the universe will soon become clear. And with every passing second, my old life feels further away.

Jacob leans forward and clasps both my hands. "I know you've had some marriage trouble lately."

"That's putting it mildly."

He nods. "I also know that you love me, and I love you too. I always will. But, Sienna, we were so young when we were together. We were never tested."

I'm not sure yet where's he's going with this, but I sense that's one of the gifts of this place: clarity and wisdom.

"Are you suggesting that if you'd lived, we would have run into problems eventually? Or broken up? Would that have been our fate?"

"I don't know about that," he replies. "But we definitely would have had disagreements. The honeymoon phase can only last for so long."

"True," I reply. "But we were so perfect together."

He raises an eyebrow, clearly unconvinced. "No one is perfect. Some of us get banged up pretty badly in life, and it's not easy to recover."

"I understand that, but—"

"It's how we learn and grow," he continues. "But growth is in the healing. That's the whole point of living—to learn how to forgive each other for our trespasses, and how to be kind, and find joy together, even through our differences."

His words sink into my heart, and I know enough to hold on to them.

Scooter is asleep on his cushion, and I feel intensely drawn to him. I rise from my chair, cross the floor, and crouch beside him. As he sleeps, I stroke his smooth ivory coat. Then I turn to Jacob in the luminous light that shimmers through the kitchen window.

"Is that why you were invited here early?" I ask. "Because you already knew these things? You were always so kind to people, forgiving of everyone's mistakes. Is that why you were put on a fast track to heaven?"

He laughs softly. "No, it's not like that, and I don't know why I was chosen to die young. But I do recognize the strengths and weaknesses I had in life. Once I arrived here, I was able to look back at my existence and see it from on high. You should try that too, and you don't need to be dead to do it." Jacob waves his hand through the air. "Just try to look at your life from an elevated perspective. See the whole of it, not just what's happening to you in the present moment, because you'll judge that based on your mood or opinions at the time. But everything changes through the years, including you. You'll lose people, but you'll also gain new family and friends. You'll be happy and sad, you'll achieve good things, and sometimes you'll stumble or screw up monumentally and be ashamed of your actions. That's why it's important to reflect, thoughtfully. Recognize your achievements but also your errors in judgment, and learn from them. Just do it all with a mind that's open to change and doing things differently, or seeing things differently."

"But I don't want to look backward," I argue. "I certainly don't want to revisit the loss of you. I just want to look ahead. I know my parents are just beyond that door. I can feel them out there. Am I right?"

Jacob looks away, and I'm not sure why he's avoiding the question.

I fondle Scooter's silky ear. "You keep talking about learning and growing. Do you think I'm not ready to be here?"

Jacob gets up from the table. He joins me on the floor next to Scooter. "It's not about being ready. Some people arrive with hardly any life experience at all. Babies . . . toddlers . . ."

"Then why do you think I'm not meant to be here now?" I feel a bit hurt, as if I'm not worthy. "Have I not suffered enough?"

"You've suffered plenty," he replies. "More than some, but less than others. You've been very blessed, Sienna. Maybe that's what you need to appreciate." His eyes grow brighter, and he speaks with passion. "You also need to be proud of yourself for surviving hellish experiences. And be grateful for every second of your life—past, present, and future—because it won't last forever. It'll fly by in an instant, and then it'll be over. So don't take it for granted. I swear to you, even through the dark times, it'll be worth it in the end. Trust me on that."

"I do trust you."

I'm also overwhelmed by feelings of connection to this man I've always considered to be the true love of my life.

"You need to trust others too," he says.

I look down at Scooter again, sleeping peacefully. I run my hand across his shoulder. "You're referring to my husband?"

"Not just him." Jacob touches my hand. "Look up, Sienna."

I do as he asks, and I realize I'm not looking at the ceiling. I see endless blue sky, cottony clouds, and luminous light. I feel the same warmth that pulled me out of the frigid waters at Peggy's Cove. That warmth gave me a reason to swim to the surface.

I gaze back down at Scooter and feel the pleasant heat from the woodstove. Steam begins to rise from the spout on the kettle.

Jacob rises and sets a teapot on the table. As he pours hot water into it, I ponder everything he's just said to me. I understand that he wants me to go back to my life on earth. He doesn't believe it's my time. He wants me to put my faith and trust in a grander plan for me.

But I haven't forgotten the bone-numbing agony of my body smashing into the rocks, or the horror of seeing blood in the water, or the burning sensation in my lungs. The notion of returning to my life fills me with terror.

Is there even a body to go back to?

I bend to kiss the top of Scooter's head, but when I sit back, I stiffen. Jacob's at the table, pouring tea for us. I want to get up, but I can't move. There's a trembling in my core, a disruption in the air. I start to feel dizzy.

Jacob regards me with concern. "Are you okay?"

I open my mouth to answer, but before I can respond, I'm ripped away from him.

At lightning speed, I'm yanked backward by a mighty force that makes Jacob's house vanish like ashes in the wind.

CHAPTER TWENTY-FIVE

Sienna

I'm dropped mercilessly into my ravaged body. The sudden jolt leaves me stunned and disoriented, but within seconds, I become aware of physical pain everywhere, from the bones in my arm to my fractured skull, my chafed flesh, my smashed rib cage.

I am alone in a dark cave, but machines are beeping.

Wait. It's not a cave.

I'm vaguely aware of a woman moving around me. My eyes are closed, but I sense her hovering like an angel, just above my face.

"Sienna. Can you hear my voice? Can you open your eyes for me?"

My mind registers her words, but my body won't respond. All I can do is listen.

"Can you squeeze my hand?"

After some struggle, I manage to bend my middle finger.

"Excellent."

I sense another presence in the room. A man. He speaks to the woman. She's a nurse. I know this because I'm finally grasping that I'm in a hospital and something terrible has happened to me, but I don't know what. I can't remember much of anything, except for where I've just come from, which leaves me heartbroken and devastated to have left it behind.

The doctor pinches my arm. He asks me to open my eyes, but they weigh a thousand pounds. It takes a while before I can push them fully open.

A white ceiling. I blink a few times, but I have no strength. I fall in and out of consciousness, and I savor the sensation of floating in space, among stars . . .

It's so quiet in space, except for the pumping of my blood through my veins and arteries, and the random movements of my cells—like tiny bubbles in the ocean of water that makes up my physical body. I could float there forever.

CHAPTER TWENTY-SIX

Amanda

I wake and go to the kitchen, where I find a note from Dad. It's written with a Sharpie and stuck to the refrigerator with a magnet.

> Good morning. I was up early so I went to the hospital to sit with Mom. Have some breakfast and come when you can. I'll be here all day.

I leave the note on the refrigerator for Connor and look down at Oscar, who's staring up at me, tail wagging. "Let me guess. You need to pee."

His eyes are intense, like two laser beams of pure desperation.

"Let's go." I lead him down the basement stairs, across the rec room to the sliding glass doors, and let him out. The subzero temperature strikes me like sandpaper, and I can see my breath. I watch Oscar trot across the patio stones to a small patch of grass under the maple tree where there's no snow. He relieves himself and hurries back. I let him in, slide the door closed, and relock it. "Good job. Now let's get some breakfast."

As soon as we return to the kitchen, the phone rings. I move around the island to answer it. "Hello?"

"Good morning. Is this Amanda?"

"Yes," I reply as my heart begins to race because I recognize that it's someone from the hospital. I'm terrified of bad news. I barely slept a wink last night, dreading the phone call I didn't want to receive.

"I'm calling from the ICU," a woman says. "We have good news for you. Your mom's awake."

"Awake?" Happiness and relief flood through me, unstoppable.

I hold on to these words for a few seconds and wrap myself up in them. But then I remember the doctors' warnings—that Mom might be left with reduced motor skills or other long-term disabilities. "Is she okay?"

"She's weak and groggy," the nurse explains, "but the doctor is with her now, and we'll know more as the day goes on."

"Is my father there?" I ask.

"He's not here at the moment, so you might want to come in. It would be good for your mom to see you."

I hate the fact that none of us was at Mom's bedside when she woke up. Where is Dad?

Adrenaline surges through me. All I want to do is get to her room as fast as possible. "We'll be there in fifteen minutes. Thank you for calling."

"My pleasure," she replies.

I hang up and run to the stairs. "Connor! Mom's awake! Get up! We have to go see her!"

CHAPTER TWENTY-SEVEN

Sienna

I'm floating peacefully among stars when a woman's voice echoes through the universe. "Your children are on their way."

The words pull me back to earth, like a magnet, to my bed in the hospital.

My children . . . Amanda and Connor . . . the heartbeat of my life.

I need to see them.

Wake up, Sienna! Wake up!

I open my eyes, and the nurse bends over me. I want to say thank you—*thank you!*—but I can't do it. I'm in some sort of suspended consciousness. I'm here, but not really here.

In the next few seconds, I begin to feel physical pain—in my head, my shoulder, and my arm. It's ghastly, and terror stabs at me because I've been through this before. A lifetime ago. I know this is just the beginning and it's going to get worse. Much worse.

"That's it, very good," the doctor says as he pinches my forearm again.

This time I force my eyes open and struggle to focus. My chest burns, and my throat stings. I become aware of a thick tube down my throat.

White-hot panic shoots through me. I want to scream, but I can't. I'm paralyzed with shock and panic.

The pain intensifies in every realm of my body. My head endures the worst of it. It's a cruel throbbing just beneath the surface of my skull that no human being should ever be subjected to. Inside the bounds of my consciousness, I'm in agony. I'm screaming my head off.

I reach for the tube down my throat and try to pull it out, but the nurse grabs hold of my wrist. "Don't do that. It's for your safety."

I shake my head from side to side on the pillow. *I don't want it! Get it out!*

The doctor bends over me. "Sienna. My name is Dr. Malik. You've been in a coma. We need to make sure that you can breathe on your own before we remove it. Can you squeeze my hand, please?"

I squeeze with all my might.

"Good. Now wiggle your toes."

I wiggle my whole feet.

"Just your toes."

I roll my eyes and fulfill his request.

"Blink three times for me. Very good."

I wait impatiently while he positions his stethoscope in various locations on my chest and listens. "RSBI is looking good. Respirator rate less than twenty per minute. Oxygenation is good. She's alert. SpO2 of ninety . . ." He rattles off a few more stats, then turns to the nurse. "Let's extubate."

Eyes wide, I watch while they pull on masks and gloves and assemble some equipment. My heart races with anxiety. I'm desperate for them to hurry and get this thing out of me, but I'm terrified.

The nurse raises the head of my bed until I'm partially sitting up. She lays a blue absorbent pad on my chest like a bib. They set up some suction tubes. The doctor asks me to take some deep breaths, and he listens to my chest with his stethoscope. "More big breaths. Good. Now I'll get you to breathe in, hold that breath, and that's when I'll pull the tube out. Do you understand?"

I nod.

"Good. Ready? Here we go. Take a big breath. Now hold it!"

He pulls the tube out. The shock of the removal makes me sit forward and cough uncontrollably.

"You're doing fine. Cough it out." He sticks a suction tube into my mouth, then sets nasal cannulas in my nostrils for oxygen and hooks the tube behind my ears while I try to calm down. He listens to my chest again and asks me to take a few breaths while he studies the monitors. "Vital signs look good."

The nurse cleans up the blue pad, and the doctor leans over me again. "Can you tell me your full name?"

The area around my vocal cords is scratchy and raw, but I manage to croak out my name.

I'm not entirely recovered from the trauma of extubation, but my children are on their way, and that's worth breathing for. I can't wait to see them. I'm glad to be back, because all I want is the incomparable joy of holding my babies close to my heart.

CHAPTER TWENTY-EIGHT

AMANDA

It's lucky I don't get a speeding ticket on my way to the hospital, because my head is firing on all cylinders. I'm in panic mode, afraid we won't make it in time, that Mom will slip back into the coma before we arrive. Or, worse, something will go wrong and she'll die.

I glance at Connor in the passenger seat beside me. "Has Dad texted?"

"Not yet."

"Where is he?" I ask irritably. "Can you at least text Becky and tell her that Mom's awake?"

He thumbs a message, and within seconds, Becky calls us. I answer on the car speakerphone. "Hello?"

"Hi, it's me. She's awake?"

"Yes!" I shout elatedly. "We're on our way to the hospital now."

"I'm grabbing my purse, and I'll be there soon as I can," she replies.

"Do you know where Dad is?" I ask. "He said he went to the hospital this morning, but he's not there. I don't even think he knows Mom's awake."

"I'll try the restaurant," Becky says. "And I'll see you soon."

~

I park the car, and we get out and sprint to the hospital entrance. The elevator ride takes forever, stopping at different floors to let people on and off. But at last, we reach the ICU and are buzzed inside.

Familiar with the routine, we sanitize our hands and don yellow gowns outside Mom's room. Her nurse comes out to greet us, and her smile is infectious. It sends an abundance of happiness into my heart.

"She's still okay?" I ask.

"Doing great," the nurse replies. "She's a fighter. She made it clear she wanted to breathe on her own, so we removed the tube, and she's able to talk now."

"Can we go in?"

The nurse speaks gently. "Yes, but keep in mind that she's been through a lot, and she's still very tired and groggy from the pain medication."

"What about her motor skills?" Connor asks, not having forgotten our initial conversation with the doctor.

"So far, so good," the nurse replies. "But head injuries can be unpredictable, so we'll need to keep a close eye on her for a few days."

I'm listening, but all I want to do is see my mother.

The nurse finally ushers us into the room, where I pull to an abrupt halt. Mom is asleep on the bed, without the breathing tube. The room is quiet, and it's a gift not to hear the ominous sound of the ventilator.

Connor and I move to either side of the bed. She must feel our presence, because she opens her eyes and looks at each of us in turn with love. I tremble and cry tears of relief. Mom holds out her arms to us, and we bend over her, crying and hugging and kissing the sides of her face.

"I love you, Mom." I cherish her lips on my temple as she kisses my tears away.

"I'm happy to see you both," she says in a weak, raspy voice.

I draw back and look more carefully at her. The cuts and bruises on her face seem insignificant now, blessedly superficial. What matters is that she's awake and she knows who we are. She's able to speak to us. But I can see that she's weary.

"Rest now, Mom." I run my hand over the bandage on her head. "We want you to get better so you can come home." She nods and closes her eyes. I glance across at Connor. "She needs to sleep, but she's okay."

He wipes his forearm across the tears on his face.

We look around for chairs and pull them close to the sides of the bed, where we sit down and hold Mom's hands.

Beyond the window glass, outside the room, a team of nurses and doctors stand in a circle and discuss something at length. The nurse in charge of Mom is sitting at a portable rolling desk, on the other side of the glass, watching us. She smiles at me, and I smile back, feeling overwhelmed by my gratitude for the care that Mom has received.

I bow my head over my mother's hand and kiss it.

Thank you, Lord, for answering my prayers.

~

One moment there is light, sunshine, and warmth. Then my cell phone rings, and the whole world turns dark.

"Hello, is this Amanda?"

"Yes."

"Hi. It's your uncle, Arthur."

I rise from the chair and leave Mom's room, searching for a quiet corner somewhere in the unit. "Where's Dad?" I ask.

He hesitates, which compounds my unease. "Sorry, kiddo. I know this isn't what you want to hear right now, but he's been arrested. The charge is attempted murder."

Dread catapults into the pit of my stomach, and I cover my mouth with my hand. "No."

"They must have felt they had enough evidence."

Evidence. I hear the word but can't register it. At least not right away. Then it hits me full force—the magnitude of what he just said to me and the image of my father pushing my mother off the rocks at Peggy's Cove, into the brutal and violent waves, to a place where the ocean is a killing machine.

"That couldn't have happened," I say. "There's no way he did that."

"I'm on my way to see him now."

"But Mom's awake," I tell him, which is not a proper response to what he just communicated, but I need to cling to something good. I can't handle a fresh new hell, nor do I want to believe this terrible thing about my father, despite whatever evidence they found.

"Did you just say she's awake?" Uncle Arthur asks.

"Yes."

"Oh, thank God. How is she?"

"Doing well so far. Sleeping mostly. But she can talk, and she knows who we are."

"Does she remember what happened?" he asks. "If she can confirm that what happened was an accident, then we can get your father released."

I face the wall and rest my forehead against it. "She hasn't talked about that yet. She's still groggy."

"Amanda . . ." He pauses, and I wait uncomfortably for him to continue. "Don't tell anyone she's awake yet, okay? We don't want the cops in there taking notes. I'm coming over right now. Just stay put. I'll see you shortly."

He ends the call, and I stare blankly at my phone. His words repeat over and over in my mind—that they have evidence to charge Dad with attempted murder.

What in the world did they discover on his laptop or in his office files? What if it's something bad? It's been years since he's felt like a real father to me. He's been a stranger, but he's been trying to do better since Mom ended up in the ICU. Or has he just been trying to cover his ass?

With a flash of panic, I walk quickly back to Mom's room. I barely know Uncle Arthur, but I'm afraid to trust anyone about anything.

I reenter the room and find Mom still sleeping. Connor glances up from his phone. "Who was that?"

"Uncle Arthur. He said Dad's been arrested."

Connor lowers his phone. "What?"

"He's on his way here, and he wants to talk to Mom and find out what really happened." Feeling protective, I sit down beside her and take her hand. "Mom? Are you awake?" She doesn't stir, so I gently shake her shoulder. "Mom?"

Her eyes flutter open, and she looks at me.

"Can you talk to me?"

She nods.

"Do you remember what happened at Peggy's Cove?"

"I fell in the water, and I drowned," she replies.

"Yes. But do you remember *why* you were in the water?"

Her eyes glisten with a mixture of sadness and fear. She slowly shakes her head on the pillow.

"Were you arguing with Dad?" I ask.

She turns her face away.

I don't want to upset her, but I need to know what happened. I need to know the truth. Leaning close, I whisper in her ear. "Mom. Did Dad push you off the rocks?"

Her eyebrows pull together with anguish, and she shakes her head. "No. He'd never do that."

"But do you remember?"

Her gaze darts uncertainly toward the window, then back at me. "I'm not sure . . . I . . ." She blinks a few times. "Everything's fuzzy. I think I might have gone to heaven."

Her words crash into me. I lose track of what I was just asking her. I glance across the bed at Connor, who stares at me with wide eyes.

Mom's chin begins to quiver, and she fights tears. I rub the back of her hand. "It's okay. We don't need to talk about this right now."

She starts to cry. "It was very beautiful."

My heart races wildly because I can't bear to think of my mother in heaven. That would mean we'd truly lost her. But this is not news to me. I was told that she'd had no pulse for at least twelve minutes before she was resuscitated on the rocks. Maybe I'd been in denial about that.

Heaven . . . "Did you see Nanny or Granddad?" I suddenly ask.

"No, but I felt them. They're waiting for me." Her brow furrows with amazement. "There was so much love there. You wouldn't believe it. I never felt anything like it."

The door to Mom's room opens, and Becky walks in. She takes one look at Mom and bursts into tears as she moves around the bed. I get up from my chair to let her take my spot, and she bends to hug Mom. They both cry and cry.

"Thank goodness you're okay," Becky says.

They keep hugging each other and crying, and I feel nothing but love in this room—and immense gratitude for Mom's return.

The nurse opens the door and peeks her head in. "There's someone outside the ICU who wants to come in, but we can only have three visitors at a time."

"Who is it?" I ask.

"Arthur Palmer. He says he's your mother's brother-in-law."

I catch Becky's gaze and shake my head.

"Ask him to wait for a bit," Becky tells the nurse, who backs out of the room and closes the door.

Mom's eyes fall closed, and I know she is tired and needs sleep. Becky kisses her on the forehead and turns to me. "Do you want to go out and talk for a minute?"

"Yes. Stay here, Connor," I say. We both get up and leave the room to stand outside the door. "Dad's been arrested," I whisper. "Uncle Arthur said they had enough evidence to charge him with attempted murder."

Becky places her hand over her heart. "Oh, my God."

"Arthur's defending him, and he's here because he wants to know what Mom remembers. He wants her to say that Dad didn't do it."

"But is that true?" Becky asks.

"I don't know. I'm so confused right now."

She ponders this. "We need to ask her."

"I already did. She says she doesn't remember. She also said . . ." I pause because I don't want anyone to think my mother is delusional. They might send her to the psych ward.

"Tell me," Becky whispers, and I trust her like I always do.

"Mom believes she went to heaven," I quietly say. "She felt Nanny and Granddad there."

Becky stares at me, speechless.

"She said it was beautiful."

Two male doctors in blue scrubs walk past, and we move closer to the wall to speak more privately.

"She *was* clinically dead," Becky whispers, and I'm relieved that she seems to have an open mind about this. "Did she mention seeing anyone else?"

Becky stares at me with desperate eyes.

"I'm not sure," I reply. "She didn't say much more than that. I'm mostly worried about what happened *before* she fell in the water, because that's what Arthur wants to know, and he'll be asking Mom the same question. But she doesn't remember."

Becky turns to scan the unit. "I'd like to talk to her doctor about her memory. Is he around?"

I spot Dr. Malik at the nurses' station, but he starts heading for the exit. I point. "That's him."

"I'll be right back." Becky hurries and catches him just before he pushes through the doors.

I watch and wait while they talk. A moment later, she returns.

"What did he say?" I ask.

"He said it's normal to forget the details of a trauma like that, and it could just be temporary. Her memory could return in the next few hours or days. Or possibly never. We just have to wait and see. But the good news is that she's stable and they'll be moving her out of the ICU tomorrow morning."

"That is good news," I reply, exhaling with relief. "But what do we do about Uncle Arthur?"

Becky ponders this. "Do you have his number in your phone?"

"Yes, he just called me." I retrieve it from my back pocket and hand it to her.

Becky starts texting. "I'm telling him that your mom's sleeping and she can't receive any visitors, and that he should go home and call later."

"What about my dad?" I ask. "He's stuck in jail."

Becky hands my phone back to me. "If there's actual proof that he pushed your mom off the rocks, then that's where he belongs."

She starts back to the room, and my emotions start to spiral because I don't want to believe that he did this. I just want my old dad back—the one who used to carry me on his shoulders and take me to swimming lessons at the pool. I want the father he once was, before he opened his restaurant.

But maybe that man doesn't exist anymore.

I hurry to follow Becky back to the room.

CHAPTER TWENTY-NINE

Sienna

I wake in the hospital bed with needles and tubes sticking out of my arms, a fog in my head. My children aren't here. It's just Becky and me.

"How long was I asleep?" I ask.

"A couple of hours," she replies. "I just sent Amanda and Connor to the cafeteria for some lunch, but they'll be back soon."

I try to shift my position, but I have no strength, and I'm afraid to disturb the needles in my veins that are taped to the tender crook of my arm.

Becky adjusts my pillow and the blue sheet that covers my battered body. I wet my dry lips, and she reaches for the cup of water with a straw and feeds it to me. While I sip from it, she talks.

"Amanda said you had . . ." She pauses. "Something like a near-death experience when you were in the water."

I finish drinking and lie back. "Yes."

"She also said that you felt your parents were there?"

I don't remember telling Amanda that, but I'm groggy because of the medications. I wonder uneasily what else I said, especially about Jacob.

"Did you see him?" Becky asks.

I slowly blink and feel a deep and profound kinship with my best friend, who knows me so well. "What do you think?"

She lets out a breath of amazement. But with the pounding in my skull, despair returns with a vengeance, and I shut my eyes. "There was a part of me that didn't want to come back, knowing what I'd have to go through, physically."

But there's so much more to it than that. I wish I could articulate what it felt like, but no words can describe the peace and joy I felt when I flew over the valley, then came to rest in her brother's backyard.

"I was so happy to see him," I say. "To feel loved like that again. I haven't felt that way since . . ." I attempt to look back at my life—at the whole of it—but everything is fuzzy. What I remember best, in this moment, is heaven.

Becky smiles shakily. "I wish I could see him too. I still miss him, and I've often wondered what our lives would look like today if he hadn't died. You and I would probably be sisters-in-law."

I turn my face toward the window. "But then I wouldn't have Amanda or Connor."

"True," she replies. "And we wouldn't want to change that."

"Never."

She holds my hand, and we sit quietly for a moment until Becky inches her chair forward. "There's something else we need to talk about. We should discuss it before you get released from the ICU and get more visitors."

"What is it?" I ask.

"I'm not sure what Amanda told you when you first woke up," she replies, "but you need to know what's been happening over the past few days."

I wait for her to explain, but she hesitates.

"Tell me."

She bows her head. "People are going to ask you what you remember about falling in the water. They'll want to know if Nate pushed you."

Pushed me . . .

My memories are sluggish, but I do recall Amanda whispering that question in my ear. She was upset, desperate to know the answer.

"Why do people think that?" I ask as I struggle to remember that entire afternoon, but it's as if there's a thick fog surrounding my brain, and I can remember only short flashes: The drive along Highway 103, sitting in silence with Nate, feeling angry, frustrated. He wanted to work things out. He believed an afternoon at Peggy's Cove would bring us closer. But to me, it was a waste of time because our marriage was already dead. There was no way to resurrect it from the grave.

Becky glances at the door, and I sense her impatience. She's worried the kids will return at any moment, and she doesn't want to have this conversation in front of them.

She continues. "He's been accused because there were witnesses that saw you arguing, and now people are following the case on social media. And yesterday, the police got a search warrant for your house because they found out that Nate's restaurant was struggling financially. I think they must have settled on a motive—that he wanted your insurance money and control of the trust fund from the sale of your company."

Suddenly I feel like a snowball rolling down a hill, growing in clumps of bewilderment and confusion. I shut my eyes and try to remember plunging into the water, but that event does not exist in my memory. I can recall only the powerful currents carrying my body down, then up, sideways, and forward. In my panic, I was desperate to take a breath . . . I sucked in water that burned my lungs . . . then I was rescued. I was drawn upward to warmth and light.

"Did he push you?" Becky asks.

Again, I struggle to recall those last few seconds. "I think . . . I think I ran away from him, and he chased me. I was angry, and I felt used. But then I don't know what happened. I only remember the wave hitting me like a truck. It slammed into me, and I was swept off my feet."

"Was it the wave that hit you, or Nate?"

I lie motionless on the bed and blink up at the ceiling. "I'm not sure."

"What you just told me, about Nate chasing after you, could be damaging if the investigators hear it. But if you think it was just the wave, you need to be clear about that."

I shake my head on the pillow. "But I'm not sure. I honestly don't remember what happened or what hit me. But, Becky . . ." I meet her gaze directly. "I'm certain he'd never try to kill me. He has his faults but—"

The door opens, and Amanda walks in. "You're awake." She cheerfully kisses me on the cheek and sits down.

"Where's Connor?" I ask.

"He ran into a friend from hockey. They're still in the cafeteria."

I try to relax, but it's not easy.

Amanda leans close and speaks quietly in my ear. "Did Becky talk to you about Dad?"

She knows. I can't bear it.

"Yes," I reply, "but I'm sure he wouldn't have done what they think he did."

"How are you sure?" she asks. "I just . . . I wanna know."

I nod because I understand. She's seeking reassurance, and I want, more than anything, to give it to her. "I know him," I reply. "And he loves me."

"But you went to see a lawyer about a divorce."

The heartache in her voice breaks my heart too. "Yes, and I'm sorry I didn't tell you about that."

"But why? Don't you love him anymore? Or is he bad, like they're saying?"

I shake my head. "Dad has disappointed us lately, but that doesn't make him a killer. I won't believe that about him."

"But the police searched our house, and they say they have proof."

It sickens me to imagine strangers going through our personal belongings, and I still can't believe Nate would ever do something like this.

"It has to be a mistake," I tell her. "Believe me, sweetheart . . . we'll get to the bottom of it."

"Will we?" she tearfully replies. "But what if you're wrong? What if he's found guilty and he goes to prison for the rest of his life?"

I honestly don't know how to answer that.

CHAPTER THIRTY

Nate

I'm awake inside a nightmare. Or maybe I'm on my way to hell.

I thought it was bad enough when LaPierre locked me into this concrete cell, but it's worse now that the sun has gone down. There's no light shining through the barred window, only a cold and bluish fluorescent glow from an overhead bulb in a cage. It's deathly quiet except for another inmate hacking and coughing, occasionally spitting.

This is a hellish place, and I don't belong here. I want to go home and get a second chance, but Sienna's in the hospital. She's bruised, broken, and battered. She's on life support, and I might never see her again. She might die, and if that happens, I'll never forgive myself. I might as well die too.

But this hell of mine can't be any worse than what she went through when she was swept off the rocks and fought for survival in the raging, ice-cold ocean waves.

God . . . I'm losing it again. My body shudders, and I fight not to sob, because no one has any sympathy here. Besides, I can't be absolved. Nor can I change what I did. I asked for money again, even after I promised to stop putting the restaurant ahead of our family. That's why she ran away from me, toward the waves.

I let out a loud, wretched sob.

"Shut up!" someone shouts.

I fight for breath and use the scratchy wool blanket to wipe at my snotty nose.

Sienna, please don't die. Please live so that I can prove that I love you more than anything. I've learned my lesson. I swear it.

CHAPTER THIRTY-ONE

Sienna

I wake at 6:30 a.m. when a nurse comes to take my blood pressure. She tells me she's finishing her shift and that the day nurse will see me out of the ICU.

"Congratulations," she says while she squeezes the inflation bulb. "You're doing well." I remain quiet while she listens with her stethoscope and reads the gauge. She peels at the Velcro and removes the cuff from my arm.

"Have you been following social media?" I ask curiously while missing my phone at the bottom of the ocean.

"Yes. It's a shame what happened to you. No one deserves that."

I take a moment to digest this. "I suppose everyone thinks my husband is guilty."

"That's what it sounds like," she replies, "but it's not for me to say. That's what the courts are for."

She finishes up and leaves the room.

Tired all of a sudden, I close my eyes and use my imagination to recall what happened before I drowned. All the events of the day. I remember, quite clearly, writing *broccoli* on the magnetic grocery list on the refrigerator when Nate walked in the door.

From there, I lie quietly and replay each moment. I see the landscape on the old Lighthouse Route. Most of all, I remember my certainty that Nate would never change.

~

The move from the ICU to the neurosurgery floor exhausts me. Not long after they situate me in a private room, a young man delivers breakfast on a tray. It's been days since I've chewed and swallowed anything, which feels daunting after having a tube stuck down my throat. But I'm tired of all these needles and tubes sticking out of me, so I pick up my spoon.

Just as I'm about to give the warm broth a try, Amanda and Connor walk in. Amanda takes a look at my breakfast tray.

"You're eating," she says. "This is huge."

"Don't get too excited," I reply as each of them greets me with a kiss on the cheek. "I haven't swallowed anything yet. I don't have much of an appetite."

"Are you feeling okay?" Amanda asks.

"I feel great," I reply, because I don't want her to worry anymore. I'm sure she's done enough of that.

They drag two chairs to either side of my bed.

"Any news about Dad?" I ask. He's been on my mind all night. Everyone seems to believe he tried to hurt me, but I don't know what's real anymore. I went to heaven, for pity's sake. Or at least I think I did. I don't know.

"Nothing this morning," Amanda replies. "Just more people expressing their opinions on social media."

"I haven't seen any of that yet. Can I look at your phone?"

"I'm not sure you want to see that stuff, Mom," Connor warns me. "It might upset you."

"I appreciate you being protective," I reply, "but I really need to know what's going on. I'd like to know what evidence the police have because I still have no recollection."

"I think that's the problem," Amanda says. "You have no recollection, one way or the other."

"But it's impossible to remember something that didn't happen," I argue.

"True," she replies, "but do you remember getting hit by the wave?"

I stop and think about it, carefully, but I still can't recall that exact moment.

"I'm sure it'll come back to me," I assure them. "Other memories have been returning, one by one. I think I just need time to recover and get off the pain medications."

An ambulance siren blares somewhere outside, and it strikes me with a sense of urgency. "What about your uncle Arthur?" I ask. "Has he been in touch?"

Amanda clears her throat. "Yes, but we don't want him to come here and pressure you to remember."

"But maybe that's what I need," I tell her. "To be pressured." We all trade glances, and I feel heat in my cheeks. "I'm worried about him. And now that I'm more coherent, I'd like to talk to the police. I want to know what smoking gun they have, if they'll tell me."

The telephone next to my bed rings. It startles me enough to make me jump, but I can't reach it.

Amanda stands and answers it. "Hello?" Her eyes meet mine. She holds the handset away from her, covers the mouthpiece with her palm, and whispers, "It's Uncle Arthur."

My breath comes short with relief and anticipation. "Tell him I'm out of the ICU and to come here as soon as he can. I want to talk to him in person."

Amanda brings the handset back. "She's feeling better, and she wants you to come here as soon as you can—"

"Ask him how Dad's doing," I interrupt before she has a chance to hang up the phone.

Amanda asks the question and relays the information to me. "He says not great."

My chest feels tight, as if there's a weight pressing down on it. I can't bear to imagine Nate in jail. Does he even know I'm awake?

Amanda hangs up. "He'll be here in fifteen minutes."

I look down at the broth on the tray in front of me and push the rolling table off to the side. "I don't think I can eat right now. I'll save this for later."

~

Arthur slowly approaches the foot of my bed. It's been a few years since we've seen each other, and I notice a difference. He's gained a few pounds and lost some hair. I hate to think it, but he's starting to look like his father.

His face goes pale at the sight of me, and he inclines his head with sympathy. "Sienna. My God."

Amanda vacates her chair at my side and offers it to him. He sets his briefcase on the floor and moves to give me a kiss on the cheek.

"It's good to see you," I say. "I'm sorry it's been so long."

"No, I'm the one who's sorry," he responds. "I shouldn't have let my baby brother get so caught up in the rat race."

I chuckle. "That's a polite way of putting it."

His gaze takes in the cuts and bruises on my face, the bandage on my half-shaved head, the cast on my arm. "Is there anything I can do for you?"

"You can tell me about Nate," I doggedly reply.

Arthur sits down, his expression unmistakably serious. "I'm not sure what you know at this point."

"I know that he's been arrested and that people think he's responsible for what happened to me. That's about it."

Arthur nods, and I brace myself. "He spent last night in jail, and now I'm waiting to hear about the discovery and a date for the arraignment. We're working on bail, but it takes time."

My lower back starts to ache, so I shift a little on the bed. "Becky told me they found evidence that incriminates him. Do you know what that is?"

"Not yet," he replies. "And frankly, I don't think it'll stand up in court because it can only be circumstantial. Unless Nate is lying to me and he took detailed notes, confessing a brilliant master plan to do you in."

"That would've been a genius move."

"If that's what they have, I'll eat my shirt." Arthur takes hold of my hand. "Unless . . ."

"Unless I tell you that I remember him pushing me," I say.

Arthur shrugs, as if he knows it's a ridiculous question, but he still wants to hear my response.

I look down at my fingers poking out of my cast. "I wish I could tell you that I remember the wave hitting me, and that Nate was twenty feet away, but I honestly don't recall that moment. I only remember the shock of realizing I was in the water."

Amanda pipes up. "The doctor said it's normal for her memories to be vague after her head injury, and that they might come back to her."

"Would it be possible for me to speak to your doctor?" Arthur asks. "You'd need to give permission for that."

"I'll give it," I reply. "No matter what happened, I want the truth."

Arthur studies my expression. "What's your gut telling you?"

My children watch me closely, and in the end, I decide to be an open book. "My gut tells me that he's become very self-centered since he opened his restaurant, that he put the restaurant before his family, and he's chipped away at the love I've felt for him. But I don't think he'd ever try to hurt me."

Arthur looks down at my good hand and speaks flatly. "Here's what I think. He needs to go on a yoga retreat to Costa Rica."

I consider this carefully, then chuckle. I realize it's the first time I've laughed since I woke up. I'm surprised it didn't hurt.

"Are men allowed to go to those things?" Connor asks, genuinely curious.

Again, I chuckle.

"Of course," Arthur replies. "Are you interested?"

Connor waves his hand in front of his face. "I'll stick to hockey, thanks."

"If it helps," Arthur says, returning to the subject at hand, "just remember that the burden is not on us to prove that Nate didn't do it. The burden is on them to prove that he did. So we'll just have to wait and see how strong their case is."

"Will you see him today?" I ask. "And does he know I'm awake?"

"I saw him last night," Arthur replies, "and I told him. But you should know . . . he was pretty down. I was worried. But that news made all the difference."

"We don't want him to go to prison," Amanda says.

Arthur rises from his chair and picks up his briefcase. "Based on what I'm seeing here this morning, I'd like to believe that the odds are in his favor. Let's go with that, okay?"

I want to trust Arthur's gut instincts, but after everything I've been through—the highs and lows of happy times followed by shock and trauma and disaster—I've learned to never take anything for granted.

~

Arthur has gone, but my children are still here, one on each side of my bed. I'm sleepy, and my head hurts, mostly because of my skull fracture, but there's also an element of stress in my pain. Since Arthur left the hospital, I've had time to lie still and reflect, to imagine Nate getting arrested and escorted to a jail cell. Spending the night there.

No amount of hurt regarding our marriage or hostility over his obsession with the restaurant can dampen my concern for him. I'm worried. All I want to do is see him as soon as possible and tell him that his family hasn't abandoned him.

~

I wake to the sound of a nurse changing an IV bag and pressing buttons on a machine. The sky out the window has gone gray, and I suspect it might snow.

"You're awake," Amanda says.

I turn my head on the pillow. "What time is it?"

"Almost two o'clock. You've been asleep for a while. They brought the lunch tray, if you're hungry."

When I try to sit up, Amanda gets out of her chair and adjusts the head of my bed. She then rolls the tray table toward me.

I examine the bowls of red Jell-O and soup with rice and tiny pieces of chicken.

"How's Oscar?" I ask as I remove the clear plastic lid from the soup.

"Good, but he misses you."

"I miss him too."

Amanda seems relaxed, lounging back in her chair. "That first night that you were gone, he ran all over the house looking for you. We felt so bad for him."

Her words stir a memory in me, or maybe it was just a dream. I returned home to say goodbye to my children before I left this world. I floated through the front door, but no one saw me except for Oscar.

"Where's Connor?" I ask.

"He went home to walk Oscar," Amanda explains. "Becky picked him up about an hour ago."

I scrape the soup bowl clean. Then I reach for the Jell-O and feel good about the return of my appetite.

"Can we talk about Dad?" Amanda asks. "I want to tell you what it was like having him at home."

I push the rolling table off to the side. "I'm listening."

"It was different," she says. "He was just . . . trying harder, I guess. He made cinnamon toast for me."

I draw back slightly with surprise. "It's been a long time since either of us made that for you."

"Yeah, I'd kind of forgotten about it," she replies, "but obviously Dad didn't. And we talked in the kitchen. It was nice. It reminded me of how he used to be."

I don't want to pry or push her to reveal every detail of their conversation. Sometimes my motherly inquisitiveness makes her shut the open door between us. "I'm glad you had that time together," I simply reply.

"Me too. Although it wasn't all warm fuzzies. I woke up because I heard him crying."

The weight of those words cuts at my heart. "Really?"

"Oscar heard it too. Dad sounded really upset. I never heard anything like that before. He was always so together, you know? Those pictures of him on the website in his chef's uniform . . . he looks so tough and determined, but that's not who he is." She stares at me, sending a piercing challenge, daring me to disagree.

I nod, and she relaxes slightly.

"You've talked to me about his father," she continues, "and I think, deep down, he's just lost. Even more so, now that he's in jail and might lose us."

A quiet pain spreads through me, slow and deep. I can't bear to think of Nate all alone, coping with this ordeal.

Amanda picks up her phone and starts swiping. Our conversation has come to a dead halt, but I understand that she needs to tune out for a moment, so I wait patiently. She swipes again, reads something, and taps a few buttons. "Oh, my God."

"What is it?"

"Connor just texted." Her cheeks flush with color, and she squints as she studies her screen.

"What's he saying?" I ask.

"Someone just posted a video on Facebook. Apparently, someone was filming when you were swept off the rocks. It's all there." She gets up and moves closer to show me her screen.

My pulse races, wild and uncontrollable, because I don't want to relive that ordeal, yet I need to know what Nate was doing when I fell in the water. I need that question answered. Unequivocally.

The video starts with an older man standing on the rocks, smiling and pointing, but then I enter the frame in the background.

"That's Dad behind you," Amanda says as we watch. "But he's not even close."

Then I disappear.

"Play it again." I watch the whole scene, from the first second I enter the frame. I'm hopping down the sloping rocks. Then a gigantic explosion of water crashes over me, and I vanish. Only then does Nate enter the frame. He runs desperately to the spot where the wave had taken me.

"Does the RCMP know about this?" I ask, dumbfounded.

Amanda starts to thumb a message. "They will in about two minutes, as soon as I text Uncle Arthur. And whatever evidence the cops think they have, I'm pretty sure this'll crush it."

With a surge of relief, mixed with nausea from watching how I'd vanished into that frothy white surf, I rest my head against the pillows and shut my eyes. All I can see, over and over, is Nate running to the edge of the rocks, coming to an abrupt halt, placing his hands on his head in despair, and then desperately pacing back and forth, scanning the churning water below.

CHAPTER THIRTY-TWO

NATE

It's remarkable how a night in jail, not knowing if you'll ever be released, can strip you down fast. It's like a glass of cold water in the face. It really wakes you up.

After the video was posted on Facebook, it took hours for Arthur to arrange my release. I didn't even know why I was being let out. No one told me anything, so I assumed bail had been granted. But when I see my brother's buoyant smile in the station corridor, I know immediately that it was something much better than bail. I stride fast into Arthur's arms and cry my eyes out.

"You're all right now," he says, hugging me tight and patting my shoulder to console me. "The charges were dropped."

So much for not showing weakness. I guess jail time stripped me of that instinct as well.

I back away from him and wipe at my cheeks. "I'm so sorry. I've been such an ass about the restaurant."

Arthur flippantly shrugs a shoulder. "At least you can admit it."

Suddenly, I'm lost for words. Clearly, Arthur hasn't changed. As a lawyer, he's tough as nails, but with me, he's still, despite our estrangement, the same teasing, affectionate brother I've always known.

We walk out, and I feel a long trail of regret behind me, but as we push through the glass doors and step into the sunshine, I promise myself that, from this day forward, I will do better with my family. And I won't let my brother drift out of my life again.

~

Arthur gets behind the wheel of his Mercedes to take me straight to the hospital. He explains about the video that was posted on Facebook.

"But what about the evidence the cops found in the search?" I ask as we pull away from the curb.

Arthur speaks bluntly. "It was garbage. They found some panicked emails you wrote about your line of credit being overdue, and then a new life insurance policy a week later, so they figured they had enough to get a guilty verdict out of a jury." He glances my way and shakes his head dismissively. "I would have destroyed them in court."

I feel incredibly blessed and fortunate as we cross the city. When we finally arrive at the hospital, we take the elevator to the neurosurgery floor. The doors slide open, and my body pounds with anticipation. I step off and search for a sign indicating which direction to go for Sienna's room number.

"It's this way," Arthur says, grabbing my arm.

My whole body is buzzing with impatience as I follow him. I can't wait to see her. I don't recall feeling like this since the day I drove to meet Sienna at Point Pleasant Park for our first date. I'd stepped out of the car with Dolly and searched the parking lot for Sienna. When at last I'd spotted her with Scooter, my heart erupted. I was a goner. She was the most beautiful woman I'd ever seen, and it was as if I'd been hit by a high-speed train. She became the center of my universe after that, and when our children were born, they expanded that universe.

Arthur is walking too slow, so I start to jog ahead until I find Sienna's room. I enter cautiously, knocking on the wall to make sure I'm in the right place, but the bed is empty. There's no one there, and my stomach drops. I swing around and nearly bump into Arthur on my way out. "She's not here."

I go to the nurses' station and find a young man sitting behind the desk at a computer. "I'm looking for Sienna Palmer, but she's not in her room."

He finally drags his eyes from the screen and meets mine. It takes a few seconds for the question to register in his brain. "Mrs. Palmer . . . yes . . ." He points down the hall. "They have her up walking. She should be down that way."

Walking . . . I can think of no better news.

I turn and stride fast in that direction. I swerve around a tall cart of linens rolling toward me and the hospital worker who's pushing it. I reach the end of the corridor and look to my right.

There she is—at the end of a long hall, dressed in her pink bathrobe and slippers, shuffling in the opposite direction. Amanda walks slowly beside her, pushing a metal IV pole with a dangling saline bag.

For a few seconds I can't breathe. I feel as if I've died and gone to heaven.

Eventually, I recover my emotions and resume my pace. They reach the end of the hall, turn around, and see me. Our gazes lock on each other, and I feel an intense longing, but it's mixed with sorrow. Sienna's eye is still black and blue, her head is partially shaved where they operated, and her arm is in a sling. She looks weary, but she's still the most beautiful woman on this planet, alive and on her feet.

It's not lost on me that our last words to each other had been shouted in anger and frustration, but that's all gone now. I feel only love and gratitude.

We come together and stand face-to-face. "I thought I'd lost you," I say, and my voice breaks.

"You didn't." She reaches her good arm out to me, and I step forward into her embrace, where I shed all my tears, sadness, and regret—and also my boundless joy.

"I'm so sorry," I whisper.

"I'm sorry too," she replies. "Thank goodness they let you go. I knew you didn't do it."

I draw back, lay my hand on her cheek, and kiss her tenderly on the mouth.

Sienna laughs softly through her tears. Then we both look at Amanda, who's standing beside us, gripping the IV pole, staring in silent awe. We reach out and pull her in for a group hug, where we cry and I mumble about how happy I am to see them both.

Eventually we step apart and begin to walk slowly back toward Sienna's room. "Where's Connor?" I ask.

"Becky came and took him to hockey practice," Amanda replies. "It's his first time back on the ice since the accident."

"That's good to hear." I want normalcy for our family. But I know it will take time for Sienna to get there, physically, and I'm not sure how I'll fit into their normal world. I've not been a part of it for quite some time. I only hope that Sienna can love me again like she used to, and that everyone can forgive me. Even if I've done nothing yet to deserve it.

CHAPTER THIRTY-THREE

Sienna

I'm back in bed, and it's dark outside the window. Arthur stayed for a while, updating us on the situation with the police, but he left soon after.

Amanda has also left the hospital. She went home an hour ago with plans to return to school in the morning.

Now it's just Nate and me. He sits beside me and raises my good hand to his lips. He kisses it for about the hundredth time.

"Amanda told me you made cinnamon toast for her," I say as we watch the night nurse write her name on the whiteboard.

"It was nice to talk to her," Nate replies. "She's grown up to be strong, just like we knew she would."

"We did a good job with her," I add.

"No, *you* did a good job. I was barely around."

I appreciate his concession, but despite recent circumstances, I can't take all the credit. "That's not entirely true. In the early days, you were around more than I was, and she remembers everything about that—the donkey rides and the Halloween costumes. Do you remember taking her and Connor out when you were Luke, Leia, and Darth Vader?"

Nate chuckles softly. "That was one for the history books."

I smile warmly as I remember them posing for pictures at the front door.

It's remarkable how memories can become lost or distorted over time. Sometimes, through the lens of unhappiness, they make you see falsehoods. Or you remember only the bad.

Other times, they bring you back to the truth.

We sit for a moment, saying nothing, just watching each other until Nate reaches for his phone on the side table.

A familiar tension heats my blood. I turn my head on the pillow and look away from him. But I don't want to fall back into those old habits where I feel slighted, when my knee-jerk reaction is to blame him and shut him out. I don't want anything to taint what happened in the hall earlier, when our eyes first met and we were overjoyed to see each other. It was happiness in its purest form, just like it used to be, in the beginning.

I look at him again, and he's scrolling. "Anything important?" I ask, hoping that after everything we've just been through, he's gained the capacity to read me better.

His eyes lift and meet mine. I cling to a fragile hope that he won't wave his hand at me dismissively.

"It's a bunch of messages from the restaurant," he explains.

"Is everything okay?"

He sets his phone on the side table again. "It's fine. The staff is sending good wishes, saying they're glad I got out of jail." He takes my hand again and kisses it. "We're closed tonight because of my arrest. You probably know it was on the six o'clock news yesterday."

I shake my head on the pillow. "I wish that hadn't happened."

"I don't," he replies. "Seeing you in a coma and spending the night in jail was a huge wake-up call for me, and I needed it."

"I needed a wake-up call too."

I find myself thinking of Jacob and his wisdom in heaven—or in my dreams, whatever that was. If there was a part of me that continued to compare Nate with the perfection of my first love, in my youth, I feel ready to let go of that, because Jacob was right. Life is messy. There's no such thing as perfect. I understand that now.

Nate gazes into my eyes. "I don't want to go back to how we were before."

"I don't either." Yet I'm still hesitant, and I have to voice that. "But will you ever be able to step back from the restaurant? You've made so many promises in the past, and I always believed you were sincere when you made them. But the next day, it was the same old thing."

"It'll be different this time," he says. "I promise."

I let out a heavy sigh. "Can you please choose different words next time? I've heard those too many times."

There's a comforting softness in his expression. "Duly noted."

The night nurse reenters the room with a cheerful smile. "How are you feeling?"

"Good," I reply.

She checks the monitors, then reaches into the shirt pocket of her scrubs to retrieve a syringe. "It's time for your pain meds, but the doctor ordered a lower dose for tonight. He wants to start scaling back so that you can get out of here."

"I'm on board for that."

She administers the medication, and after she leaves, I find myself studying the hints of gray in Nate's hair and the lines around his eyes. His cheeks are stubbled because he hasn't shaved in a while. I notice traces of gray in his beard as well.

"Can I talk to you about something?" he asks.

"Of course." It's been so long since we've communicated openly with each other, without walls of defense between us and weapons armed for our own agendas. I'm determined to be receptive and nonjudgmental.

"When I was in the car with Amanda," he tells me, "she made a comment about Martina, something about her not being able to survive a night at the restaurant without me."

"That's interesting." Clearly my daughter had my back while I was comatose. "Tell me more."

Nate turns my hand over in his. "I hope you never imagined that there was anything going on between us, because there isn't."

After some contemplation, I decide that I believe him, but that doesn't mean the problem doesn't exist. As far as Nate's concerned, there's been nothing to worry about, but only because he's been obsessed with other things. He's been oblivious to the needs of his family, just as he's been oblivious to the flirtations of his house manager.

"I believe you," I say. "I trust that nothing's ever happened, but I've also seen the way Martina looks at you, and I've seen her texts. She's very flirty."

Nate grimaces and speaks apologetically. "She is, but I honestly think that's just her personality."

A bitter laugh escapes me before I can stop it. "I don't think so, and obviously Amanda doesn't think so either."

Nate stares at me with a blank expression, but there's nothing blank about what's going on in that head of his. I know him too well. I see the wheels turning.

He reaches for his phone and starts tapping and swiping. I wait patiently but recognize the effects of the pain medication the nurse just administered. My eyes are growing heavy.

"I'm reading some of her texts," Nate says. "She *is* kind of flirty."

"You don't say."

He continues to scroll. "She uses a lot of heart emojis. No one else does that except for you. Although not so much lately."

I let my eyes fall closed and leave him to evaluate the situation. I'm just starting to drift off when he gets up from the chair.

"I'm going to give her a quick call and deal with this," he says.

My eyes fly open, and part of me wants to suggest that he think on it first and strategize, but I'm too tired to talk anymore.

He leans over me and kisses my cheek. "Get some rest. I'll be back in a few minutes."

I nod, fall fast into sleep, and float into my dreams, where I'm in our kitchen, cooking, while Oscar sniffs around my feet, waiting for food to drop.

~

The sky outside the window is growing light. "Good morning," Nurse Katie softly says.

"Good morning," I reply.

"Do you need some help getting to the bathroom?"

She must be reading my mind, because I don't trust myself to walk steadily just yet. "Yes, please."

She raises the head of my bed and lowers the side rail. Only then do I realize we're not alone. Nate sits up in the visitor's chair in the corner by the window and stretches his arms over his head.

"You stayed all night?" I ask.

"Yeah. Becky was with the kids."

I realize this is a new reality for me—having an attentive husband who prioritizes me over everything else.

"Did you sleep okay?" I ask. "That chair doesn't look too comfortable."

"Compared to my night in jail, this was a five-star hotel."

The nurse supports me under my good arm as I swing my legs to the floor. "We're all glad to see you out of there," she says to Nate. "I love your restaurant, by the way. That's where my fiancé proposed to me."

He sits up a little straighter. "No kidding. When was that?"

"About six months ago."

"What did you have?" he asks. "I hope it was good."

"Honestly, I don't even remember. I just remember the candlelight and how it reflected off my ring."

I give Nate a private smirk because I know that response will drive him mad. For him, it's all about the food.

He simply grins and shrugs at me. Maybe there's hope for him after all.

~

When I emerge from the bathroom, the nurse is gone and Nate is sitting forward on the edge of the chair, elbows on knees, reading his phone. He looks up and immediately slides the phone into his back pocket. "I need coffee. Do you want anything from the cafeteria?"

I take in his appearance—the greasy hair, a faint sheen of oil on his face, and his wrinkled clothing. "You haven't been home in two days. Why don't you go take a shower, change, have breakfast, and come back later?"

He looks down at himself. "Is it that bad?"

"Kind of," I reply with affection as I climb into bed and glance at the clock on the wall. "The kids probably haven't left for school yet. If you go now, you'll see them. And if you feel like it, you could let Oscar out. Or, better yet, take him for a walk. He'll be your new best friend."

Nate adjusts the blue sheet on my bed to make sure it covers my feet. "I could use a friend. Are you sure you'll be okay for a while?"

"Positive. They'll be bringing breakfast soon."

Nate hesitates, and I appreciate this side of him—a caregiving side that I haven't seen in years.

I use my good hand to fan my face. "Please go, because you're starting to reek."

He smiles. "Message received, loud and clear." He moves to collect his jacket from the chair and promises to return before lunch.

~

It's surprising how busy and exhausting it can be, lying in a hospital bed all day. The nurses come in to change my bandage, the doctor makes his rounds with a group of medical students, and three bouquets of flowers arrive.

By noon, I realize I'm famished, which is a welcome sensation, knowing that my appetite is returning to normal. Compared with my husband's cooking, the food on the tray is below par to say the least, but I enjoy it, nonetheless.

As soon as I'm done, Nurse Melanie walks in. She's young and fit, and I suspect, by the look of her biceps and quads, she lifts weights.

"Time to go for a walk." She lowers the side rail on my bed. "It's the best thing for you right now, to get moving again."

I eagerly toss the covers aside because I want to get better so that I can go home. Besides that, her enthusiasm is contagious.

~

I'm on my second lap around the ward when I glance at a clock and notice it's past one o'clock. I recall that Nate promised to be back before lunch, and again, I find myself leaning into old insecurities. With every passing moment, I feel more and more certain that he's gone to the restaurant and gotten himself caught up in something.

But then I hear his jovial voice behind me. "Look at you!" He appears at my side, freshly showered and dressed in a clean pair of jeans and the off-white fisherman's knit sweater I gave him for Christmas a few years ago.

He kisses me, and his cheek is smooth. He smells of shaving soap. "Sorry I'm late, but I went to the mall to get you a new phone." He raises a small reusable shopping bag. "I set you up with a better plan than before, and I also got new phones for the kids. Believe it or not, it'll be even cheaper than before."

I blink a few times in astonishment. "You're joking. They'll be ecstatic."

"Maybe it'll earn me some points with them."

"Oh, it will." We start walking slowly while I wheel the IV pole beside me. "Thank you so much for doing that. I'll be glad to have a phone again so I can keep in touch with them."

"And your husband," Nate reminds me.

"Of course. You too."

An alarm goes off in one of the rooms, and a nurse exits a different room to attend to it. After she passes us, Nate says, "I didn't go to the restaurant, but I was on my phone a lot in the mall, dealing with stuff."

"What kind of stuff?" I ask.

He halts abruptly, meeting my gaze head-on. "Martina emailed me her resignation."

Stunned, I freeze mid-step. "She did what? Did she at least give you two weeks' notice?"

"No, but it's fine," he replies and drops his gaze to the floor. "Maybe this is a sign that I should take some time off and keep the restaurant closed. Maybe indefinitely. I don't know yet. All I know is that I want to focus on us."

My thoughts flash back to the early years of our relationship, when we were young and madly in love. We bonded over our dreams and ambitions. He supported me in mine, and I supported him in his. We were a great team. Until we weren't.

"Why did she quit?" I ask, curious about her email.

"Because she's a spoiled diva," Nate replies.

I can't help but laugh with satisfaction, hearing him say this. "Please, give me the dirt."

Nate's lips curl into a smile. "If I must . . . when she announced her resignation on the group chat, a few of the employees sent me private messages, saying they were happy to see her go. Graham called her a manipulative attention-seeker, and one of the bartenders said she always had to be in the spotlight and that she took credit for other people's accomplishments."

"Interesting," I say. "But why did she quit?"

Nate holds nothing back. "Because I called her last night and asked that she keep to a professional tone with her texts, and to not use heart emojis. I didn't threaten to fire her or anything. I just wanted her to stop doing that. But I guess she was offended."

I hate to admit it, but this news gives me immense pleasure. "She packed up her toys and stormed off?"

"Pretty much." Nate and I start walking again. "Now I'm without a house manager."

"I could do that job, you know," I tell him. "I know how to run a business, and the kids are more independent now. It might be good for me to get out there in the world again. And good for us."

He nods nostalgically. "We always did make a good team."

We stroll the hospital corridor in silence for a while, and I think of everything we've been through over the past few days.

"I need to tell you something," I say.

Nate regards me with a serious expression.

"I'm not sure if Amanda told you about this," I continue, "but when I was in the water . . . or after that . . . I don't know exactly . . . I had a near-death experience."

Nate stops short. A deep crease forms between his brows. "Oh, my God. What happened?"

I shrug because it's impossible to explain, but I start walking again and do my best. "After I drowned, I saw a light at the water's surface, and I swam toward it."

He slowly digests this.

"It felt very real," I continue, "but now that I'm back here, it feels like a dream. But it was a good dream."

Head down, he nods. "What else happened? What was it like?"

I'm starting to feel tired, so I gesture toward my room. "Let's go back. I need to lie down. Then I'll tell you the rest."

He escorts me down the hall and helps me into bed, tucks the thin blanket around me, and pulls a chair close.

"Did you see Jacob?" he asks.

I'm not surprised by the question because my husband of many years knows all the depths of my soul. Nothing, not even our recent differences, can erase that. "Yes."

He nods with understanding, but I sense a fear in him.

I tip my head back on the pillow and stare up at the ceiling, and all at once, I'm back there in my imagination, in Jacob's kitchen. I hear his voice in my head.

We definitely would have had disagreements . . . No one is perfect. Some of us get banged up pretty badly in life, and it's not easy to recover . . . It's how we learn and grow. But growth is in the healing. That's the whole point of living—to learn how to forgive each other for our trespasses, and how to be kind, and find joy together, even through our differences.

"It was nice to see him," I admit. "But it made me realize that my life with you has been so much more than a brief spark of first love. You've loved me for two decades, and you've given me children. We bought a house together and built two businesses. Our life has been full of highs and lows, but you've always been there, in for the long haul. So now, I want you to know that if I ever made you feel like I was comparing you to Jacob, or if you felt like you couldn't compete with a ghost, I'm sorry. I never wanted you to think you weren't good enough or that you didn't measure up to some impossible standard. You got enough of that from your father."

Nate sits forward and rests his elbows on his knees. "I did sometimes feel like you were holding on to him, that you thought he could do no wrong."

"He couldn't," I reply. "Because he didn't live long enough to make any mistakes. But he would have made plenty, I'm sure, if he'd survived."

I glance at the sky outside the large window. The sun is just moving into view. It's going to be blinding in the next few minutes.

"Something else I've learned from this," I say, meeting Nate's gaze, "is how trauma can push you off your path and take away your faith in good outcomes. I think I was always waiting for the other shoe to drop with you, and when you got busy with the restaurant, I latched on to that as the beginning of the end. I imagined us falling off a cliff."

Nate steeples his fingers and presses them to his forehead. "Funny. When you first mentioned trauma, I thought you were referring to me and my relationship with my father—how that planted an expectation of failure in me. But you're talking about your fall from Cape Split."

"Yes, but it's no different from what you went through as a child. Trauma put fear in both of us, I think. And on the day you missed my father's funeral, for me, it felt like the beginning of the earth collapsing."

Nate hangs his head low. "I'm so sorry. If it helps you to know, I've always regretted that. I should have been there."

Another alarm goes off in the room across the hall. No one comes to answer it, and we sit uneasily, listening and watching, until it finally stops chiming.

Nate says something out of the blue. "I think I should see a therapist."

"Really?"

"Yes," he replies. "I think I might actually *enjoy* trash-talking my dad with someone who's willing to listen for a full hour."

I laugh. "I'd be more than willing to listen to you trash-talk your dad. You wouldn't even have to pay me."

He smiles. "Yes, but you've already heard it all. I think I need fresh ears."

I nod approvingly. "Then let's look into that."

His phone chimes, and he pulls it out of his back pocket. "It's Connor. Oh, wow."

"What is it?"

Nate reads, taps, and scrolls. "The video of you getting swept off the rocks is everywhere. It's on CBC, Fox, and CNN. Even the BBC." He swipes and scrolls some more, then rises from the chair to show me his screen.

We watch and listen to a panel of experts on one of the news channels. They're discussing how social media groups can become pitchfork mobs. They refer to Nate's arrest and show photos of the Oblique website and Nate in his chef's uniform, leaning confidently over the stainless steel worktable in the kitchen.

"Babe, you've gone global."

Nate shakes his head in disbelief. "But they're showing my perp walk. God, I'm in handcuffs. This is terrible."

"But justice prevailed," I remind him.

His phone rings, and he checks the call display. "It's Graham." He accepts the call. "Hello? Hey." Nate wanders away from the bed and stands at the window. "Really? Wow. No, I don't think I can do that." He looks back at me. "I really need some time off." He listens, his eyes trained on mine. "Yeah, that's great. It's really good news, but let's just take some time to regroup, okay?" He pauses. "Sure. Yes, I agree. I just . . . I'm not right in the head yet. Thanks. We'll talk more tomorrow."

Nate ends the call and stares at his phone for a few seconds.

"What's happening?" I ask.

He returns to his chair, takes my hand, and kisses it, yet again. "Nothing. Just a bunch of phone calls about when the restaurant will reopen."

"Phone calls from who?"

"Reservation requests," he explains, "and some reporters."

I feel a rise of excitement in my chest, and I lay my hand on his cheek. "Sweetheart . . . this could be huge for you. You should go."

He blinks a few times, looking confused.

I smile warmly and feel goose bumps all over my body. This is his dream, and I've wanted it for him since the first time we met. It hasn't always been easy, climbing this hill, but he supported my dreams with my business, and he gave me two beautiful children. It's *his* turn now, and he needs to take it while the stars are aligning.

"Babe, go open your restaurant," I say. "I want you to. You have to go and milk this publicity for all it's worth."

He stares at me and slowly processes my words. Then a smile spreads across his face. He rises from the chair, and I sit up as he bends to kiss me on the mouth.

"I love you," he says.

"I love you too."

As he backs away and grabs his jacket off the chair, I feel a lightness in my bones, a glowing sense that all is right with the world.

"Whatever happens," he says, "I just want you to know . . ."

I wait with bated breath for him to finish that thought.

"It's all for you. Everything I am and everything I do, from this day forward, is for you."

I feel like I'm dreaming. Happiness bubbles up in me—not a fleeting, surface-level joy, but a quiet and profound contentment that fills every space inside of me. It's a feeling of being whole, of knowing, at last, that everything was always meant to be just as it is. There is no more longing, no more searching, no more aching for what was or what could have been. I want only what I have, here and now.

I want Nate.

EPILOGUE

One year later

Graham pokes his head into the back office. "Does he have any idea?"

"None at all." I roll my chair back from the desk. "He thinks I came in early to work on payroll, so he volunteered to walk Oscar."

Graham looks down at the stack of glittery party hats on my desk. "He's going to hate those, you know. They're very off brand."

I raise a finger. "That's why we're doing this during brunch, before the restaurant opens. We'll have all the streamers taken down before the doors open for dinner."

Graham offers to blow up the balloons, which I appreciate. He takes them out to the dining room to summon help from Becky, who's out there hanging streamers.

I roll my chair back under the desk and find myself staring at the framed group selfie of me, Nate, and the kids, and Oscar in my arms, with a gigantic pine tree behind us. It was taken last year when we went on a camping trip to Kejimkujik National Park to connect with nature. It was a planned celebration of my full recovery.

We've come a long way. Today is Nate's forty-fifth birthday and also a significant milestone because it's been twenty years since he announced to his family that he was quitting law school. Since that day, he's succeeded beyond his wildest dreams, and I, too, have been blessed with a new career I didn't even know I wanted.

Shortly after Martina resigned, and not long after I was discharged from the hospital, I decided to step into the role of temporary restaurant manager until Nate could find a replacement. At first, I worked from home, because those were the early days of my recovery. But the demands of the job turned out to be good for me, physically, and good for the restaurant as well. My past experiences running my own company were invaluable to Oblique.

(Not to toot my own horn, but I did a much better job than Martina ever did with the financials, along with everything else, except maybe flirting with the older male patrons.)

My phone rings, and it's Arthur. I answer the call. "Where are you?"

"Alex and I just picked up the kids," he replies, "and we're parking."

"Wonderful. But make sure you park down the street because he knows your car."

"Will do. We'll see you in a few minutes."

I end the call and text Amanda. Where are you guys?

She immediately responds. Jeff just arrived and Dad is feeding Oscar. Then we're heading for the car. ETA: Fifteen minutes. I'll text you when we're two minutes away.

I thumb a reply: Awesome! Make sure you come in the back door so that he doesn't see the decorations out front. And tell Connor not to let anything slip. He's terrible at keeping secrets!

I set down my phone and prepare to wrangle everyone into the walk-in cooler.

~

The cool, crisp air inside the cooler was refreshing at first, but we've been hiding in here for almost two minutes, and we're all starting to shiver.

I'm at the back. Hugging my arms around myself, I rise up on my tiptoes and look for Graham. He's at the front, just inside the door, and he wraps his arm around Becky and rubs furiously at her upper arms to warm her. They've become close friends since I began working at Oblique, which is fine with me because he's a good man. Being an incurable romantic and an optimist, I can't help but anticipate something more happening between them. Eventually.

A drop of condensation lands on top of my head, and I look up. I hear voices and drop my gaze. It's Nate and the kids in the kitchen.

The air inside the cooler is dense and still, filled with the muted hum of the cooler's motor working to keep the temperature low. We all remain silent, despite our shivering. Then the latch clicks and the door swings open.

"Surprise!"

Nate jumps back and lays his hand over his heart. He starts laughing. "Thank God!" he says. "The kitchen was empty, and I didn't know where everyone went. I thought you'd all quit on me!"

"Never!" Graham shouts. He steps out of the cooler and hugs Nate. "Happy birthday."

Becky hugs him next.

"Happy birthday, Flapjack," Arthur says, and Alex, Andy, and the twins hug him, followed by the employees.

I stand back and watch it all with profound contentment.

"I didn't expect this," Nate says, and then his eyes meet mine. "Babe. Come over here. Let me kiss you."

Everyone cheers and whistles as he takes me in his arms and kisses me—hard. I laugh when he steps back.

"I'm a lucky man!" he shouts.

I glance to my left and notice Jeff giving Amanda a kiss on the cheek. She looks up at him with affection, and it's sweet. First love is so important, and thankfully, the bar has been set high for my daughter.

"Wait until you taste the cake," Graham says to Nate. "Mary Jane did something special. You might want to consider it for the new menu."

Nate raises an eyebrow at his talented pastry chef, who's been with us since the beginning. "I'm eager to dig in," he says.

He holds his hand out to me, and we all saunter to the dining room for the first official reboot of the Palmer Birthday Brunch tradition.

~

Tonight, the restaurant is crowded as always. The lights are dimmed, and the white marble bar is aglow above warm ambient lighting, topped with gleaming glassware and bottles of premium spirits. It's past nine o'clock, and every guest on the reservation list has been seated. The pressure is off, so I move discreetly between candlelit tables, checking on plates and drinks and making sure all guests have everything they need and desire.

This is the time I like best. For me, as house manager, it's the other side of the uphill climb. The reward. The fulfillment of joy, laughter, and good conversation among our guests. I delight in watching each of them marvel at the exquisite culinary presentation on each plate that is set down in front of them. This is a setting for special occasions, and my husband has created a dreamy and intimate background for moments that will live forever in our guests' memories.

Isn't that what makes life meaningful? These precious moments of joy and love, to be remembered and appreciated?

I'm grateful that life, though tough and cruel at times, has taught me this.

~

The front door of the restaurant opens. It's almost ten o'clock, and the kitchen won't expect any additional orders, but sometimes patrons come in off the street to make reservations for another night, or they're simply looking to have a drink at the bar.

An older couple has entered, so I cross the dining room, reach the podium, smile, and say hello. Only then does a stark recognition hit me. Time seems to pause, hanging motionless for a breath. Those cold eyes have been imprinted on my brain forever. The man before me is not a stranger.

"We'd like a table for two," he tells me.

He doesn't recognize me, which confirms so much about the hollowness of his heart and the apathy of his character.

I clear my throat and reach for the leather binder on the shelf beneath the podium. "I'll check and see if we have any availability."

I flip through the pages, but I already know that we are full to capacity—but there's always space for an extra table to be brought out for unexpected VIPs.

But Bill Palmer is not a VIP. Not in my books. He's my father-in-law, but he has never met my children, and he's the reason my husband has been in therapy for the past year.

"Will you excuse me for a moment?" I ask. "I'll have to speak to the chef."

"Of course," he replies with a patronizing look in his eyes.

As I turn and walk past the bar toward the swinging doors to the kitchen, I suddenly remember a very different kitchen . . . I see an antique woodstove and a farmhouse sink. I see Jacob, who never harbored any hate or judgment toward anyone. He was a warm and loving soul with a forgiving heart, and I loved that about him.

I push through the door to the kitchen, where Nate, with extreme care and delicacy, is positioning seared scallops on two plates. I don't want to disturb his focus, so I wait patiently as he arranges the scallops in elegant patterns, each one placed atop a velvety cauliflower puree. He adds a drizzle of rich, vibrant herb oil and stands back to evaluate his creation.

"We have a VIP in the door," I tell him.

His eyes lift. He signals Thomas, one of our servers, to collect the plates.

"Who is it?" Nate asks.

Without hesitation, I state plainly: "Your father."

Nate hesitates, his gaze flicking away for half a second before settling back on me. A crease forms between his brows, slow and tense. "Who's he with?"

"A woman. His wife, I assume. Your stepmother."

Nate has never met his stepmother. Neither have I.

Nate places both fists on the stainless steel table and bows his head. "I wasn't expecting this tonight."

"I know. I'm so sorry. He's probably here because it's your birthday. And maybe he saw the review in *The Globe and Mail* yesterday."

I know all too well how deeply Nate's sense of self-worth is tied to earning that man's approval. We've had many conversations about it, over the years.

I want him to walk into my Michelin-star restaurant, have the best meal of his life, and ask me to come to the table so that he can tell me how good it was, and that he was wrong to doubt me, and I did well.

Nate hasn't earned a Michelin star. The inspectors still haven't come to Nova Scotia, and maybe they never will. But Oblique is the best restaurant in the city, and everyone knows it. Nate knows it. I know it. His father must know it too.

Nate hangs his head and shakes it while I wait for him to decide about setting out the VIP table. Finally, he lifts his gaze and speaks to me firmly, with conviction.

"Tell him we're full."

I freeze, stunned yet pleased. We stare at each other for a few intense seconds until I smile. "I'll take care of it."

Nate nods and mouths to me, "I love you." Then he turns his attention to three sparkling dessert plates with crisp, golden pound cake. They are placed in front of him to await a final flourish of hand-piped chocolate, impossibly thin and intricate.

I push through the swinging doors to the kitchen and walk past the bartender, who is filling a cocktail shaker with ice. A sense of quiet satisfaction rises in me as I approach the podium to turn Nate's father away. If he wants to come back another night, we will most certainly welcome him. But he will need to make a reservation, just like everyone else.

~

Later, after closing, Nate and I shut off the lights in the restaurant, step outside, and lock the door behind us. The night is clear, the moon full and bright, as we walk silently, hand in hand, along the sidewalk. Not a single breath of wind touches the air, and I feel a lightness in my chest, a fresh optimism because I believe, in my core, that Nate has finally let go of the past. His father has no more hold over him.

Before we reach the car, Nate pauses to look up at the stars. "It was a really good night," he says, tracing the constellations with his eyes.

I stare at his handsome face, at the elegant slope of his nose, and at the lips I've memorized without ever meaning to. I'm so very proud of him.

"It was an amazing night," I reply. "The lobster ravioli was a culinary triumph."

His eyes meet mine, and he slowly shakes his head, as if spellbound. "*You* were the best part about it."

For a second, I forget how to breathe, and heat rises to my cheeks. All I can do is move toward him, cup his face in my hands, and lay a soft kiss on his lips. "You make me so happy."

He pulls me into his arms and holds me—warm and steady, safe and sure. Then he whispers in my ear, "Let's go home."

I step back, and as I place my hand in his open palm, I am grateful for the clarity in my heart. Everything has become so clear to me lately, ever since I was pulled from the mighty ocean waves at Peggy's Cove. All I want now is this messy life that Nate and I have built together and our timeworn, weathered love—because somehow, we've managed to survive what should have undone us. Through our healing, we've grown into something new, and it's wonderful.

Tonight, under the stars, standing in the calm after all the chaos, I know this: *I choose you, Nate. I will always choose you, for better, for worse. Today, tomorrow, and forever.*

Acknowledgments

I am deeply grateful to my early readers, Michelle Killen and Stephen MacLean, whose invaluable feedback on the first draft helped shape this work into what it has become. My heartfelt appreciation goes to my extraordinary agent, Paige Wheeler, for her unwavering support and advocacy. I am equally indebted to my exceptional editor, Nancy Holmes, for her insightful comments and suggestions while leading the book through the editorial process. Thanks also to Megan McKeever, whose keen editorial eye elevated every page. Finally, my sincere thanks to the entire team at Lake Union Publishing for their dedication, care, and professionalism in bringing this book to life.

Questions for Discussion

1. In chapter 2, when Jacob and Sienna reach the summit at Cape Split, Jacob says, "Maybe, as we get older, we develop a clearer sense of danger because we become more aware of our mortality." Discuss this concept, and share times in your life when you took risks or when you were perhaps not fully aware of your mortality. Have you become more aware of it over time? If so, was it a specific event in life that gave you a keener awareness? Or do you believe we all gain this wisdom with age?
2. Before her fall from the mountain, Sienna thinks, *I've been blessed. But why? Was I simply born under a shining star? Or did some powerful force from above consider me deserving? If so, I don't understand the reason. I only know that I've been incredibly lucky. I met the love of my life in my own neighborhood, at the exact right time. God has been very good to me.* Knowing what the future holds for Sienna, discuss this belief she holds.
3. There are many instances in the novel where Scooter, in life or in dreams, provides emotional support for Sienna. Which one resonated the most with you, and why?
4. Nate and Sienna bond over a shared desire to follow their creative passions in their careers. They encourage each other to follow their dreams. But later in life, Nate's

passion for his career causes problems in their marriage. Did you feel Sienna was being fair when she let that chip away at the love she felt for him, and was she justified in speaking to a lawyer about a separation?

5. In chapter 9, Sienna remembers her relationship with Jacob and says, "When it grew dark, we stretched out on the grass, stargazed, snuggled, and talked more about our hopes and dreams for the future. To this day, I consider that night to be the most romantic experience of my life." She then compares her feelings to what she has with Nate, which she calls "a quieter kind of love." She admits she's not sure how true love is supposed to feel. Discuss how first love can be romanticized later in life and how memories of past relationships can affect a marriage, positively or negatively.
6. After the accident at Peggy's Cove, public speculation online arouses suspicion about Nate as a murderous husband. Was there ever a moment when you, as a reader, doubted his innocence? Did you feel that Amanda's thoughts and behaviors, in response to the backlash against her father, were warranted? How did you feel about Becky's handling of that situation?
7. Do you believe that near-death experiences are proof of heaven or an afterlife? Discuss.
8. In the epilogue, Nate's father walks into Oblique and requests a table. How did you feel about Nate's decision to turn him away? Would you have preferred for Nate to entertain the possibility of a reconciliation? How does his decision tie into the novel's message that "there is growth in the healing"? What about forgiveness in the healing process? Do you think Jacob would have advised Sienna to handle that situation differently?

About the Author

Photo © 2013 Jenine Panagiotakos, Blue Vine Photography

Julianne MacLean is a *USA Today* bestselling author of more than thirty novels, including the popular Color of Heaven series. Readers have described her books as "breathtaking," "soulful," and "uplifting." MacLean is a four-time Romance Writers of America RITA finalist and has won numerous awards, including the Booksellers' Best Award and a Reviewers' Choice Award from the *Romantic Times*. Her novels have sold millions of copies worldwide and appear in more than a dozen languages.

MacLean studied in Nova Scotia, earning a degree in English literature from the University of King's College in Halifax and a business degree from Acadia University in Wolfville. She loves to travel and has lived in New Zealand, Canada, and England. The author currently resides on the east coast of Canada in a lakeside home with her husband and daughter. Readers can visit her website at www.juliannemaclean.com for more information about her books and writing life and to subscribe to her mailing list for all the latest news.